AN UNFORESEEN KISS
Captivating Kisses
Book 4

Alexa Aston

© Copyright 2025 by Alexa Aston
Text by Alexa Aston
Cover by Dar Albert

Dragonblade Publishing, Inc. is an imprint of Kathryn Le Veque Novels, Inc.
P.O. Box 23
Moreno Valley, CA 92556
ceo@dragonbladepublishing.com

Produced in the United States of America

First Edition August 2025
Print Edition

Reproduction of any kind except where it pertains to short quotes in relation to advertising or promotion is strictly prohibited.

All Rights Reserved.

The characters and events portrayed in this book are fictitious. Any similarity to real persons, living or dead, is purely coincidental and not intended by the author.

ARE YOU SIGNED UP FOR DRAGONBLADE'S BLOG?

You'll get the latest news and information on exclusive giveaways, exclusive excerpts, coming releases, sales, free books, cover reveals and more.

Check out our complete list of authors, too!

No spam, no junk. That's a promise!

Sign Up Here

www.dragonbladepublishing.com

Dearest Reader;

Thank you for your support of a small press. At Dragonblade Publishing, we strive to bring you the highest quality Historical Romance from some of the best authors in the business. Without your support, there is no 'us', so we sincerely hope you adore these stories and find some new favorite authors along the way.

Happy Reading!

CEO, Dragonblade Publishing

Additional Dragonblade books by Author Alexa Aston

Captivating Kisses Series
An Unexpected Kiss (Book 1)
An Impulsive Kiss (Book 2)
An Innocent Kiss (Book 3)
An Unforeseen Kiss (Book 4)

The Strongs of Shadowcrest Series
The Duke's Unexpected Love (Book 1)
The Perks of Loving a Viscount (Book 2)
Falling for the Marquess (Book 3)
The Captain and the Duchess (Book 4)
Courtship at Shadowcrest (Book 5)
The Marquess' Quest for Love (Book 6)
The Duke's Guide to Winning a Lady (Book 7)

Suddenly a Duke Series
Portrait of the Duke (Book 1)
Music for the Duke (Book 2)
Polishing the Duke (Book 3)
Designs on the Duke (Book 4)
Fashioning the Duke (Book 5)
Love Blooms with the Duke (Book 6)
Training the Duke (Book 7)
Investigating the Duke (Book 8)

Second Sons of London Series
Educated By The Earl (Book 1)
Debating With The Duke (Book 2)
Empowered By The Earl (Book 3)

Made for the Marquess (Book 4)
Dubious about the Duke (Book 5)
Valued by the Viscount (Book 6)
Meant for the Marquess (Book 7)

Dukes Done Wrong Series
Discouraging the Duke (Book 1)
Deflecting the Duke (Book 2)
Disrupting the Duke (Book 3)
Delighting the Duke (Book 4)
Destiny with a Duke (Book 5)

Dukes of Distinction Series
Duke of Renown (Book 1)
Duke of Charm (Book 2)
Duke of Disrepute (Book 3)
Duke of Arrogance (Book 4)
Duke of Honor (Book 5)
The Duke That I Want (Book 6)

The St. Clairs Series
Devoted to the Duke (Book 1)
Midnight with the Marquess (Book 2)
Embracing the Earl (Book 3)
Defending the Duke (Book 4)
Suddenly a St. Clair (Book 5)
Starlight Night (Novella)
The Twelve Days of Love (Novella)

Soldiers & Soulmates Series
To Heal an Earl (Book 1)
To Tame a Rogue (Book 2)
To Trust a Duke (Book 3)
To Save a Love (Book 4)
To Win a Widow (Book 5)
Yuletide at Gillingham (Novella)

King's Cousins Series
The Pawn (Book 1)
The Heir (Book 2)
The Bastard (Book 3)

Medieval Runaway Wives
Song of the Heart (Book 1)
A Promise of Tomorrow (Book 2)
Destined for Love (Book 3)

Knights of Honor Series
Word of Honor (Book 1)
Marked by Honor (Book 2)
Code of Honor (Book 3)
Journey to Honor (Book 4)
Heart of Honor (Book 5)
Bold in Honor (Book 6)
Love and Honor (Book 7)
Gift of Honor (Book 8)
Path to Honor (Book 9)
Return to Honor (Book 10)

The Lyon's Den Series
The Lyon's Lady Love

Pirates of Britannia Series
God of the Seas

De Wolfe Pack: The Series
Rise of de Wolfe

The de Wolfes of Esterley Castle
Diana
Derek
Thea

Also from Alexa Aston
The Bridge to Love (Novella)
One Magic Night

PROLOGUE

Brownstone—March 1800

EDEN SNOW SAT in bed, nibbling on the toast points her maid had brought for breakfast. She was rarely hungry in the mornings and alternated between a single poached egg or a few toast points, accompanied by a cup of tea.

She took the last sip of her tea before setting the tray aside, ready to dress for the day. Polly helped her from her night rail and into a riding habit, taking time to braid Eden's hair in a long, single braid.

"There you go, Miss Eden," the servant said. "Are you off to visit your mother?"

She nodded, sadness filling her. Within a week, Eden and her father would be leaving for town in order to attend the upcoming Season. Her mother, who was bedridden, would remain behind at Brownstone. She had never been separated from her mother and while she looked forward to attending the various social events, Eden knew how much she would miss her guidance as she navigated the waters of the Marriage Mart during her come-out.

Still, Papa would be there to help advise her. Eden was as close to her father as she was her mother. Being an only child, she had gravitated to her parents and spent a huge portion of her day with one or both.

While she was eager to get to know some of the other young ladies making their come-outs, she wasn't sure exactly how to go about making friends. She had never had any previously. Because of her mother's health, Eden had always chosen to keep close to Brownstone, only venturing into the village with her father upon occasion or for church on Sundays. Her world had been a very small one compared to what would await her in town.

Miss Barnes, her governess, had left them at the beginning of the new year. She had said she was no longer needed since Eden was now grown, and Miss Barnes had taken a new position with a family with two little girls, ages four and six. Eden still missed her former governess terribly and wrote to Miss Barnes once a week. She doubted she would be able to keep up with that correspondence, though, because Mama said Eden would be too busy once the Season began.

She left her bedchamber and headed toward her mother's rooms, entering the small sitting room which was never used since Mama never left her bed. The door to the bedchamber was slightly ajar. As Eden started to open it, she heard Mama's voice mention her name. Something caused her to wait a moment, not wanting to interrupt the conversation.

"You must speak with Eden today, John," her mother said firmly. "She must understand it is imperative that she wed by the end of the Season."

"I think you are worried for nothing. Eden has plenty of time to choose a husband. If none of the gentlemen are to her liking this year, why, she can do a second Season as she looks for a husband."

A long pause sounded, and she felt guilty for eavesdropping on her parents, but she wondered what her mother was talking about and decided to keep her presence unknown for the time being.

"You, of all people, John, know how life can change in an instant. I would not see our only daughter left unprotected."

She leaned around and saw her father's head fall into his wife's lap. Mama stroked his hair tenderly.

"I will never forgive myself for what I did to you, Mary," Papa said, raising his head, tears staining his cheeks.

Mama cupped his cheek, her thumb wiping away his tears. "How many times have I told you, my darling, that it was not your fault what happened to me?"

"But I knew you were timid around horses. You only agreed to learn how to ride in order to please me, and look what that got you. If I hadn't made you go out that day . . ." His voice trailed off.

Eden knew about the accident. How her mother's horse had bolted with an inexperienced rider on its back, racing across a field and jumping a fence. Mama had been thrown from the horse, her spine severely injured in the fall as she hit the ground. She had lost all feeling from her waist down.

Eden had only been six months old.

Despite Mama's disability, Eden had never lacked for attention from her mother. Mama remained a bright light in both her and her father's lives. She chose to be happy that she had only hurt her spine and not died in the fall. She always told Eden to cherish each day, saying that no matter how sad you might feel, there was always someone else with deeper, more serious problems, and that Eden should always be grateful for what she had.

"If you wish, I will speak with her this morning before the two of you ride," Mama said.

"How I wish you could come to town with us, Mary," Papa said, the anguish obvious in his voice.

"You know travel is impossible for me. You will need to write to me every day. Tell me of Eden's suitors and all the events you escort her to."

"It will be so very hard to be parted from you, my love. We have spent every night of our marriage together under this roof. To be apart for months and months is almost more than I can bear."

"You will be doing it for our Eden, John. For her future happiness."

"You are right, as always," he said, resignation in his voice. "I will leave you now so that the two of you might chat. I will reiterate to

Eden what you tell her today."

She watched her father place a tender kiss upon Mama's brow, and Eden quietly slipped from the sitting room, heading back into the corridor, where she gathered her thoughts.

Why did she need to wed during her first Season? Even Mama had told her that some girls, including herself, took more than one Season before they settled into marriage. Mama had seemed adamant, however, that her daughter wed.

She reentered the sitting room just as Papa came through the bedchamber door.

He smiled at her. "I will head to my study. When you and your mother have finished your visit, come and get me. We will go for our daily ride."

In spite of her injuries, Mama had insisted that Eden learn how to ride. From a young age, she had been placed in the saddle and never showed any fear of horses, thanks to her parents keeping the precise nature of her mother's accident from her until she was older and already an experienced rider. She grew to love her hours in the saddle. Even her father said she rode superbly, and he was known as the best rider in the area.

"All right, Papa. I will see you soon."

Entering the bedchamber, she went to Mama's side, kissing her cheek before taking the chair next to the bed. She had spent so many hours in this room because Mama never left it. Even afternoon tea was served here so that the three of them might be together.

"Well, it is less than a week until you leave for town," Mama said brightly. "Do you have any more questions about the Season?"

"I cannot think of a one," she said honestly. "You have told me about so many of the different kinds of affairs which are held. You have explained the social rules and how I must follow them to the letter. I only wish you could come with us, Mama," she said fervently.

"You know that is not possible, my child. My condition has deteriorated over the years. You probably do not recall, but I used to be carried downstairs for tea and dinner."

That surprised her. "You did?"

"Yes. You were still very young then. Your father would lift and carry me. I even had a bath chair he would set me in on the terrace so I could enjoy a nice day. It came to be too much for me, however. It is easier to remain in this bed."

Mama took Eden's hand. "But how I wish I could go to town with you. See all the beautiful gowns you will wear. Meet the men who will woo you." She squeezed Eden's hand and released it. "There is something important we must discuss, Eden. I know you will write to me of what you do in town and the gentlemen you are interested in. I will do my best to give you advice from a distance, but you will need to choose a gentleman to wed by Season's end. It is imperative that you do so."

"Why, Mama?" she asked, perplexed. "You and Papa were a love match. I would seek that for myself, and it might take some time. Papa has been so devoted to you all these years, never leaving your side. I want a man who also would be that faithful to me."

Her mother's face grew stern. "Love matches are rare, Eden. Very few exist in Polite Society. I would tell you not to fill your head with ideas of love. Instead, look for a good man. A kind one. He may not be the most handsome or possess the most wealth, but character is what is important. In fact, many men are overlooked because young ladies are ore dazzled by titles and riches."

"I will give every gentleman fair consideration, Mama." She covered her mother's hand with her own. "Why do you feel I must wed this first Season when you did not?"

"I did not want to have to say this to you, Eden, but life can change in an instant. I am the best example of that. One day, I was a young woman, practically a newlywed. In love with my husband and the mother of our first child. The next, I could not stand on my own two feet, much less take a single step. I could not give your father the heir he deserved. Because of that, you know his title will go to your cousin."

Eden shivered involuntarily. Cousin Edgar was selfish and rude. He was an only child and had been spoiled from the moment of his birth. Her uncle had lost his wife in childbirth and because of that, Uncle Snow focused every minute of each day on his only son. She hated that Edgar would one day assume her father's title as Viscount Brownley.

"While your father remains in excellent health, you never know when an accident or sudden death might occur. That would leave Edgar as the viscount, and he has only been interested in himself. Though he would be charged to care for the two of us once he becomes the viscount, I doubt he would do so in a proper fashion, Eden. Because of that, I want you protected. If you are wed, you will have your husband to look after you and your interests. Then it will not matter who the viscount is once your father is gone."

"But you said so yourself, Mama. Papa has robust health."

Her mother's expression grew solemn. "As I did before I took that fall from my horse."

She gazed at her mother, who suddenly appeared more fragile than she had only yesterday.

"Mama, are *you* well?"

Mama gave her a rueful smile. "As well as one who is bedridden can be, my dearest. But I am serious. Do this for me. Find yourself a husband. Marry him. And then bring him here to Brownstone to meet me."

Eden swallowed. It hurt to know that her mother would not be able to attend her only child's wedding. That her world was confined to this one room.

"I will do as you ask, Mama. I will be diligent in regard to finding a husband, and I will have Papa get to know the gentlemen I am especially interested in. He can help guide me through the Season and into a marriage."

Her mother took Eden's hands, kissing them tenderly. "Thank you for doing this, dearest." Her eyes bright with tears, sparkled. "Oh, I cannot wait to receive letters from you, telling me of all the wonderful balls and garden parties."

"Do not forget card parties," she said, smiling.

Her mother had taught her how to play various card games, as well as chess, and they had passed many hours engaged in both.

"You are rather clever when it comes to games," Mama praised. "Gentlemen will be flocking to partner with you. Go. Your father is waiting for you."

She rose, brushing a kiss against her mother's cheek. "Rest for now, Mama. I will be back to see you soon."

Eden went downstairs and claimed her father, thinking over what Mama had said. If Cousin Edgar could not be trusted to look after her, she worried about what might happen to Mama. She determined to find a generous man who would allow Mama to be brought into their household once her father passed.

They headed to the stables, where a groom saddled their horses for them.

"Where shall we ride today?" Papa asked.

"Let us go to the top of the ridge," she suggested.

They did as she requested and dismounted, walking to the edge and gazing out over Brownstone.

"I will miss home and the country while we are in town," she said wistfully. "And Mama."

Papa's fingers closed around hers. "We both will be a little bit lonely without your mother's calming presence in our lives."

After several minutes spent in peaceful silence, looking over the land, they returned to their horses. Papa tossed her into the saddle and mounted himself.

They cantered down the hill and through a valley, and Eden cried, "I will race you!"

She took off, tearing across the field, Papa's horse galloping close behind. Then she heard a sudden cry and wheeled about. Her father's horse was collapsing, and Papa sailed over the horse. Her heart was in her throat as he hit the ground hard. The horse was in distress, making terrible noises, but Eden blocked out the sounds, leaping from her horse and racing to her father.

He lay at an awkward angle, his neck twisted. She turned him over gently and saw his eyes wild with fright. His breath rattled loudly.

"Papa!" she cried, clasping his shoulders, feeling helpless.

The light began fading from his eyes, and she begged, "Papa. Please. Don't leave me. Please."

With his dying breath, he managed to say, "Tell Mary . . . I . . . love her."

Then he ceased breathing.

Eden let out a howl of hurt, falling atop his prostrate body, clutching him, pleading for him to open his eyes. To come back to her.

She pushed to her feet, hearing the weak cries of his mount. Going to the animal, she stroked the horse's side, seeing that its leg was broken, its eyes full of pain.

Knowing she needed to put the horse out of its misery, she returned to Papa. He always carried a pistol with him when he left the house, a habit he had picked up from his own father.

Eden's fingers found the weapon, and with tears streaming down her face, she went to his horse. Bending, she kissed its snout.

"I am so sorry. So very sorry."

The single gunshot erupted, disturbing the peace of the country day. She knew it would bring others to them. She stroked the horse a final time, the pistol falling from her hand. Returning to her father, she lifted his head and placed it in her lap, sobbing quietly.

A few minutes later, their steward and one of their tenants arrived on horseback. The two men quickly assessed the situation, and the steward asked her to come with him, saying that her father's body would be cared for.

"No," she said resolutely. "I must stay with him. Place him atop my horse. I will take Papa home."

She lifted her father's head and eased away from him, placing his head back on the ground. Eden watched as the two men lifted him and placed Papa face down over her saddle. She took up the reins and slowly walked the horse back to the stables. The tenant rode ahead to let others know to expect her.

And their dead master.

By the time she entered the house, the doctor met her. She had forgotten this was his usual day to call upon her mother and supposed he had come from upstairs.

"Are you all right, my lady?" he asked, concern in his voice.

She shrugged, feeling all the life had gone out of her, as well.

"Can you tell me what happened?"

"Papa's horse suffered a broken leg," she said dully. "It stumbled, and Papa was unexpectedly thrown from the saddle. I think . . . his neck was broken." She began weeping, adding, "I had to shoot the horse. It was suffering so much."

"I will go and examine his lordship," the doctor said gently. "I would like to give you something to help you sleep."

"Not yet. I must go and tell Mama what has happened."

Feeling ancient, Eden climbed the stairs slowly, wondering how she would break the news to Mama. She couldn't help but think how ironic it was that both her parents had suffered falls from their horses. One had been left unable to use her legs, while the other had lost his life.

A sudden fear seized her. Only this morning, Mama had voiced her worries regarding the death of her husband—and what it would mean for her and Eden. Her cousin Edgar would now become Viscount

Brownley. Would he turn her and Mama out? And what about her come-out?

Her heart pounding, she pushed open the door to her mother's bedchamber and found Mama sleeping. Eden took the chair beside the bed, worry filling her.

After sitting for some minutes, she could wait no longer and gently shook her mother.

Mama stirred, opening her eyes. "Eden, darling." She frowned. "What is wrong? You have been crying."

Her tears had ceased once the dread filled her, but she had always looked terrible for hours after she cried.

"I have some bad news, Mama," she said quietly. "It is about Papa."

Her mother sucked in a quick breath. "Oh!" she cried, as understanding clearly filled her. "He is gone, isn't he? How?"

She nodded. "His horse broke its leg. Papa was not prepared for the suddenness of it. He fell from the horse." Her eyes filled with tears. "Mama, he broke his neck in the fall. He is . . . no more."

Mama turned white and began to tremble all over. "My worst fears have come to pass. Edgar is now Lord Brownley."

"You do not think he would turn us out, do you?" she asked, afraid of the answer her mother would give.

"I cannot predict what evils lurk in his mind, Eden. But he must be notified at once."

After her uncle's death two years ago, Edgar had left Cambridge, where Eden gathered he had not met with much academic success. Edgar had gone to London and taken over his father's rented rooms. Her cousin had even made a trip to Brownstone, encouraging his uncle to reopen his shuttered townhouse so he might live there. It had remained unused in all the years after her mother's accident. Papa had refused Cousin Edgar's request, telling him that the townhouse would come to him in good time.

The townhouse had remained closed until only yesterday, when some of their staff had traveled to town in order to prepare for her and Papa's arrival next week. They were to air out the place, remove the dustcovers from furniture, and clean everything from windows and rugs to linens.

Now, Edgar would get his wish. He would have the London townhouse and everything else that belonged to the viscountcy.

"I will write to him now and send the message at once," she told her mother. Kissing her brow, she added, "Try to get some rest." Then she remembered something important.

"Mama, Papa lived for a few seconds after the fall. He told me to tell you that he loved you. His last thoughts were of you."

She left the room as her mother began to wail, the news of her husband's death finally sinking in. Though Eden, too, wished to give in to her own sorrow, she must be the strong one now. Papa had always taken care of her and Mama. It was now up to her to care for her mother.

After composing the brief letter informing Cousin Edgar of her father's untimely death, she found their butler and asked that a footman ride to town to deliver the note in person.

"Of course, my lady," the butler said, pity in his eyes.

The doctor entered the house again and asked, "Might we speak in private, Miss Snow?"

"Yes," she said, leading him to what had once been her mother's parlor. The room now sat unused.

After they were seated, the physician said, "You were correct. Lord Brownley did break his neck. I do not believe he suffered, though."

She kept quiet about the last half-minute of her father's life. Let the man think her father had died instantly. It would do no good to say otherwise.

"My lady?" the doctor asked, looking mournfully at her. "I must share something with you." He hesitated. "It is not good news."

A coldness swept through her. Stiffly, she said, "Tell me. Now."

"Your mother has lost weight recently. I have been worried about her. I have discovered that... well, I will not go into complicated medical terms, but you must be made aware that she hasn't long to live."

Her throat tightened, even as acid filled her belly. "How long?" she demanded.

"I would venture between three and six months."

"I see."

"I will share this with the new Lord Brownley. Once he takes up his position."

"Do not do that," she said firmly. "He may have inherited my father's title, but he is not family. I do not wish for him to be privy to such information. Do you understand?"

"Yes, my lady."

"What can be done for her?"

He shrugged. "We can keep her comfortable. Your mother has never been one to complain, but I fear the pain will grow great."

"You must teach me to do whatever else must be done to care for her," she said.

"A few drops of laudanum will help ease Lady Brownley's suffering when the time comes. It can be placed in a drink or soup." The physician hesitated. "A time will come when she may refuse to eat or drink, yet she will still be experiencing pain. Only then will you need to place a drop directly upon her tongue."

Eden thought she would ask Cousin Edgar if they might move to the dower house. It would give her mother privacy in which to spend her final days. In fact, she decided to have the servants ready the dower house immediately. That way, the manor house would be vacated by the time her cousin arrived at Brownstone. Surely, Edgar would not toss them from the dower house. This way, she and Mama would be out of his way. Out of sight, out of mind.

At least Eden told herself that would be the case.

"I will also call every week, as I have. More often if she needs to see me."

"Thank you. Come to the dower house in the future. I will care for Mama there."

After he left, she found their butler. The housekeeper had been among those servants who had gone to town to ready the townhouse. Eden explained how she wished for the dower house to be cleaned and readied so that she and her mother might move in promptly.

"I am guessing that my cousin will prefer his privacy," she explained, but she saw the butler knew why she did what she did.

"I will see to it at once, my lady. As well as to Lord Brownley. I have sent for the vicar. He should be arriving shortly."

She realized she would need to be the one who planned Papa's funeral service. It would simply be too much for Mama to handle.

"That was quite thoughtful. Thank you."

As Eden waited for the clergyman to arrive, she decided to cherish the days she had left with her mother.

And try not to worry about her own future.

Chapter One

Millvale, Kent—May 1807

VALENTINIAN WORTHINGTON, THE former Marquess of Claibourne, watched as his father's coffin was lowered into the ground in the Willowshire churchyard. He was now the Duke of Millbrooke.

And totally unprepared to fulfill his ducal responsibilities.

It wasn't that he did not possess the intelligence or that he lacked empathy for his tenants. Val had simply been prevented from ever having anything to do with his future, thanks to his father's iron grip on the dukedom. While he had never sought to usurp his father's authority, Val would have liked to have become involved to some extent with the various properties owned by the Worthington family. He had longed to be made aware of their investments, as well as to have a clear picture of the financial situation he would one day inherit when the title fell to him.

He wasn't a fool, having moved in Polite Society for several years now after leaving university. He knew sometimes the heads of families made unwise business decisions or even gambled away family fortunes. To the world of the *ton*, these matters could be hidden. Bills from tradesmen would go unpaid. Food and wine merchants might be left in the lurch. Sometimes, years could go by without entitled noblemen paying for any goods and services, the head of the family simply ignoring a downward financial spiral.

What would he find now that he had access to any secrets his father might have kept?

The duke had always brushed off Val's concerns when he voiced them, telling his son and heir apparent to simply enjoy the bachelor life. Millbrooke had held strong opinions and even stronger convictions, and Val knew there would be no going against his father. So, he did as requested.

He enjoyed himself. Probably more than he should have.

His reputation was that of a charmer. Val Worthington was downright irresistible, to both men and women. He had an aura about him which drew others to him like a moth drawn to a flame. Everything came easily to him, from academics to sports. His school chums were merely acquaintances, though. He never let any of them get too close to him, except for his cousin. Con was like a brother to Val, and they had been close for almost twenty years. They had gone away to school together. Even shared rooms during university and even afterward in town. They had also made their way through women of the *ton*, albeit with discretion.

Family was important to him, though, and he was close to his three sisters. Ariadne had made her come-out last Season, wedding the Marquess of Aldridge. She now lived at Aldridge Manor in Surrey and had given birth to their first child last week. Val had yet to meet little Penelope. With his father's recent death, he wasn't certain when he might be able to do so.

Not only would he need to learn everything about being a duke, he would also need to prioritize the wellbeing of his mother and sisters. Mama had taken her husband's death hard. Thankfully, Aunt Agnes had been with them in town before the start of the Season when his father had died suddenly. She had accompanied them back to Millvale. As his mother's closest friend, Mama would lean on Aunt Agnes in the coming days and weeks.

He was more concerned about the twins. Lia and Tia were meant to make their come-outs next month. Obviously, that would not occur since their house was in mourning. He knew how much the pair had looked forward to the Season and hopefully finding their husbands. They would most likely mourn the loss of a year away from Polite Society more than the death of their father. Millbrooke had been cold to all three of his daughters.

While the duke favored his son and heir apparent, Millbrooke was a man who kept everyone at a distance, other than his sister. Val's Aunt Charlotte, mother to Con, Lucy, and Dru, always had a special closeness with her brother, and the family joked how Aunt Charlotte was even more formidable and stubborn than the duke himself. Lucy would make her own come-out this Season. He supposed Dru would do so the following year. At least Tia and Lia would have that cousin to share in the social whirl.

The vicar finished his prayer, indicating the service was all but concluded. He nodded to Val, who went and scooped a handful of dirt, tossing it atop the coffin now resting in the ground. As he moved away, others in attendance did the same. He moved toward the carriage and entered it, the coachman taking him back to Millvale. He had called for his horse to be readied to ride to the funeral service, but Quigby, Millvale's longtime butler, had pulled Val aside, telling him it would be more fitting for a duke to arrive in his ducal carriage for the service.

To him, hearing that felt like the last of his freedom slipping away. From now on, he would be judged differently because he was a duke. He must maintain a certain standard. Be a leader in Polite Society. Even take on a bride. After all, a duke needed an heir—and hopefully, a spare—to keep order in the family. He had thought he had years before he would need to wed. Now that, too, was something pressing upon him.

As he returned to Millvale, he knew to prepare himself for the onslaught which would follow. Neighbors from the area, along with various residents of Willowshire, would soon be descending upon the house to offer their condolences to the family. Cook and her staff had been busy the past two days, preparing for the numerous guests.

He arrived home and entered the house. The twins met him. Women rarely attended funeral services, and he had asked them their preference. Both had admitted that they wished to remain home, with Tia, as usual, being the most vocal. She had confessed that she did not want to go to the church and graveyard because she would have to muster tears. She said their father had rarely spoken a word to either her or Lia, and she did not feel any sadness at his passing. Though left unsaid, it was obvious that Tia was resentful in having to postpone the Season she had looked forward to, all because of their father's untimely passing. Lia had silently nodded, agreeing with her sister, so Val had not pressed them to accompany him.

Mama, who was visibly upset, had been in no condition to go with him. He only hoped she might rally and be able to receive their guests.

"Did everything go well?" Tia asked him.

"Yes. Mr. Clarke did a nice job with the eulogy. A good number of others were present. We need to prepare for a large crowd to arrive soon."

Lia touched his sleeve. "How are *you*, Val?"

She was the more intuitive of the two, so he wasn't surprised by her question.

"I am still in a bit of shock," he admitted. "Things will change quickly now. I know that I have much to learn."

He mentally berated himself because he could have been more prepared. As Marquess of Claibourne, he'd held a small estate of his own. Because of his father's encouragement, however, he had merely hired a competent steward and let the estate manager deal with all matters. Instead of spending more time at that country estate, preparing himself for the eventual day he would become the duke, he had enjoyed his time in town, carousing as most young men of his social standing did. Regret filled him now for being so shallow.

Lia squeezed his arm. "You will make for a wonderful duke, Val," she assured him.

"You are very smart—and very stubborn," Tia teased. "You will learn what you need to and then act accordingly."

"Where is Mama?" he asked.

"In the drawing room," Tia told him. "With Aunt Agnes. I am so glad she returned from town with us."

Val had always liked his aunt Agnes. She had married one of his father's cousins and had been widowed many years ago by her husband's early death in a carriage accident. It had also claimed the life of her second son. Lucius had been only eight years of age. The earldom had gone to Aunt Agnes' older boy. Hadrian was ten when he came into his title. He had learned that Hadrian now went by Tray, being the Earl of Traywick. Val couldn't blame his cousin. Hadrian wasn't a modern name. In fact, none of the cousins had fashionable names. All ten of them had been named after Roman and Byzantine emperors and empresses since his father, Aunt Charlotte, and their cousin, his uncle George, had all been fascinated by history. Several of the cousins, including Val himself, went by more diminutive forms of their pompous names.

He noticed Quigby hovering in the foyer and told the butler, "Tell Cook and Mrs. Quigby to get ready. The hordes will descend upon us soon."

"Yes, Your Grace," Quigby said, making a quick exit.

"Oh, dear," Lia fretted. "I suppose we are to call you Millbrooke now."

He touched her cheek. "Only when others are around. I will always be Val to my sisters."

"I am glad of that," Tia declared. "I know it defies convention, but I do not think I could ever call you Millbrooke, Val. Millbrooke is Papa." She frowned. "You are nothing like him."

He caught her hand and squeezed her fingers. "I hope to be a good duke. Not that our father wasn't, but I wish to be my own man and cut my own path."

"You will need to wed now," Lia said, ever practical. "Perhaps you should return to town and attend the Season. I heard Mama and Aunt Agnes discussing it. They said that men are not bound by the same constraints of mourning as are women."

"Hah!" Tia said. "I am usually the one eavesdropping and not you, Lia." She looked to him. "Is that true? Will you leave and go to town without us?"

"No," he assured them. "I have far too much to learn and do to go gallivanting about at balls and Venetian breakfasts. Besides, the Season is the same each year. I have attended it before and will not miss it. Millvale and my other properties and investments will keep me busy."

"Until next year's Season," Lia said. "Then you must go and find a bride on the Marriage Mart, Val."

"We will all three do next Season together," he declared. "Ariadne has already conquered Polite Society. It will be time for the rest of us Worthingtons to do the same."

He couldn't help but think as the daughters of a duke, the twins would be in high demand. As much as he had scrutinized gentlemen seeking Ariadne's favor, he would be twice as busy, responsible for his unwed sisters, as well as perusing the Marriage Mart for a bride for himself.

"I do want to go see Ariadne and Penelope," Lia said. "Is it possible to visit family while we are in mourning?"

"Yes, but her loyalties now lie with Lord Aldridge. She may grieve for Father some, but most likely, she will go to the Season with the marquess. Perhaps you can visit her and meet Penelope sometime this autumn. We might even ask her to come and spend a quiet Christmas with us."

"I like that idea," Tia said. "You should go see Mama before everyone arrives."

"I will do so now."

Val made his way upstairs and entered the drawing room. He saw his mother and aunt in quiet conversation. They rose as he approached.

"Oh, Millbrooke, how did the service go?" Mama asked.

He had already tried to convince her to refer to him by his Christian name, but Mama was a stickler for protocol. She had told him he was Millbrooke now and would forever be Millbrooke.

"Everything went smoothly, Mama," he said, kissing her cheek.

"I am glad to hear that. Mr. Clarke wasn't too longwinded, was he? He has a tendency to wander with his words."

"No. It was a lovely service."

"If you will excuse me, I must go and freshen up before the other mourners arrive."

He watched her go and then turned to his aunt. "How is she?"

"Lost," Aunt Agnes said. "Alice's entire world revolved around your father. I fear it will be some time before she finds her footing."

"I cannot thank you enough for coming to Kent with us. I do not wish to impose upon you, but do you think you could stay a while? Mama is going to need you. As her closest friend, you know her the best."

"I am glad you brought that up, Millbrooke."

"Val," he insisted.

She smiled, her eyes bright. "Val," she corrected. "I was going to ask you if I might stay for an extended period. I agree that having my company will help your dear Mama."

He took her hands in his. "You are always welcome at Millvale, Aunt. For as long as you wish."

"I do not want to impose upon your hospitality, but if I am to be here for any length of time, I wonder if you might allow me to bring Justina and Verina here."

"I have not seen my cousins in a good many years. Of course, feel free to have them come and stay. I believe it will be good for Lia and

Tia to have their cousins' company."

"I will write to them and let them know. I had previously written to tell them of your father's death." She paused. "Would you mind if their governess accompanies them?"

"Millbrooke is a large household. I think we can find room for my cousins and their governess."

Aunt Agnes looked relieved. "Miss Snow is a gem. She has been with us for almost five years now. It will be good for the girls to continue their studies while they are here. It would also give them—and my nieces—a chaperone, in case they wished to go riding or call in the village to have tea or do a bit of shopping. I do not know how long it might be before Alice wishes to get out and about."

"Send the letter at once to inform them we are expecting them at Millbrooke with open arms." He paused. "Is this Miss Snow chaperone enough to see them here, or should I send someone to accompany them?"

She thought a moment. "Miss Snow is five and twenty, the same as you, Val. Though gently bred, she has a maturity about her. I believe that Miss Snow, along with a maid, would be good enough. I will write to her separately and convey my expectations."

"What about the cost of undertaking such a journey?" he asked.

"Since I go to town every year for the Season, I have always provided adequate funds if for some reason I might need the girls brought to me. Kent is not that much farther than London. Miss Snow has enough to see to transportation, staying overnight at inns, and the cost of meals."

"That is good to know." He had always thought Aunt Agnes both practical and nurturing, and he was happy to have his two cousins join them at Millvale.

Smiling, she enveloped him in an embrace. "Thank you for allowing my girls to come and be with me. It is one thing to leave them behind during the Season, but it is something else altogether to leave them alone for months while I am at Millbrooke."

Val thought of Ariadne's idea of bringing children to town. His sister had voiced this to Con and him. All of them had felt neglected, being left in the country each year while their parents left for town for several months. Ariadne said she wished for the Season to be not only about attending social affairs. She wanted it to be time spent with family. The ten cousins had only come together once in all these years, about a decade ago, and Ariadne was of a mind to be close to her own children and have those children be raised, in part, alongside their cousins.

He had thought it a unique idea, and he had readily gone along with it. Now, Ariadne already had her first child, and Val would be looking for a duchess who would give him heirs. Their lives were rapidly changing, but he agreed with Ariadne that family was of utmost importance. He would enjoy spending time with his children. Having watched how little women were valued in Polite Society, he wanted more for his own girls.

The first mourners arrived. Soon, the drawing room was filled with people he had not seen in years. It still seemed odd to hear everyone address him as *Your Grace*. His carefree bachelor days were at an end. It was time to become a responsible duke and take up the mantle as head of the Worthington family.

Val only wished he had a better grasp on his duties and finances. When their guests left in a few hours, he would write to his father's solicitor. He wanted a clear picture of where he stood. If he must wed for a dowry—or if he might have the chance to wed for love. He had not been raised in a household where his parents loved one another. Marrying for love was almost unheard of in the *ton*, but his sister had done that very thing. She and Julian were madly in love, and seeing their happiness made him want the same for himself. Of course, being a duke, every unwed woman in Polite Society would set her cap for him. He would need to fight off the eager mamas thrusting their daughters into his path.

Val hoped his solicitor—and even banker—would have good news for him. He would rather wed a woman of his own choice than be forced to go after the largest dowry available.

He would make his plans on the morrow—and then begin this new chapter in his life.

Chapter Two

Val sat patiently as Fisham shaved him. He had brought his valet with him to town, and they had arrived late yesterday afternoon in anticipation for his meeting this morning with Creighton. Val had written to his father's solicitor, telling him he wanted a full accounting of his financial holdings, including all properties which he owned and every investment he was involved with. Creighton had said he would prepare all the documents for perusal and spend as long with him as Val needed in order for him to understand his situation.

He had done much of this prior to coming to town with Masters, Millvale's steward. For days, he had gone over ledgers from the past five years with the estate manager, gaining a better understanding of the crops grown by his tenants and how the estate was managed, as well as the yields of each harvest. Once he was on solid footing regarding the records of the estate, he and Masters had gone about the land for several days, meeting various tenants and allowing Val to look over things the steward was involved with. He supposed he would need to travel to each of his country estates in order to obtain a full picture of their workings, as well, but he would save that trip until a future date.

"That should do you, Your Grace," Fisham said cheerfully. "You're ready to meet with Mr. Creighton."

Even though his valet now addressed him properly, Fisham still had a lightheartedness about him, as if he were not that impressed that his employer was now a duke. He appreciated Fisham all the more for doing so. It seemed that other servants walked on eggshells about him. He knew the same would be the case once he mingled with others in Polite Society.

Val dreaded returning to the social affairs in town, simply because he was now a duke. Other men would fawn over him, agreeing with every opinion expressed from his lips, merely because he was a duke. What would be worse would be the women flocking to him. They would never see the man—only the lofty title he held. In some ways, he wished he did not have to look over the Marriage Mart in order to find himself a duchess. It might be easier to investigate his neighborhood in Kent and see if any titled noblemen had eligible daughters of a certain age that would make for a good duchess.

Rising, he said, "Thank you, Fisham," knowing his own father had never thanked a servant his entire life. He had told Val to barely acknowledge servants. That they were here to see to their employer's needs and did not require any thanks beyond the salary they received. It was one of many ways he intended to be different from his father.

"I will most likely spend the bulk of my day with Creighton, so you are free to do as you please."

"When might we return to Millvale, Your Grace?"

"If all goes well and I have my questions answered, I wish to do so after breakfast tomorrow morning."

The valet said, "I will make certain things are ready for our departure." He left the room.

Val glanced about the large bedchamber, which had belonged to his father. It had seemed incredibly odd, coming to these rooms yesterday, rooms which were now his. He had not been familiar with them because the duke was a very private man and had not even asked his own son into this inner sanctuary. Val had spent time with his father in the study downstairs, however, and he needed to go through it and see what papers had been left behind. That would be for another trip, however. Or perhaps Fisham could bundle things up for them to take back to the country and Val could study what was brought back at his leisure.

He went down the main staircase, thoughts of his father still with him. He paused on the landing, looking over the foyer, which was similar in size to his aunt and uncle's townhouse. It had only been three weeks since he and his family had gone to take tea with Uncle Arthur and Aunt Charlotte before this Season began. Lia and Tia had been on the verge of making their come-outs, as had his cousin Lucy. Val and Con were going to look after the three girls as they had Ariadne last year, making certain no rogues took advantage of them and that all three made acceptable matches with men of good character.

Then the world as he had known it ceased to exist.

Vaguely, he remembered ripping off his coat, placing it under his father's head. The duke had made strangled noises, then gibberish spilled from him. That was when Val had known for certain that his father had suffered an attack of apoplexy. Con had raced off for the doctor, while his aunt Charlotte had quickly taken charge of the situation. Mama had been like a lost sheep, trailing behind as they took her husband's body upstairs to make him more comfortable.

Pushing aside these recent, terrible memories, he made his way to the breakfast room.

Parsons greeted him. "Good morning, Your Grace. The newspapers are on the table for you. What might you care to eat this morning?"

Knowing he might be tied up all day with Creighton, he said, "Make it a hearty breakfast, Parsons. Eggs. Sausages. Ham. Bread and cheese."

The butler nodded to a footman, who quickly left the room to report to the kitchens with the order. In the meantime, a second footman approached, pouring tea for Val. He would have preferred coffee but merely nodded his thanks, taking up the first newspaper and skimming through it and then the second until his breakfast arrived.

He couldn't help but be drawn to the gossip columns, full of Society news, making an attempt to disguise who they spoke of by using only initials. He began reading about Lady P and Lord G and knew exactly whom they referred to, as would any member of the *ton*. Suddenly, something which he had always been so interested in seemed petty and insignificant. Who cared if Lady P and Lord G had been spotted in a compromising position at the previous night's ball?

Val finished his breakfast and had Parsons summon the carriage. Going outside, he climbed into it. It was incredibly grand, totally befitting a duke, as was the team of matched bays which pulled it.

As he rode down the streets of London, he thought of how lucrative the past few harvests at Millvale had been. His greatest fear was that he would need to wed a woman with a large dowry and not one of his choosing—or liking. So far, Millvale provided him with a steady income, but it remained to be seen what else his father had been involved with.

Once more, Val tried to tame the anger within him at being left out of anything regarding his ducal responsibilities. Yes, he had enjoyed life—perhaps a little too much—just as his father had instructed him to do. The only true duty he had been given had been to help Ariadne in choosing her husband, and his sister had managed to find a good man all on her own without any help from her brother. Yet now, he wished he had been more insistent about learning more in regard to the family's finances and investments. Then again, his father was not one who easily shared any kind of information and had always pushed aside all Val's requests to discover more of what lay in his future.

At least he knew that Creighton must be an excellent solicitor. Millbrooke would not have retained him for so many years if he had been deficient in any way.

He arrived at Creighton's offices and went inside.

"The Duke of Millbrooke, here to see Mr. Creighton," he told the first clerk he saw.

Immediately, the flustered man leaped to his feet. "Yes, Your Grace. You are expected. One moment. I shall bring him to you."

The clerk vanished. Moments later, a man of average height and build, looking to be in his mid-forties, appeared.

"Good morning, Your Grace. I am Creighton. May I extend my condolences to you in the loss of His Grace?"

"Yes, thank you. It was . . . quite sudden."

"If you would follow me, Your Grace, I spent all of yesterday organizing your papers in a logical fashion in order to present things to you."

They moved to a room with a large table in its center, six chairs about it. Neat piles stood atop it, with about two dozen stacks total.

"Would you care for something to drink?" asked Creighton.

"Not at the moment," he replied. "Perhaps some coffee in a couple of hours."

The solicitor's eyes flicked to the clerk who had followed them. "Make certain coffee appears in exactly two hours," he instructed.

The clerk nodded and closed the door behind him.

"You may have already found copies of many of these documents, Your Grace," Creighton began. "Naturally, my clerks always create additional copies of the originals."

"I have yet to go through my father's papers, so I am seeing all of this for the first time."

Creighton looked at him sympathetically. "You seem a most capable man, but I realize you must be somewhat apprehensive, having no knowledge regarding your financial affairs. Before we begin, let me assure you that the picture is quite rosy. Your estates flourish. His Grace chose wise managers and received the best of advice regarding his investments, which are quite diverse. You hold interests in everything from shipping to textiles to rum and tea."

Val relaxed upon hearing this. "Then thank you for the overview. It has put my mind at ease."

"That is good to hear. Shall we begin?" The solicitor reached for a stack of documents. "The first thing I wish to draw your attention to are the marriage settlements between your parents. Her Grace is to be taken care of."

"Summarize these settlements for me if you would, and then you may speak more about them in detail."

Creighton told him of the annual sum which was settled upon the duchess, to be paid in quarterly payments. Val thought the amount generous and would not have to supplement the allowance. It would see to all of Mama's needs regarding her wardrobe and other miscellaneous expenses.

"Since there is a dower house at Millvale," Creighton continued, "Her Grace is to be allowed to spend the rest of her days in it. You are to adequately staff it for her, paying the salary for those servants."

He frowned. "Must I send Mama there? She is suffering a great deal. I would not wish to banish her from her home. Besides, my aunt is now staying with us, and Aunt Agnes has sent for her daughters to come to Millvale. My own two sisters, who remain at home, are also in mourning. I would prefer us to remain together as a family, supporting one another and gathering strength."

The solicitor nodded approvingly. "It is always up to you, as the Duke of Millbrooke, to see to your family's needs. These settlements merely ensured that Her Grace had a place to go if she survived His Grace." He paused. "I think it not only wise but generous of you to wish to have Her Grace in the same house with you during these first difficult months after His Grace's passing. However, the day will come when you take on a duchess. *She* will be the one who is to run your household, not the dowager duchess."

He supposed in other families having two duchesses in a household might cause problems, but he could not envision any that would be raised between Mama and the wife he chose. Of course, if any did arise, the solution would be to have Mama move to the dower house. Val would want his duchess to fully be in charge of his households and not have the servants with divided loyalties among two duchesses.

"Continue," he said.

For the next several hours, Creighton walked him through the numerous documents. Val had always been good with numbers and could see just how shrewd—and profitable—the investments which had been made on his father's behalf were. By the time he concluded his time with Creighton, he knew without a doubt that he must be one of the wealthiest men in England. It also would give him the freedom to take a bride of his choosing and not have to consider her dowry, for which he was grateful.

"If you wish, Your Grace, I will have my clerks make copies of every document you see here. I am not aware of where His Grace stored his. They could be here in town or at his country seat. They might even be in a haphazard fashion."

"It would save me a great deal of time if you would embark upon this project, Mr. Creighton. I plan to keep everything well organized and in one place for safekeeping and accessibility."

"With fresh copies, it would help you have a clean start as to your business affairs."

"Any documents I do find, I will hold and then burn once I receive updated copies from your office. This way, I will know I have access to everything I need."

"A wise decision upon your part, Your Grace. You might choose to hire a secretary to handle both your business and personal affairs. I know His Grace did not retain one during his last several years, but you might find having one very helpful."

He would consider doing so next spring when he returned to town for the Season. He knew from experience just how hard it was to keep up with the many invitations received, much less have to worry about business affairs on top of that. By next year, he would be familiar with all the workings of his estate and beyond, having access to the complete picture. Only then would he hire a secretary, one whom he could trust.

After thanking Creighton for his time, he saw it was half-past three when he left the solicitor's offices. He ordered his coachman to take him to Lord Aldridge's townhouse. He knew by now that Ariadne and Julian would be in residence, along with little Penelope. He was eager to meet his first niece.

Half an hour later, he arrived at the marquess' townhouse. He presented his card to the footman who opened the door, having had the forethought to set aside his Marquess of Claibourne calling cards, replacing with them ones he found in his father's desk drawer.

"Come in, Your Grace," the footman said.

A butler joined them, and the footman handed the card over to him.

"I am in town for the day and hoped I might see my sister and brother-in-law if they are in town," he told the butler.

"They have just begun tea, Your Grace." Looking to the footman, he added, "Retrieve an extra cup from the kitchens and bring it to the drawing room at once."

The butler smiled. "If you will come upstairs, Your Grace, I will take you to Lord and Lady Aldridge."

The look on Ariadne's face was priceless when he entered the drawing room. She sprang to her feet, dashing across the room, throwing herself into his arms.

"Val!" she cried. "What a delightful surprise." She kissed both his cheeks and took his hand, leading him back to where her husband and the teacart sat.

Julian rose, offering his hand to Val. "It is good to see you, Val. I am so very sorry to learn of your father's passing."

"Sit, sit," Ariadne insisted, handing over her own cup and saucer to him. "How is Mama? I have written to her but only received a few lines from her."

"She is heartbroken, Sis," he shared. "Thank goodness, Aunt Agnes returned to Millvale with us. They have been close friends for many years, and I know she is a comfort to Mama."

"Will she stay a while? If not, perhaps we should go to Millvale ourselves."

"That will not be necessary," he assured his sister. "In fact, Aunt Agnes has sent for Verina and Justina. I believe they will be with us through the spring and summer. Possibly longer."

Concern filling her eyes, Ariadne asked, "And how are the twins? Oh, I know they were so looking forward to making their come-outs this spring. They must be so disappointed."

He shrugged. "They are experiencing mixed emotions. You know they were never close to Millbrooke. Lia has accepted the situation, as her practical nature is wont to do. Tia, on the other hand, is always a little more fiery. She is upset their plans were so abruptly ended to mourn a man they saw little and spoke even less to."

"I knew it would hit them both hard. Tia, in particular, though I daresay that Tia is one who might choose to enjoy a few Seasons before she settles into marriage. Lia, on the other hand, is more nurturing in nature. I believe she will be eager to wed and begin a family of her own."

"Speaking of families. I am ready to meet my niece."

While his sister's face softened, Julian's smile broadened.

"Penelope will be down any minute now," his brother-in-law shared. "Her nursemaid brings her to us once she has awakened from her nap each afternoon."

"Will you allow my brother to hold his niece?" Ariadne asked, her brows arching.

Julian laughed. "I suppose I could share our daughter for a few minutes."

He laughed. "Considering I intend to be her favorite uncle, I think that wise."

A few minutes later, the nursemaid appeared in the drawing room with Penelope in her arms. Without asking, she handed the babe over to her father. Julian looked as if he were very comfortable holding her.

He looked to Val. "I had never been around a babe until Ariadne produced this creature of perfection. At first, I was a bit afraid to hold her, fearing she was too fragile for my big, rough hands." He kissed Penelope's head tenderly. "But now, it is second nature."

Ariadne chuckled. "I have to fight my own husband to get time with her."

"Are you ready to hold her?" Julian asked.

"Teach me what I need to know."

Julian placed Penelope in Val's arms, emphasizing that her head and neck should always be supported. He looked down at the tiny babe, who had big eyes, and she studied him with curiosity. Val found himself cooing to her, telling her all about himself and her other aunts who would be jealous that he had met her before they had.

"You must come to Millvale, Penelope," he said. "Your grandmama will be happy to meet you."

She gurgled at him, and then she smiled. Something tugged at his heart, and he knew without a doubt he was ready for children of his own. Not simply because he wished for an heir, but because he simply wanted them for themselves.

Glancing to Ariadne, he asked, "Why did our parents have so little to do with us, Sis? I look at Penelope and think she is wonderful."

"I know. We were never a priority for them. At least I grew closer to Mama because of making my come-out last spring, but I never really knew much about Papa."

"I spent more time with him than you girls did, but I cannot say I truly knew him." He kissed his niece's brow, causing her to gurgle.

"Your idea of bring our children to town each spring when the Season begins is a good one."

"I am glad you think so. Having had Penelope, I cannot ever imagine leaving her at Aldridge Manor for a day, much less for several months."

Val nodded, standing and handing his sister her babe. "Parents should see their children often instead of abandoning them to come to town each Season. I also like the idea of my children being close to your children. Cousins should know one another. They should be not only family, but friends, as Con and I always have been."

They talked a while longer, and then he told them he was going back to Millvale tomorrow morning.

"Should we come soon?" Ariadne asked.

"No. Enjoy the Season. Mama will be happy with Aunt Agnes as company, not to mention her nieces. I think it will be good for Lia and Tia to have their cousins with them. They will form strong bonds over the next few months together. And Verina will then make her come-out with the twins next year."

"I assume you will look after our sisters as you did me," Ariadne said. "Help them in finding a husband."

He chuckled. "I will try. You seem to have found Julian all on your own, with no help from Con or me." He looked to his brother-in-law. "But with three of them making their come-outs, I will need to count on you and Con to help them find advantageous marriages with men who are respectful. After all, you are family, Julian."

"I appreciate that, Val. Having no family of my own, your accepting me into yours means a great deal to me."

"Goodbye, Sis," he said, kissing Ariadne's cheek and then Penelope's. "Keep writing Mama. I will encourage her to write you, as well. And the twins."

They walked him out to his carriage, and Julian wished him a safe trip back to Millvale. He waved goodbye, blowing a kiss to his niece.

She had no idea who he was now, but Val planned to be an active part of Penelope's life and all his nieces and nephews, as well his own children. His parents had done him and sisters a disservice, not getting to know them. It was a new day dawning in his family, and Val planned to lead the others in this endeavor.

He only hoped he would make the right choice when he selected his duchess—and that she would agree to become actively involved in the raising of their children and in her new family's lives.

Chapter Three

Eden added up the sums with her pencil, scribbling figures for the cost of their journey from Cumberland to Kent. She had kept a running total of what she had spent and would present the information to Lady Traywick when they arrived at Millvale. The carriage jostled her, so she paused a moment, looking across at her two charges. Lady Verina was ten and six, while Lady Justina was a year younger. The girls were asleep, their heads resting against one another.

Oh, how she had come to love them. They had been ten and eleven when she had come to Traywick Manor, having lost their father and brother in a carriage accident when they were but two and four years of age. Neither remembered much about these two loved ones, having been so young at the time of their passing. They were close to their older brother, Lord Traywick, who had inherited his father's title at the tender age of ten. Though the earl was away at university for much of the year, he would join in on the girls' lessons at times when he was home for the holidays or accompany the three of them when they went out riding. Lord Traywick had one year left at university, and then he would join his mother in town for the Season each year.

She thought it would be good for the girls to have their brother as an escort to the various social events when they made their come-outs. The earl could also look closely at the suitors his sisters attracted. Verina was a very pretty girl, and by the time she made her come-out, Eden thought she would be beautiful. Verina was also a little too trusting, so having both her mother and brother guide her through the Season would be ideal.

Justina, on the other hand, was strong-willed for one so young. Eden did not envy Lord Traywick having to rein in his sister when she was introduced into Polite Society. If she were this opinionated and stubborn at ten and five, Justina would be quite hard to handle by the time her own come-out occurred.

Sighing, she thought how she had never been able to make her own come-out. After she retreated to the dower house with Mama, the new Viscount Brownley, barely one and twenty, had made it perfectly clear to them that they were a burden he had no interest in bearing. Mama had spoken up, telling Brownley that she would not be around much longer, which had silenced the entitled dolt. Shamed, he had retreated, not calling upon them again until after Mama's death five months later.

It had been a difficult time. Not only did Eden have to watch her mother slowly slip away one day at a time, Brownley provided nothing for them. Polly had come with them and stayed in the dower house, helping Eden to physically care for her mother. Both she and Polly had also split the housekeeping between them, and Eden had learned to become self-sufficient. Cook would send meals when she could, but for the most part, she merely sent food, which Eden and Polly, between them, had learned how prepare.

When she sent word of Mama's death to the house, Brownley had finally visited. Eden had sternly told him that he would pay for Mama's burial in the Snow family plot, and so Mama was laid to rest next to Papa. Her cousin also told Eden she had one month to vacate Brownstone lands. Knowing this was coming, she had actually obtained employment.

Eden, using the last of the pin money she and Mama had saved, took the mail coach to Carlisle in Cumberland. She had continued her correspondence with Miss Barnes, her former governess. While Miss

Barnes thought the Lake District beautiful and enjoyed teaching her two young charges, the governess missed Kent—and the local vicar. Mr. Mason convinced Miss Barnes they were meant to be man and wife, despite both being in their early forties, so when Eden found herself in need of employment, Miss Barnes suggested that her former student take her place in Carlisle. The governess even spoke to Lord Kessley, her employer, about the arrangement, and he had agreed.

Miss Barnes remained with Eden for a week, helping her settle into a new household and her role as governess to two young girls. Then she departed for Aylesworth and her vicar.

Only then did the trouble begin.

It had nothing to do with governessing and everything to do with Lord Kessley. Eden took to teaching and quickly grew fond of the earl's two young daughters. She also liked Lady Kessley, a timid creature who liked to read and sew. The countess gave Eden two hours each afternoon to herself so that she might spend time with her daughters.

She had enjoyed that free time in the beginning. Strolling in the gardens. Reading in the library. Even going out on horseback. But Lord Kessley began showing up wherever she was. At first, she was polite to him. After all, he was her employer. Then he began overtly flirting with her, and she tried to remain cold and distant, not wanting to encourage his advances. Still, he pursued her, trying to charm her, which she was having none of.

He finally caught her alone in the gardens one afternoon. She had seen a guest arrive and go into the viscount's study and felt safe enough to walk the gardens. She had taken to staying in her cramped room and reading there each afternoon, trying to avoid his company. That afternoon, though, she was eager to get some air with the viscount being occupied. His guest must have left soon after his arrival—and some servant must have revealed where Eden had gone—because Lord Kessley showed up while she sat in the gazebo.

At first, he had asked about his daughters' progress, and she was lulled into thinking he truly cared for them. When his questions turned more personal in nature, she rose, telling him she was uncomfortable and wished to return to the house. He had caught her as she hurried away, slamming her against a tree. Pressing his body against hers, the bulge in his breeches hard. He had forced kisses upon her, kisses she neither wanted nor liked.

When his tongue slipped into her mouth and his hand went under her dress, Eden had had enough.

She bit him. Hard.

He had jerked away, raging at her. He had even slapped her, the sting painful. Eden had raced away, panicked. Hurrying to her room, she had locked the door, studying her image in a small hand mirror. The imprint of his hand remained for a good while, even as dread built within her.

Knowing she could not stay in this household any longer, she packed her things, waiting for the summons she knew would come. She had returned to the schoolroom, the girls jabbering away, and Eden tried to conduct a new lesson, hoping to keep things normal. The housekeeper herself had appeared in the doorway of the schoolroom, telling her that the earl had requested her presence in the library. The woman's eyes held sympathy in them, and she realized that this was not the first time a governess had been dismissed.

Both Lord and Lady Kessley waited for her, the countess wringing her hands, her gaze focused on her lap, not wishing to meet Eden's eyes. The earl smirked at her when he addressed her.

"It has come to my attention that you are lacking, Miss Snow," he began. "Your former governess, Miss Barnes, had a great deal of experience. I was reluctant to let her go and have you as a replacement, seeing as this is the first post you had ever held. Against my better judgment, I allowed Miss Barnes to leave and decided to employ you for a trial period."

Nothing about a trial period had ever been voiced, and she raged inside as the viscount rewrote the past.

"While I know my girls have already developed tender feelings for you, you are not a good fit for them and are not meeting their educational needs," he had continued. "You are to be immediately dismissed. I see no need to provide references when you have done such a poor job."

"It will be almost impossible to gain another post without references," she had said. "Neither you nor Lady Kessley has expressed any doubts about my performance. Until now."

He had eyed her maliciously. "I am sure it is hard for you to recognize how you might come up short, Miss Snow. Lady Kessley and I wish for better for our girls. I will graciously have someone take you into Carlisle tomorrow so that you might catch the morning mail coach."

The earl had eyed her, defying her to speak. Though she had received her first quarterly payment, he mentioned nothing of the upcoming one due her. She doubted even if she asked for a portion of it that he would acquiesce.

"Then I will finish this afternoon's lessons," she said, her head held high.

"You are not to see them again," Lord Kessley said, cutting her to the quick.

"Not even to say goodbye?" she asked.

"You are done. Go to your room," he ordered.

Eden had done just that, crying quietly, worrying who the next governess would be. The housekeeper had a tray sent to her room for dinner, and she picked at it. She had very little money and no idea of where to go. With no reference from Lord Kessley, it would be next to impossible to find employment.

The next morning, Lady Kessley had come to Eden's room. She gave her a few pounds and apologized, saying she knew nothing was her fault. That her husband had already run off two other governesses. Miss Barnes had been older, past forty, and the countess thought that had solved their problems.

"My mother lives in Keswick," Lady Kessley had said, handing Eden a folded note. "Her address is on the front. Go to her. She has just written to me about a friend of hers who is in need of a governess. I have told her you would be a good choice. Mama will see that you get the post."

She'd had enough money to reach Keswick. Barely. And she had gone to the countess' mother, giving her the note. The woman's lips had pursed, and she had murmured something about her son-in-law up to it again. Still, she had arranged for Eden to meet with her friend.

And Lady Traywick had saved her.

Justina and Verina had been present when she called upon Lady Traywick for tea. It was obvious she took to the girls and they to her. When tea ended, the countess had offered Eden the position, which she had gratefully accepted. She had now spent five years watching the two sitting across from her start to grow into being young women. She had also gained confidence in her governessing skills and knew when the time came and Lady Justina made her come-out in three years, she would be able to find another position with ease.

She returned to her journal and finished adding up the costs of the trip to present to Lady Traywick. The older woman had always shown great kindness to Eden, treating her more as a relative than the hired help. She doubted Lady Traywick would even look at the figures Eden now tallied, but she wanted her employer to know she had been responsible with the funds she had been given in which to make this journey.

The carriage bumped again, waking both Verina and Justina.

"How much longer?" Justina asked. "It seems as if we have been on the road forever."

"I agree," Verina said. "It has been a week, Miss Snow."

"We last changed horses at Maidstone. There will be one more change, and then we should arrive at Millvale," she replied. "I believe we should reach His Grace's estate in time for tea this afternoon."

"Oh, a decent tea," Verina said, sighing. "I am so ready to be in one spot again. One bedchamber to sleep in. Not living out of a trunk. My limbs are tired, and I haven't even moved much at all today."

"I hate long carriage rides," Justina declared. "When I wed, I will make certain that my husband lives close to town. I cannot imagine having to go back and forth for days on end on the road as we have done this past week. No wonder Mama has always left us at Traywick Manor when she goes to the Season."

"It must be the reason we never visited with our cousins more," Verina pointed out. "Millvale is in Kent, and we know now how far it is from our home. And Marleyfield is in Somerset. That is also a long way from Traywick Manor and the Lake District."

"I think it will be fun to see our cousins again," Justina said. "I remember Val and Con being the oldest. They managed to be in trouble that entire week we cousins were together." She paused. "Do you remember Tia and Lia?" she asked her sister.

"A little. They were a couple of years older than I was. I recall Dru the most. She was only a year older. You and I played with her more."

"I think it so sad that their father died so suddenly and made them miss their come-outs," Justina said.

"They cannot help that their father passed when he did," Eden said gently. "They will be sad about his death and the fact they are missing their come-outs. It will be good that they will have the two of you to talk with. Be generous with your time and nurturing with your spirits."

"Their mourning period will be up by next spring," Verina said. "That means Tia and Lia can make their come-outs, along with Cousin Dru. She should be doing so." She looked to her sister. "Perhaps Mama will let us come to town with her next spring. I know we cannot attend any events since we will not be out, but it would be good to be with Mama and perhaps see something of our cousins."

"I would like that so much," Justina declared. "Miss Snow, perhaps if you suggest that very thing to Mama, she will allow us to do so. Mama trusts you implicitly. If you say it is good for us, she will let us accompany her to town. You would come, too. Have you ever been to town?"

"We should concentrate on other things for now," she said crisply. "However, I do think it would be a good idea for you to have some time in the city before you are officially seen at events. There are all kinds of lessons that we could do while there. And it would be helpful for Justina to see what Verina goes through as she makes her come-out in two years' time. It would prepare you more thoroughly for your own. When the time comes, I will speak to Lady Traywick about this."

"Thank you, Miss Snow," the sisters said in unison, chatting happily about what they would be doing at Millvale and how they would become reacquainted with their cousins and aunt again.

These girls were so happy. This would be a good trip for them, and time spent bonding with their cousins would be nice. Whether Verina and Justina knew it or not, their presence would lighten the sadness felt by their aunt and their cousins.

And the duke, she supposed.

Her charges had barely mentioned His Grace. He had been so much older than they the only time this group of cousins had been brought together. Eden couldn't help but wonder how this new duke was settling into his role as head of the family, especially because his father's death had come so unexpectedly. Then again, it was none of her business. A duke would have nothing to do with a governess. She might see him occasionally in passing, but he would be far too busy to take notice of her.

At least that's what she told herself.

It had been a blessing to be at Traywick Manor all these years, with no gentleman to avoid. Lord Traywick was six and ten when Eden had arrived. He was a happy young man and a good brother to his sisters. She had never felt threatened by his presence. Going to a new household, however, where a powerful duke resided, did give her pause for thought. She did not want to have anything to do with this duke. She would go out of her way not to draw his notice. Eden was far too happy with her current post to want to leave it.

She only hoped the Duke of Millbrooke would be respectful and behave himself in a gentlemanly fashion, especially with his mother, aunt, and so many young ladies present in his household.

Let me be safe, she thought as the carriage rolled on, bringing them closer and closer to Millvale.

Chapter Four

They arrived at Millvale, all of them glancing out the window at the beautiful estate, full of rolling hills with green grass and large trees shading the lane they drove up. Eden had thought Traywick Manor gorgeous, but then again, this was the country seat to a duke. She had heard Kent was the loveliest county in England. After driving through it and now being at Millvale, she tended to agree.

"Do you think Val will act like a duke?" Justina mused.

Verina nodded. "He must. After all, he is one. I do understand what you are saying, though. He was a lively boy. But dukes must be sober. They are the leaders of Polite Society, only slightly lower than a prince in rank."

"Remember, even though he is your cousin, you are to address him as Your Grace at all times," she reminded her charges. "He may give you leave to call him Millbrooke in private, when it is just the family gathered together, but even his mother will address him formally now that he is the head of the family."

"More of those rules," Justina said, shaking her head in disgust. "I am glad Verina will make her come-out before I do. I do not like rules."

"You are a well-behaved girl, Justina," Eden said. "It will not be hard for you to follow rules when you make your come-out. It will be helpful that Verina will have made her debut before you, however. You will be able to learn from her experience. And speaking of rules, I shall be calling you Lady Verina and Lady Justina from now on. I know I have relaxed when it has just been the three of us, but living in a duke's household, we must be on our best behavior."

"Do you wish you could have made your come-out, Miss Snow?" Verina asked.

She had told the girls the barest details of her background, merely saying that she was genteel but had become impoverished. They had been respectful and not pressed her overmuch as to why. Since she was a governess, they would at least understand she had to earn her living.

"You know I have told you it was not possible for me to make my come-out," she told them. My father was killed in a riding accident. I cared for my mother, who was quite ill herself. When she passed, then I came to look after the two of you."

She had always left out the part about her odious cousin's demand that she vacate Brownstone, as well as the fact there had been another household between her own and theirs. The thought of even mentioning the loathsome Lord Kessley caused her belly to roil.

"I would wager that you would have captured the heart of several eligible bachelors," Justina ventured. "You are quite pretty, Miss Snow. Some would even say beautiful. Though you dress rather plainly."

"As is befitting for a governess to two young ladies," she said, smiling brightly.

Oh, but how Eden wished she could have worn the ballgowns she and her mother had dreamed of her wearing. To dance with titled noblemen. To flirt a bit. Perhaps to have even engaged in a stolen kiss here and there.

She shook her head, pushing aside those girlish dreams. She would live vicariously through Verina if Lady Traywick allowed Justina and her to come to town. By the time Justina made her come-out, though, Eden would be gone, working in another household. The thought saddened her, and she told herself to live one day at a time and not borrow trouble. The future would come, and she would be prepared for it, but she should enjoy what happiness she had today. She had two sweet, kind girls to teach, and Lady Traywick was wonderful to her, treating her almost as a member of the family.

That would change during their stay at Millvale, however. While she always took her meals with the girls and Lady Traywick, it would be different in a duke's household. She supposed she would either eat in the servants' hall or have a tray in her room. If given the choice, she would opt for the tray. Some servants were uncomfortable around a governess, who was consider an upper servant, and Eden would not want to make trouble while here at Millvale.

"I see the house!" Justina cried. "Oh, my. Look at it. It is enormous!"

Her charge was right about that. The house was the largest she had ever laid eyes upon, reminding her again that they were now on a duke's property.

"I hope we can go riding while we are here," Verina said.

"Most likely, the duke's stables will be large. I will speak to your mother about it. She can convey to His Grace your wish to ride. And your two cousins might also enjoy riding. If they do, I am happy to chaperone you all on rides together."

"Are they expecting us?" Verina asked. "I do not see anyone outside yet."

"I gave Lady Traywick an idea of when we might arrive, but I was not able to provide the exact date. You saw how the roads were. Unpredictable, at best."

"Wait, I see Mama!" Justina said, her excitement obvious. "And I think that must be Aunt Alice with her."

Eden liked how close these girls were to their mother. It reminded her of her own relationship with her mother. From what Lady Traywick had mentioned on previous occasions, that was rare within the *ton*. She had been close to both her parents and hadn't a clue why other parents and children were not. Eden supposed life had worked out as it should have because she would not have ignored her children as other parents did. Being a governess gave her the opportunity to be around children and watch them mature.

The carriage began to slow and then came to a stop. Lady Traywick rushed to the door, waiting as the footman opened it.

"My girls!" she said, holding her arms wide.

Justina bounded from the carriage first, with Verina close behind. Both of them embraced their mother, who was now crying tears of joy at being reunited with her daughters. She had witnessed similar scenes between the three each year the countess returned from the Season.

"Oh, I am so happy you came," Lady Traywick said, looking up as Eden was handed down by a footman. "And Miss Snow. I am grateful to you for having brought my girls to me."

"I was happy to do so, my lady," she said demurely. "It will also be good for them to continue their lessons while they are at Millvale."

"I could not agree more. Come, say hello to your aunt."

Eden stood beside the carriage as this reunion occurred. Footmen lowered the trunks on top. Bessie, the maid who had accompanied them from Cumberland, climbed from where she had sat next to the driver. The maid would care for the girls during their stay at Millvale.

"They're happy to see her ladyship," she remarked to Eden.

"Yes, they are."

"This will be a real adventure for us, won't it, Miss Snow?"

"It will, Bessie. We are blessed to have been able to come to Kent."

"I hope the housekeeper won't put me in a closet. Looking at this house, there's plenty of room."

"I am certain you will be taken care of accordingly."

She watched as the wan duchess greeted her nieces and then motioned for them to accompany her inside.

A woman whom Eden suspected was the housekeeper came toward Bessie and her. "Good afternoon. I am Mrs. Quigby, the housekeeper at Millvale."

"I am Miss Snow, governess to the two young ladies, and this is Bessie, who will be the maid taking care of them."

"I have rooms for you both," Mrs. Quigby said genially. "Bessie, you will be sharing with one of our new maids. Miss Snow, you will have a room to yourself. Come inside and let me show you where you will be as soon as I get the young ladies settled. Quigby will take you to the kitchens for now. I'm sure you could use a cup of tea."

"Thank you, Mrs. Quigby," Eden said.

The housekeeper led the new Millvale guests upstairs, while the butler took them to the kitchens. Cook greeted them, settling them at a table and getting them a cup of tea.

"I'm readying tea now for the family," Cook said. "Didn't know for certain when you would arrive. Give me a minute to get that together, then I'll give you each a slice of ginger cake."

"That would be lovely, Cook," she said, seating herself at the table and mixing a bit of cream into her tea. She noted no sugar present and knew some households kept it in reserve for the family only.

Cook chatted with them as she arranged items for the teacart, telling them a little about the house and grounds, as well as naming several of the other servants. Eden merely enjoyed her tea and the fact that she was no longer bumping along roads in a carriage. She was glad Lady Traywick had written they would most likely stay until the end of summer because she was not looking forward to making the long journey back to Traywick Manor anytime soon.

Quigby made another appearance, asking, "Is tea ready, Cook? Her Grace is taking the others to the drawing room now."

"Yes, the teacarts are ready to go."

The butler signaled two maids who had accompanied him, and they rolled both carts away.

"Now, let me get you some cake," Cook said. "Then I want to get off my feet for a few minutes and join you."

Soon, they had plates before them, and Eden thought the ginger cake moist and tasty. She was only a few bites into it when Mrs. Quigby appeared, looking a little flustered.

"Miss Snow? You are to join the family in the drawing room," she said, seeming out of breath, and Eden thought she must have run from the drawing room to the kitchens.

"That is not necessary," she said.

"The young ladies are insisting," the housekeeper said. "Lady Traywick, too."

Feeling awkward, she rose and excused herself, following the housekeeper.

On the way, she said, "Often, it is just Lady Verina and Lady Justina and me. We take tea and our meals together. I was not expecting to do so here at Millvale."

Mrs. Quigley stopped. "It is most unusual. No governess I have ever known has socialized with the family."

"I will join them for tea today, but I will speak with Lady Traywick and help her to understand the circumstances are different here than at Traywick Manor."

"It would be best if you did," the housekeeper agreed.

The housekeeper started up the stairs, and Eden followed her, her belly churning violently. She prayed that the others had started tea without her. Keeping a duke and his family waiting was the last thing she wanted to do. This incident would only draw unwanted attention to her. She wished she would have thought to talk to the girls about this.

They reached the drawing room. "Slip inside," Mrs. Quigby advised, and Eden did so, heading across the room to the far side where the large group was gathered.

She saw Lady Traywick and Her Grace seated together. Verina and Justina sat on a settee, as did two other girls, whom she assumed to be Lady Tia and Lady Lia, the cousins and sisters to the new duke.

On another settee sat an incredibly handsome man. He caught sight of her, watching as she walked the length of the room as the others chattered away.

Then he rose, and the others noticed her as she arrived.

"Miss Snow," the duke said. "Won't you join us?"

Nerves flitted through her as she saw the only place to sit was beside him.

"I should not be here, Your Grace," she said firmly, letting her governess persona out in order to remedy the situation. "I was having tea in the kitchens with your cook. The ginger cake is lovely."

His eyes gleamed, giving her a sick feeling. "I have always been fond of ginger cake myself. But you must stay. My aunt and cousins say you always take tea with them. Dine with them, as well."

Her heart fluttering now, Eden knew she must stand her ground, even if this man were a duke. She had let one nobleman take advantage of her before. She would not show any sign of weakness with this one.

"I should have explained to my charges that while we are a more relaxed household at Traywick Manor, especially when Lady Traywick is in town for the Season, things are vastly different here at Millvale."

His gaze pierced her. "And how would you know how things are at Millvale, Miss Snow? Please, stay."

In that moment, she understood that despite the fact he had used the word *please* in his request, she was being given a command. Not wishing to appear to rock the proverbial boat, she nodded.

"Of course, Your Grace. Thank you kindly."

Eden took a seat, and the duke sat beside her. He was a large, muscular man, and he smelled heavenly. A clean, crisp citrus scent that filled her nostrils and made her almost giddy.

The duchess handed a cup and saucer to her, and she thanked her.

"We told Val that you always have tea with us," Justina told Eden. "That it would be wrong to keep you away."

Trying to keep her hands steady so that she did not dump tea on herself—or the duke—she said, "Remember that we spoke of formalities, my lady."

Justina brightened. "Oh, Val does not wish us to call him His Grace. Verina and I told him you had instructed us on the correct forms of address, but he simply wishes to be Val to us."

She couldn't help but turn to look at him. "Your Grace, I know you are new to your title, but your cousins should be more respectful of—"

"You are right, Miss Snow, in pointing out that I have not been Millbrooke for long. I am already weary of hearing *Your Grace* a hundred times a day. When only my family is present, I wish to be called Val." He paused, smiling at her. "For Valentinian. You see, our parents named each of us after emperors and empresses."

"Yes, I am well aware of your family's tendency to do so. My charges and I have even studied various Roman and Byzantine rulers and their wives, becoming familiar with those each of the cousins have been named after."

He smiled at her, his teeth white and even, his cheekbones sharp and prominent. "I might wish to sit in on one of these history lessons. I have always enjoyed learning."

She felt her face flush with heat and quickly looked back to her tea, taking a sip, willing herself to calm down. He was a terrible flirt, and she was having none of it.

"Well, I shall address you as Millbrooke," Her Grace said. "It is simply how things should be. A mother should use her son's title. It is a point of pride."

"I find I am growing comfortable calling you Millbrooke, as well," Lady Traywick said.

One of the duke's sisters smiled at Eden. She had auburn hair and deep, blue eyes. "We have not been introduced yet, Miss Snow. I am Lady Lia, short for Cornelia." She indicated her sister, whom Eden recalled was her twin. The other girl favored Lady Lia in the face, but she had strawberry blond hair and eyes as blue as a summer sky.

"This is my twin, Lady Tia, a diminutive for Thermantia," Lady Lia concluded.

"It is a pleasure to meet both of you, my ladies," she said.

"I think only we young people will be calling my ducal brother Val. And then, it will only be in private at occasions such as tea." Lady Lia smiled. "My cousins insisted you join us this afternoon. I hope you are comfortable doing so."

Her head held high, she merely said, "I appreciate the invitation."

Eden remained quiet the rest of tea, letting the others talk as the cousins got to know one another. She was very aware, however, of the duke sitting next to her. He was so large that he took up a good deal of the settee, causing their thighs to press together every now and then. He generated an enormous amount of heat, much as if she sat next to an open fire, and she wished she could fan herself. Having no fan with her, she suffered in silence.

As tea concluded, Verina and Justina asked Eden to accompany them to their room so she would know where it was located.

"We can see if you are close to us, Miss Snow," Verina said.

"I have yet to be taken to my room, my lady. We shall see."

The duke rose, so they all did. "I have some business to attend to. I will see you all at dinner." Then he looked to her, and Eden felt her cheeks heat. "You should be given a bedchamber next to my cousins, Miss Snow. They seem to depend upon you a great deal. If Mrs. Quigby has not done so, see that remedied."

"Yes, Your Grace," she replied, afraid to meet his gaze, much less tell his housekeeper which room she should be given.

"That would be more convenient," Justina said. "And where are we to have our lessons, Miss Snow?"

"After I have seen your bedchamber, we can go and look at the schoolroom."

"That won't do," said the duke, frowning. "My sisters have not used it for years. It is set up for much younger children than Verina and Justina."

Boldly, she asked, "Then where would you suggest I hold lessons, Your Grace?"

He smiled. "Why, I believe the library would be appropriate, Miss Snow. In fact, I will show it to you now before you take off with my cousins. Come along." To his cousins, he added, "I will send Miss Snow to you directly once she sees if the library is an appropriate place for your lessons."

Turning, he held his hand out, indicating for her to leave, and she stepped from the settee, walking beside him the length of the room.

When they reached the corridor and were out of sight, however, Eden said, "I prefer not to go anywhere with you, Your Grace. Please give me directions to the library, and I will determine its suitability for my charges."

"You are a prickly thing," Then ignoring what she had just said, he said, "The library is this way, Miss Snow."

The duke moved away from her, and Eden followed him, walking a good ten feet behind him, determined not to show weakness and assert herself once and for all.

Chapter Five

Miss Snow intrigued Val.

More than she should have.

She had entered the drawing room, catching his eye immediately. Hers was a fresh, natural beauty, using no enhancements as some women of the *ton* were wont to do. She dressed plainly, her honey-blond hair pulled back severely, which only emphasized her beautiful bone structure and hazel eyes. He'd had an immediate longing to take down her hair to see how long it was.

This was madness. He was a duke. A man rarely affected by any woman. She was a governess. They had only just met. There could be no relationship between them, especially because she served as a teacher to his two young cousins.

Then why was he so taken with her?

Possibly because she was unattainable. She was an employee of his aunt's. Nothing more, nothing less. Val had always been drawn to a challenge. Knowing he could not have any kind of relationship with her only made him want to do so, though. He would have to be careful. Not only did he have the eyes of his sisters upon him, but his cousins were also present. He would need to watch his step and not give these girls even the hint of impropriety on his part.

As he strode down the corridor, hoping she followed him to the library, he wondered how Miss Snow had wound up in her sad situation. From his understanding, most governesses were impoverished gentlewomen who'd had no chances of making a match. Since they had not wed and oftentimes no one in their families wanted them underfoot, they had been sent out to earn their living as governesses or companions.

But who would not have wanted this magnificent creature?

He liked that she had stood up to him. For all his affability, Val was a stubborn, determined man, one used to having his way. His own family knew not to cross him—and that was before he even became a duke. And yet, here was this beautiful stranger, in a lowly position. She had not wanted to be present at tea and voiced her opinion that she would look at the library on her own.

Well, Miss Snow would simply have to deal with the fact that he was a duke and destined to get his way. If he wanted to show Miss Snow the bloody library, then that is what he would do.

Still, he couldn't help but wonder about her background and why she had not wed. Since Aunt Agnes had mentioned to him that they were the same age, Miss Snow would have made her come-out while he was at Oxford. Val could not imagine her not receiving a plethora of offers. His aunt had also said that Miss Snow had been with them for five years or so. Either she had not had any offers or she had rejected them. Even with her great beauty, if she had no dowry to back it up, many gentlemen would not have given her a moment's thought. Perhaps even her family had been too poor for her to do a Season and had sent her directly to work.

Val determined to learn something of her while they were alone, especially since she would be residing under his roof and in his care.

When he reached the library door, he paused before it. Glancing to his right, he saw Miss Snow had followed him. Her face was hard to read, however. She would make for an excellent player at cards because of that.

"This is the library," he announced, opening the door and ushering her inside.

He watched as she walked about the room, standing with his hands behind his back, admiring the slender curve of her neck and the look on her face as she studied all about her. Miss Snow moved up and down the length of the room, and he tried to see the library through her eyes.

It had several groups of seating throughout. One table was exclusively used for chess, and the chessboard was set up on it, ready for two players to go toe to toe. Two other tables were used for cards, one on the far side of the room, one sitting beside a window looking out over the front lawn. Other groupings of seats, as well as two chaise lounges, also stood in the room.

Miss Snow stopped at an atlas resting on a stand, turning a few of its pages. Then she took her time perusing the shelves of books, ignoring his presence. It gave him more time to study her, however. He liked the graceful way she moved. The curve of her breasts and hips. How a solemn look crossed her face when she investigated something.

Finally, she made her way back to him.

"I hope you will consider using the library for your lessons, Miss Snow."

"It would be a wonderful place to engage my charges in their lessons," she admitted, her tone neutral. "We could use some of the tables for when the girls are working on everything from conjugating verbs to perfecting their handwriting. The room receives good light, which is always a plus in my book. It is a good library, as well. Not so extensive as to be overwhelming, but it possesses a great number of decent books within it, particularly regarding history and geography."

"I am glad you think the room appropriate."

"I must insist upon one rule, Your Grace."

"And what that might be?" he inquired, biting back a smile at a woman demanding something of him.

"That the library must remain undisturbed while lessons are in session. While Verina has excellent concentration, Justina sometimes lacks focus. If her cousins or others come and begin conversations, I am afraid I would lose her attention." She paused. "If that proves to be inconvenient, I can always use the schoolroom or even a small parlor for the girls' studies."

He thought this her way of keeping him out of the library, especially since he had expressed an interest in sitting in on a lesson every now and then. For some reason, she did not want him around.

And that only made him more curious about her.

"No, Miss Snow, the library is the best place for lessons to occur. I will make certain that Mama and my sisters understand that you need to be left alone so that my cousins are not distracted." He wondered if she noticed that he had not included himself in that group.

She inclined her head. "Thank you, Your Grace. If you will excuse me."

"Wait," he said, and she froze, her gaze falling to the floor. "Since you are to be at Millvale, I would like to know a bit about you."

Her head tipped up, their gazes meeting, and he saw fire in her eyes. It surprised him.

What surprised him more was that he liked her all the more for it.

"Begging your pardon, Your Grace, but I am not in your employment. Lady Traywick hired me. You seem to be close to your aunt, and I would suggest that you trust her judgment. She believes I am qualified to teach her daughters. That is all that matters. There is no reason for you to know anything about me. We will not be speaking to one another again, and we will only see one another in passing, if that."

Val was attracted to both her looks and her spirit. "Why do you say that, Miss Snow? We will see each other at tea every afternoon, as well as at meals."

The fire remained in her eyes as she responded. "This afternoon was an exception, Your Grace. I will not be taking tea with the family, nor will I be dining with any of you. As I mentioned earlier, it is a quiet life at Traywick Manor. For the months of the Season while Lady Traywick is gone, it is just the girls and me. Yes, I have shared meals and tea with them, but they need to prepare themselves for moving amongst Polite Society. Being in a duke's household for an extended period will be good exposure for them. I am no longer of that world. I will make this clear to Lady Verina and Lady Justina. Now, if you will excuse me."

"I will not," he said quietly, his tone still commanding.

Her eyes widened in surprise and she started to speak, then she closed her mouth. He couldn't help but look at her lips. They cried out to him, begging to be kissed. He was at a loss as to why she affected him so. They might be the same age, but he was a duke, brimming with power and youth, while she was a governess, already on the shelf. Val had always been able to have any woman he desired. Yet suddenly, he wanted a woman entirely inappropriate for him. It was not as if she were loose in her morals and would be willing to have a quick romp in the hay. This was a woman who would cling to her dignity and never make a false step as far as a man was concerned. Her entire livelihood depended upon it.

And tempted by her beauty as he was, he had never taken advantage of anyone, male or female, in any kind of situation.

"I still wish to know something of you, Miss Snow," his tone brooking no exceptions. He was determined to learn about her and how she came to be in her present situation.

She managed to look defiant and resigned at the same time, no small feat. "I am the daughter of Lord and Lady Brownley. My father's country seat was in Buckinghamshire, near Aylesbury."

Val knew of the current Lord and Lady Brownley. The viscount was but a couple of years older than he was, and Brownley and his viscountess had wicked reputations, even for Polite Society. Brownley was the kind of man who would have tossed out a relative such as

Miss Snow without a second thought. Anger seized him, his gut telling him that is what happened to this lovely young woman.

Calming his temper, he asked, "I assume your parents are no longer with us since I have met Lord and Lady Brownley, and they are not much older than the two of us."

For a moment, he saw her mouth tremble and thought she might burst into tears. Instead, she rallied, glaring at him, her hazel eyes going from green to amber.

Her voice tight, she said, "My father perished in a riding accident when I was ten and eight."

Immediately he thought that was what had prevented her from having a Season and finding a husband. Of having the life she was meant to have, instead of teaching the children of members of Polite Society.

"My cousin Edgar claimed his title since I am an only child. He was Papa's nephew."

"And your mother?" he prodded softly, sympathy filling him.

She winced. "Mama herself was in a riding accident when I was still an infant. She became bedridden after it. Around the time we lost my father, our local doctor diagnosed her with a terminal illness. I took Mama to the dower house and nursed her until her death."

Miss Snow had tears misting her eyes now, and he reached out and took her hand, squeezing her fingers gently. The governess bit her lip in an effort to maintain control, which only sent a rush of desire through Val.

"I am sorry to hear of your parents' passing. You speak of them with great tenderness."

"Yes," she said, her voice barely above a whisper. "I was always close to them both. Papa never seemed to care that I was a girl. He always took me out and about on his estate with him, and I got to interact with his tenants and understand what it was like to be a viscount. I also spent hours each day with my mother, reading to her.

Massaging her limbs. Papa and I even took tea in her bedchamber each afternoon because she was unable to leave her bed."

She swallowed, and he could see how painful these memories were for her. Losing her parents had obviously changed the entire trajectory of her life.

"I may have lost my own father, but at least I still have Mama here with me. I will admit that we are not all that close, but I do respect her."

Realizing he still held her hand, he squeezed it a final time and released it, feeling bereft even as he did so.

"I wish for you to feel at home at Millvale, Miss Snow, during your stay here. I believe it will be good for my sisters to have their cousins with them during their time of mourning. You, as well. They are missing their older sister. Ariadne wed during her come-out season and has recently given birth to her and Lord Aldridge's first child."

He smiled. "I met my niece only yesterday. I even held Penelope in my arms."

The governess looked startled by his statement and blurted out, "A duke . . . held a babe?"

"My sister and her husband have unusual ideas about how they wish their children to be brought up. The marquess dotes upon his daughter and already holds her far more often than her mother does. Poor Ariadne has to almost fight him for a chance to hold Penelope."

Her eyes grew round in wonder. "That is most unusual, Your Grace."

"Ariadne and I have talked, along with our cousin Con, about how we felt abandoned each year when our parents traveled to town for the Season. It is my sister's desire that all ten of the cousins in our family—as we wed and have children of our own—bring those children to town with us for the Season. That way, we will be able to see our children daily, and they will, in turn, be able to spend time with their cousins."

He paused "We believe family is of utmost importance."

For the first time, Miss Snow gave him a genuine smile. "That is a most unique attitude to hold, Your Grace. You seem to be a man of good character. I am sorry I have been abrupt with you and have not spoken to you in a more respectful manner. I will manage to curb my tongue in the future."

He chuckled. "Frankly, Miss Snow, I like the fact that you have stood up to me. Everyone is so bloody obsequious to me now. In fact, I dread returning to town next Season, simply because all others will see is the newly-minted duke—and not the man behind the title."

"With your ideas, Your Grace, perhaps you and your sister can change a portion of Polite Society," she suggested. "As a duke, you will have your choice of a duchess. My only advice to you would be to select her wisely, making certain she is a woman of good character who values family in the same fashion as you do.

"Now, if you will excuse me, I must go and find where my charges have been placed."

"Do not forget to see Mrs. Quigby and ask for a room nearby. There are plenty of guest bedchambers. You could be placed next door or across the hall from them. In fact, I shall see to that myself. I do not wish to put you in an awkward position, making demands of my housekeeper. Mrs. Quigby is a most conventional woman."

Her cheeks pinkened, making her even more attractive, something Val had not thought possible.

"Please, Your Grace. Do not go to such lengths on my behalf. You mentioned that you had work to do, and I do not wish to keep you from it."

"Nonsense, Miss Snow," he said jovially. "I will come with you now and check to see that my cousins have settled in, as well as see to your own bedchamber."

He saw she wanted to fight him on this but was wise enough to give in. They left the library and went to the wing housing guests at

Millvale. He discovered his cousins were sharing a bedchamber as a maid and Mrs. Quigby unpacked for them.

"Thank you for such a lovely room, Millbrooke," Justina said enthusiastically.

He caught Miss Snow nodding approvingly at her for using his title in front of the two servants.

"Aunt Agnes mentioned you have always shared a bedchamber at Traywick Manor. I see you are happy to stay together. I hope this room will be large enough to please you." He looked to his housekeeper. "Mrs. Quigby, Miss Snow has yet to be shown to her room. I would hope it would be close to my cousins since they are so dependent upon her."

The housekeeper frowned slightly and then said, "Miss Snow has been given a bedchamber, Your Grace. It is not in this wing, however."

He assumed the governess was to be sent to the attics, where other servants had their rooms. Clucking his tongue, he said, "That will not do, Mrs. Quigby. My cousins look upon Miss Snow much as an older relative. Please place her as close to Lady Verina and Lady Justina's bedchamber as you can."

"Yes, Your Grace," Mrs. Quigby said. "I will see to it at once."

The housekeeper left the room, and his cousins began showing their governess the room. He watched the interaction between them and realized what he had said was true. Verina and Justina thought of Miss Snow as an older, wiser relative, perhaps a cousin or even sister. He witnessed true warmth between the trio and was happy Aunt Agnes had found someone so nurturing to look after her girls.

"I will be off," he told the three. "I will see you all at dinner this evening."

He watched Miss Snow's brows knit together and waited for her to protest. She kept silent, however, and he nodded to them.

Val had gone halfway down the corridor when he sensed her presence. Turning, he paused, and she caught up to him.

"Your Grace, you have been more than gracious to me, but I must insist that I do not dine with the family. I am but an upper servant. I have neither the wardrobe, nor the inclination, to be present at a duke's table."

In a way, he thought it was a bit of her pride speaking. Wanting to still see her and have Verina and Justina comfortable in his household, he said, "Then we will compromise, Miss Snow. You will agree to take tea with us each afternoon, and I will allow you to dine on your own. Is that acceptable to you?"

She nodded, gratitude appearing in her eyes. "I can accept that, Your Grace. Thank you again for the use of your library for our lessons."

"I wish for your stay at Millvale to be a happy one," he told her. "Do you ride with my cousins?"

Her face lit up, and her radiant smile warmed him in a way he had never felt before.

"Oh, yes. I have always been fond of being in the saddle. Thankfully, my charges enjoy riding, as well."

"Good. I hope you will make full use of my stables then. My sisters also enjoy riding. Perhaps you would be agreeable to taking them out when you, Justina, and Verina ride together."

"I am happy to do so. Thank you again. For everything."

Val watched the governess turn and return to his cousins, the gentle sway of her hips hypnotizing him.

He felt the first battle between them had been fought—and that they both had turned out with a share in the victory.

Chapter Six

EDEN AWOKE IN the incredibly comfortable bed, relishing the feel of the mattress and luxurious sheets.

She had the Duke Millbrooke to thank for being placed in such a room.

Despite her first impression of him as simply being a handsome rogue, Millbrooke had proved to have some depth to him. She doubted even a handful of men in the *ton* had even held a babe, much less one not their own. Agreeing with his sister's idea of bringing their children to town during the Season was almost unheard of, but the duke seemed eager to go along with it. She guessed he was a man who would do nothing halfway, even in the raising of his children. Where most titled gentlemen saw their children only rarely, Millbrooke would stand out for his belief in actually having a close relationship with his children.

In some ways, the duke reminded her of Papa. Her own father had been handsome, attentive to both his child and invalid wife. He had never made Eden seem less because she had not been born a son, and he certainly continued to love and be faithful to his wife despite the fact she could not move from the waist down and would never bear him an heir. Papa had let Eden and Mama know how precious they were to him, and she could see His Grace also cared a great deal for his own family. She almost envied the lady who would become his duchess. Not only would she hold a grand title and be a leading figure in Polite Society, but she would also have a handsome husband who truly cared for his children.

"Enough," she said aloud.

Thinking about the duke this much was merely borrowing trouble. While she believed Millbrooke to be an honorable man, she did not travel in the world he ruled. Instead, she merely flitted about its edges, helping to educate his two cousins. At least he had had Verina and Justina's interests at heart. The duke was providing a wonderful place for them to continue their studies, and he had also offered the use of his stables to them.

As she washed and dressed, she even had gotten over her upset of being made to come to tea each afternoon. She reflected on tea yesterday, recalling how she had quietly listened to the conversation about her. Eden planned to do the same for future teas. She supposed Lady Traywick would try to draw her into the conversation more. Yesterday, her employer had been too excited to be reunited with her daughters to give Eden much consideration. At teatime, she supposed she might share, along with the girls, what they had been studying or where they had ridden. Small contributions would be enough of an effort on her part.

As for her other meals, she did not mind eating alone in her bedchamber. Quigby had given her the choice last night of dining in the servants' hall or having a tray brought to her room. She had opted for the latter, thinking the Millvale servants might be uncomfortable speaking in front of her. After all, she was a stranger to them. Dining in her guestroom gave her a nice respite. She was with her charges a great part of the day. She could eat in solitude, reflecting upon the day as she planned lessons for tomorrow. It would also give her time to read for her own enjoyment. His Grace's library had some excellent choices in it, and she did not think he would mind her borrowing a volume to read, as long as she returned it to the shelves.

She sat at the dressing table, a luxury she did not have at Traywick

Manor, and undid the braid she slept in each night, brushing out her honeyed hair, which she thought was her best asset. Her mother had loved to brush Eden's hair, and she closed her eyes as she ran her brush through it, her scalp tingling, recalling how much she enjoyed the attention from Mama.

Her mind wandered, and suddenly, she pictured the Duke of Millbrooke brushing it.

"Bloody hell!" she said, upset at the image, and even more upset at herself for daydreaming about something so foolish.

Placing her brush on the table, Eden stared into the mirror, wondering if the duke had found her attractive. Her hazel eyes were almost amber now, far lighter than the shades of brown and yellow they usually were. The only time her eyes went this amber was when she was upset. She silently chastised herself, then she decided not to be so hard on herself. She might be on the shelf, but it did not mean she couldn't look at and appreciate a handsome, virile man such as Millbrooke.

It had to be because she saw so few men in her life. Traywick Manor was full of women. Lord Traywick was away much of the year, though he would be leaving university after his upcoming final year of study. The guests Lady Traywick invited to visit were almost always ladies. They came for tea or to discuss a book they had all read. They talked about gardening and children and parish matters. Occasionally, the countess had guests for dinner. Eden rarely went down for those events unless the numbers were not even, and she was asked to come in order to round them out. Even so, she slipped away to her room when the ladies left the gentlemen to their port and cigars.

So, she was not used to being around titled gentlemen. And Eden could daydream all she wanted, but the Duke of Millbrooke was not for her. No man was. Millbrooke would peruse the Marriage Mart next spring, while she would continue to work with Lady Verina for another two years and Lady Justina for three. After that, Eden would need to find another family. Hopefully, they would take to her and her to them, and she would have several years of polishing new young girls into young ladies.

It was a bit sad, living such a transient life. At least she had been at Traywick Manor a good five years and had a few more years to go. Perhaps she should look for a position with even younger children next time, so that she might remain in the same household for even longer. Her thoughts drifted back to her first pupils, girls who had been only four and six years of age. They had been sweet-natured and so eager to learn. Their father had ruined Eden's time with them, and it still angered her that he had forced her from the household as if she had done something wrong instead of him.

At least she had felt safe at Traywick Manor all these years, and that feeling now extended to Millvale. If the duke had had foul intentions toward her, he would have acted upon them yesterday while they were alone in the library. Instead, he had put up with her insubordination—to a degree. She truly hoped he understood her apology to him was heartfelt. She had been raised to have exquisite manners and knew not to cross, much less insult, a duke. Millbrooke was likeable. And handsome. Not to mention the first male she had been around in a long while. Naturally, she would be drawn to him.

But her interest had to stop now. She did not want to give off any signal to him that he might misread. She was no lightskirt. She must earn her living, and that meant acting beyond reproach. Her reputation was everything. Being dismissed from Lord Kessley's household after a few months was one thing. Thanks to Lady Kessley's sympathy, Eden had been put in contact with Lady Traywick and been offered a post. To lose another position—and after so many years—would be disastrous. She would curb her tongue.

And keep her thoughts about the dreamy duke to herself.

A knock sounded, and she went to the door, finding no one in the corridor. Confused, she closed the door, only to hear a rap again. This time, she realized it came from within the bedchamber and found a door she had not previously spotted. Opening it, she saw Justina standing there.

"It is a connecting door, Miss Snow," her charge said. "Val asked at dinner last night in which room Mrs. Quigby had placed you, and he is the one who told us that these two rooms connect. Verina would not let me knock on it when we came up for bed, though."

"I did not want to awaken you if you were asleep," Verina said from where she sat, brushing her hair. "Would you mind helping me, Miss Snow?"

"Certainly," she responded, crossing the threshold and accepting the brush Verina handed to her. After smoothing the girl's locks, she created several braids and then pinned them atop Verina's head.

"You always have a way with hair, Miss Snow," Justina complimented.

"I think you should try a new hairstyle on your own hair," Verina added.

"Why?" she asked. "No one cares what my hair looks like anyway. After all, I am only the governess."

"You are a very pretty governess," Verina corrected. "And you tell Justina and I that we should always look our best and put our best foot forward. You should do the same."

"Yes, you should," seconded Justina.

"Very well. Let me go back to my bedchamber."

Both girls followed Eden into the room, watching her as she unpinned her hair.

"Your hair is a beautiful color, Miss Snow," Verina said. "It is too bad that you were not able to make your come-out, for you would have had numerous gentlemen vying for your hand."

She had shielded them from the whole, harsh truth, that of her wicked cousin booting her from her childhood home. Eden knew they would have to grow up at some point, but she wished to keep such evil from the pair as long as possible. It had surprised her, though, when she had shared as much as she had about her past with Millbrooke. She wondered why he was easy to talk to.

"You are woolgathering, Miss Snow," Justina teased.

Eden blinked. "You are right. I am not quite certain where my thoughts wandered off to."

They watched as she sectioned her hair, braiding her long strands and then pinning them up.

"You look lovely," Verina praised.

"If you ever get tired of being a governess, you could be a lady's maid," Justina declared.

"Hush," Verina told her sister. "Miss Snow is a governess. She is not a servant."

Justina's eyes welled with tears. "I did not mean to insult you, Miss Snow," she apologized.

"There is nothing wrong in being a lady's maid," she assured the girl. "They do honorable work, but I understand what Verina meant by her remark. As a former gentlewoman, it is more proper for me to take on the role of governess or companion because of my background and breeding."

"Would you ever wish to be a companion, Miss Snow?" Justina asked. "I ask because after Verina and I make our come-outs, you will have to leave us. Perhaps you could stay and be a companion to Mama. I think she would like that."

That situation would be ideal. Lady Traywick's nature was kind and undemanding. It would also give Eden a chance to see the marriages that Justina and Verina made and the children they would birth. It would be the closest thing to having a family as she would ever have.

"That is in the future," she said dismissively, not wanting to let the pair know just how desperately she might want that very situation. "I am concerned with the present. Your present. Today, we will return to our usual routine. Spelling. Poetry. History."

"But we just arrived at Millvale," Justina whined. "Tia and Lia mentioned last night at supper that we take a ride about the property today. Val said that you would chaperone us. He told us that he had given you permission to use the stables and the four of us would be allowed to ride out with you."

She swallowed the unnamed emotion thickening her throat. "While it is lovely that His Grace is allowing us the ability to continue our rides, he also knows we are to use the library for our lessons. You know we do those in the morning and ride in the early afternoon."

"I told Val as much," Verina said. "That our routine was to do lessons first and then have the afternoons to ride and be outside. I explained that some of our lessons occur in nature. He thought that very clever of you, Miss Snow."

Rising, Eden said, "Off you go. Down to the breakfast room. Your cousins are probably waiting for you. Tell them that we will ride together at half-past one this afternoon if that is convenient for them." She paused. "Once you finish breakfast, come to the library. I will have your lessons ready by then."

Justina sighed dramatically, while Verina laughed at her sister. Both girls left using Eden's bedchamber door. She went to the adjoining door and closed it. Though it had a lock on it, she would not use it now. The girls might need her at some point, and she wanted them to have easy access to her.

A knock sounded at her door, and she answered it, finding a maid with a breakfast tray.

"Come in," she said, and the servant went to the small table by the window, resting the tray upon it.

"I'll fetch it when you're done, miss."

Eden lifted the silver cover, finding eggs and ham on a plate and a cup of fresh strawberries accompanying it. A smaller plate held buttered toast points with a crock of orange marmalade. She smeared the marmalade on one and bit into it.

"Heavenly," she proclaimed.

The eggs and ham were cooked perfectly, and the strawberries were a delightful surprise. She finished her meal and then set the tray outside her door, hoping that would be more convenient for the maid. After making her bed, Eden retrieved the satchel she had brought and carried it downstairs to the library. She removed journals for the girls since the first assignment she would give them today would be to write about their impressions of Millvale.

Since Justina's mind wandered more easily, she placed hers on the table more in the center of the room and Verina's on the table by the window, along with freshly-sharpened pencils. They would practice their handwriting with ink another day.

While waiting for her charges to appear, Eden scanned a shelf of books. She pulled a volume of William Blake's poems and set it aside to take to her room later.

She was examining a book of Wordsworth's poems when a voice nearby asked, "Are you a romantic, Miss Snow, and always reach for poetry?"

Her heart sped up as she turned, clutching the volume to her. With all the calm she could muster, Eden said, "Good morning, Your Grace."

Chapter Seven

Val entered the breakfast room and went straight to the buffet. He had asked Mrs. Quigby to discuss with Cook to serve one each morning. Especially with additional guests in the house now, it simply made more sense than each of them ordering breakfast individually. He would have thought it would have been something Mama suggested, but she still seemed too wrapped up in her grief to notice much of anything going on about her.

He filled his plate and took a seat at the round table, a footman immediately pouring coffee for him. This was the calm before the storm, being by himself. His mother usually breakfasted in her room, and Aunt Agnes had taken on the task of joining her closest friend each morning. His sisters, though, always came down to breakfast, and he assumed his two cousins would, as well.

His only regret was that Miss Snow would not be joining them this morning.

Val wondered why he was so taken with the governess. Of course, any man who met her would be charmed. She had a remarkable, fresh beauty which would draw men to her. He liked more than her looks, however. He liked how spirited she was, despite the fact that she had had a difficult time once her parents had passed. It took a mature person to handle the situation dealt to them, especially one where a person's place had fallen in the world. Miss Snow seemed to be fully in charge of her emotions and happy to be on the path she now walked.

Tia and Lia entered the room together, talking and laughing as always. He was fortunate to be close to all his siblings. Over the years, they had spent many good times together. He had grown closest to Ariadne, but he was growing closer to Lia and Tia again, simply from living in the same household with them since their father's death. He had not seen much of the twins after he left university because he had spent so much of his time at town and not at Millvale. Val had become frustrated when his father would not allow him any say in the estate, much less permit their steward to share information with him regarding the tenants and crop yields.

Because of that, he had avoided Millvale.

It was good to be back, however. As much as he had enjoyed town over the years, he had forgotten about the serenity of the countryside. While he promised himself he would find a bride of his own on the Marriage Mart next Season, he also wanted to make certain the twins made excellent matches of their own. He would lean on Con's advice for all this. Once the current Season ended, Val would extend an invitation to his best friend to come to Millvale and spend a few weeks. He missed his cousin's company greatly, having seen him daily for years.

As his sisters seated themselves, his cousins entered the breakfast room. They were sweet girls and certainly looked up to their governess. Miss Snow had done a fine job, along with Aunt Agnes, in molding Verina's and Justina's characters. He thought of their brother, Tray, whom Val had not seen in many years. Hadrian had become the Earl of Traywick upon the death of his father. His younger brother had also perished in the same carriage accident, and Val felt now that he had been remiss not reaching out to his cousin sooner. He would write to Cousin Tray today, inviting him, too, to Millvale. Since the spring term of university would be over by early June, he hoped Tray would accept the invitation.

His cousins joined them after filling their plates at the buffet, and

Justina said, "Miss Snow said we are to keep to the schedule we usually follow at home. Lessons in the morning, with riding in the early afternoon. Sometimes, Miss Snow also holds additional lessons for us after our ride, when we are outdoors."

"What lessons do you partake in outdoors?" Lia asked, adding milk to her tea.

"All kinds," Verina responded. "Miss Snow has a particular interest in gardening, and she takes us through our gardens, teaching us about different plants."

"Sometimes, she even has us digging in the dirt alongside the gardeners," Justina declared. "All while we conjugate Latin or French verbs aloud!"

"She also has taken us fishing, as well as riding," Verina added.

While Lia wrinkled her nose, Tia's enthusiasm bubbled over. "I have never gone fishing," she said. "I didn't know girls did so. Did Miss Snow's brothers take her fishing?"

"No, Miss Snow is an only child," Verina shared. "It was her father who took her. Since he had no sons, he leaned heavily upon Miss Snow, and she accompanied him everywhere on the estate."

"Miss Snow told us that you had said we could use your stables, Millbrooke," Justina said. She looked to the twins. "We will ride today at half-past one. I hope you might join us."

Both Lia and Tia agreed to do so, and Val decided to speak up.

"If you do not mind my company, I would like to join you. Show you bits of the estate."

"Yes, please do so, Millbrooke," Verina said.

"We ride often with Val now that he has returned to Millvale," Lia said. "My, we will make a merry party with the six of us on horseback."

He remained quiet after that, ignoring the girls' chatter and giving his attention to the newspapers Quigby had placed on the table for him. Once he finished his breakfast, he excused himself, taking the newspapers with him, fully intending to go to his study and enjoy reading them in greater detail.

Instead, his feet took him in the direction of the library—and Miss Snow.

He entered, seeing her skimming her finger along the spines of books. He wondered if she did so in order to locate things for her charges to read or if she looked for something for herself. He noticed a volume of Blake's poetry sitting out and then watched as she pulled a slender volume of Wordsworth from a shelf.

"Are you a romantic, Miss Snow, and always reach for poetry?"

She whirled to face him, and her cheeks tinged with a blush, Still, she looked composed and calmly said, "Good morning, Your Grace."

"I thought I would come and see if you are settling in at Millvale, Miss Snow. How is your room? Is it to your liking?"

"It is very nice." Mischief dancing in her eyes, she added, "I believe much nicer than the one I was supposed to stay in."

They both chuckled, and he asked, "What will you be teaching my cousins today?"

She went to a table and picked up a book sitting on it. "I have them write in their journals almost daily. I think it is good for the girls to get down their thoughts and reflect upon their day. It also lets them practice their handwriting. A good hand is something every lady should possess, as they will correspond with others throughout their lives. They may even wish to write out their own invitations to events they host instead of leaving it to be done by a secretary."

She set the journal on the table again. "Today, I am asking them to write about their first impressions of Millvale. Justina will take the assignment literally. She will go into great detail about the land and the house and all the rooms she has seen. She will even detail the color of the bedclothes. Verina will go in a different direction. She will write about her impressions of her aunt and her cousins."

"So, you do not tell them exactly what to write about."

"No. I simply provide a topic and allow them to interpret it as they wish."

Miss Snow brushed her fingers against the journal again, and he thought he saw her fingers tremble.

Was she nervous in his company?

Most likely, she was. Although he was the same man he had always been, Val knew the fact that he was now a duke changed his relationship with the world and those in it. Even his own peers would appear nervous around him, so it stood to reason that a lowly governess would, as well. Miss Snow had probably fretted about the conversation between them yesterday when they were alone. She had said she was going to be more respectful, but Val did not wish for her to be afraid of him.

Wanting to put her more at ease, he asked, "Beyond journaling, what else will my cousins study today?"

"We will speak of geography, especially since this is their first time in Kent. Truly, their first time to travel anywhere beyond Traywick Manor and its nearby village. We talked about the route we would take before we left. Now that the girls have traveled it, we will look more closely at the counties and towns we passed through. We will also work on maths, a topic neither one is fond of."

"I heard you will ride this afternoon. My cousins were most excited about that and invited my sisters to go along with them." He paused and then added, "I invited myself to accompany you since you are touring the estate for the first time. I hope to show all of you a bit about Millvale which you might not see on your own."

She made a small sound of distress and then bit her lip as if upset with herself for doing so. "Whatever you wish, Your Grace. Your cousins are your guests."

"You, too, are my guest, Miss Snow," he insisted, wanting to make her feel welcome.

Anger sparked in her eyes. "No, you are wrong about that. I am a servant of one of your guests, brought along to make things run more smoothly. I know Lady Traywick wishes to spend a good deal of time with Her Grace and help her through all she has suffered because of His Grace's death. That means even though Lady Traywick missed her daughters and wished for her girls to be with her during her extended visit to Millvale, they would be left on their own often with little to do.

"It was my role to act as chaperone to accompany them to Kent, and I am now present to help occupy their time and give lessons while we are here. While academics is important, Lady Traywick also knows that I am preparing her girls for their eventual debut into Polite Society. I give music lessons to Lady Verina and Lady Justina, and I have taught them to dance, as well. We work on needlework together, and they both are practicing the art of serving tea to others."

She straightened her shoulders, her gaze meeting his. "I know my exact role, Your Grace. It is not one of a duke's guest. Though I enjoy what I do a great deal, I am working the entire time I will be at Millvale. Now, if you will excuse me, it is almost time for the girls to appear for their lessons."

Her outburst, though contained, stunned him.

"I did not mean to offend you, Miss Snow," he said quietly. "And despite the fact that you are a governess, you are gently bred. I do look upon you as a guest and hope your stay in my home will be a pleasant one. If anything is not to your liking, please speak up. To me. I will address the issue at once."

She looked at him as if he'd gone mad. "You have no idea what you are saying. Dukes do not trouble themselves if a governess is put out over something, and governesses are wise enough to know they live on the benevolence of their employers. I could hate everything about Millvale. The food. The bedclothes. The servants' attitudes toward me. And I would never dare complain to anyone, much less to *you*, of all people."

Miss Snow pursed her lips, and for a moment, all Val could think was how he wanted to kiss the frown from her face.

She must have had an inkling of his thoughts because she gave him a withering look.

"I suggest you take your role more seriously, Your Grace, and quit trying to flirt with me. There is a protocol which you are to follow, and getting to know and please your cousins' governess is simply unheard of. Your duties lie with your family and your tenants. Please, do not give me a second thought because I am not a woman you can ever hope to seduce."

Val wanted to say he had given her more than a second thought. A third. A fourth. A tenth. But that would only prove what she had dared enough to speak aloud to a duke. Without realizing it, he had been subtly flirting with her. Oh, not the charming words and wistful glances he gave other women in the *ton*, but a different kind of flirting. At least it had seemed so to her.

She was right. No duke would be concerned with the wishes and wellbeing of a governess. Most would not ever bother to speak to one. He knew his own father had rarely conversed with his sisters' governess and the few occasions he did so, he addressed her as Nixon—and not Miss Nixon.

He wanted to tell Miss Snow that he meant no disservice to her. If anything, she intrigued him as no other lady of his acquaintance ever had. He most certainly did think of her as a lady, despite her protests to the contrary. From her regal bearing to her beauty and intelligence, Miss Snow was every inch a lady.

And he could not help but toy with the idea of just how fine a duchess she would make.

Just then, Justina and Verina entered the room.

"Oh, this will be a wonderful place for you to conduct our lessons, Miss Snow," Verina said, gazing about the room. She moved to the windows. "And what a lovely view."

Justina said, "Lia and Tia have promised to go riding with us, Miss

Snow. Val, too. He is going to give us a guided tour of his estate."

He chuckled. "Well, not all of it. Millvale is rather large. But we will ride out and see a good bit of it today before we return home for tea." He glanced to Miss Snow. "You will be joining us for tea, won't you?"

Her chin raised a notch. "Certainly, Your Grace. I look forward to it. Your cook did such a marvelous job at yesterday's tea, especially those raspberry tarts."

"They were wonderful," Justina said, taking a seat at the table in the center of the room. "I assume I am to sit here, Miss Snow." She glanced to Val. "Miss Snow understands that my mind wanders. If I sat by the window, I would be staring out, conjuring all sorts of things in my mind that have nothing to do with the lessons at hand."

He stepped to her and placed a hand on her shoulder. "There is nothing wrong with daydreaming, Cousin. Sometimes, you learn a great deal about yourself through it. Daydreams can turn into real dreams. Goals which you set for yourself."

Val squeezed her shoulder, letting his hand fall to his side again.

Justina frowned. "I have never really thought to have any kind of goal, Val. Mama—and Polite Society—expect me to wed and have children. What might I want beyond that?"

"That is for you to decide." He paced to Verina. "The same for you. Yes, I will help you, along with your brother, to make an advantageous match if that is what you want, but I want you to be happy with the husband you choose. And if you wish to do more with your life than simply be a wife and mother, that is for you to decide. You might wish to paint. Help others through a ladies' auxiliary."

He saw Justina pondering his words and added, "Why, my sister Ariadne, who is now Lady Aldridge, has purchased an orphanage with her husband. They spend a couple of days a week there, teaching the orphans. Ariadne has birthed one daughter, Penelope, and she and Lord Aldridge plan to have more children. She also enjoys the time spent with the orphans and feels she is contributing to the good of them and others by doing so."

He smiled at Justina. "It is up to you to fill the pages not only of your journal, but your future."

Val looked to Miss Snow, and the governess' lips were slightly parted in wonder. Something in him wanted to make her see him as more than a duke. See the man behind the title.

And want that man.

He cleared his throat, pushing aside his own fanciful thoughts. "I will leave you to your governess. Let us met at the stables at a quarter past one. That way, I can walk you through and show you the horses which are available for you during your stay. I will need to know your level of experience and the type of horse you are comfortable atop of."

"Both Lady Verina and Lady Justina are excellent riders, Your Grace," Miss Snow informed him. "They will be able to comfortably handle any mount they are given." She paused. "We will arrive at the stables at a quarter past so that your grooms will have time to saddle all our horses. It will also allow the girls to meet and bond with the ones they will ride."

"Bond?" he asked, puzzled by her words.

"Yes. I have taught my charges that it is important—just as it is with new people you meet—that they establish a relationship with a new horse they are to ride."

"It is important to always learn a horse's name, Val, and ask about their temperaments," Verina informed him. "Miss Snow also has us bring a treat for our horses. Hopefully, your cook will provide us with something we might take with us."

"I see. Then I will speak to Cook now and see that we have some apples for our horses. I will bring them myself to the stables and distribute them once everyone is present."

He looked to Miss Snow before she could protest. "I know that is not *necessary* for me to do so, but I am happy to take on the role. My own mount will be excited to receive a treat himself." Facing his cousins, he added, "Enjoy your lessons this morning. I will see you in a few hours."

Val left the library and went directly to the kitchens. He told Cook that he would return at one o'clock and asked her to have a basket of apples ready when he did.

"For what, Your Grace?" she asked, her brows knitting together quizzically.

"Miss Snow has said that it is important for our horses to receive a treat. I am abiding by her wishes."

Cook grinned. "Then the apples will be ready for you, Your Grace."

He retreated to his study, the newspapers still tucked under his arm. He set them on the desk and took the chair behind it, placing his fist atop and crossing his ankles.

Miss Snow continued to draw his interest. He'd thought to possibly look over the neighborhood to see if he might find a suitable wife amongst the families living here.

Why not Miss Snow?

Her manners were exquisite, at least when she wasn't chastising him. She was quick-witted and beautiful, Of course, she had not made her come-out into Polite Society and worked to earn her living, but he respected her for doing so. And after all, he *was* a duke. Dukes seemed to be able to make their own rules, as well as breaking other rules of the *ton*. He pictured Miss Snow wearing the Worthington diamonds to the opening ball of next Season, her hair piled high on her head, her ballgown simple and elegant, as the woman herself.

Being wed to him, she would instantly be welcomed into Polite Society.

Val wasn't ready to commit to such a wild idea, much less offer for Miss Snow, but he felt himself leaning in that direction. He had always been a man who went after what he wanted—and got it.

And in this case, he was beginning to want Miss Snow.

Badly.

Chapter Eight

What the bloody hell was she going to do?

Eden knew that a governess could not afford to be interested in any man, least of all a duke. She waffled between thinking the new Duke of Millbrooke was simply a good man concerned about her welfare versus one who wanted to engage in an illicit affair with her. Her experience with men was severely limited, which made reading the duke's intentions all the harder for her to discern.

Being around a good, kind father for eighteen years, she had thought all men were as decent as Papa. Then when her selfish, immature cousin became the new Viscount Brownley, he held party after party, inviting friends with loose morals to overrun Brownstone. She'd remained locked inside the dower house for days at a time, not even allowing Polly to go between it and the main house for fear of what might happen to the maid. Her opinion of so-called gentlemen had dipped badly, worsened when Brownley had driven her from the only home she had ever known.

And finally, Lord Kessley. A man who thought merely because he held a title, he could hold sway over her. Eden was doing well, managing her life and earning a living, despite all her many setbacks. She refused to let the Duke of Millbrooke interrupt her peaceful, productive existence.

She gave Verina and Justina their assignment, and both girls eagerly picked up their pencils and began scribbling in their journals. Eden moved to claim the volume of Blake's poetry and sat in a chair where she could observe her charges, while pretending to read.

There was no doubt about it. She was in a pickle. She had drawn the interest of His Grace and needed to remain disengaged from him. The problem was, she was attracted to him. She closed her eyes a moment, but Millbrooke's image was burned into her memory. His height and broad shoulders. Those emerald-green eyes and his citrus cologne. The immaculate tailoring which showed off his muscular frame to perfection. Even the strong jaw and those cheekbones which could cut glass. He was a handsome devil, emphasis on the devil part of it. She could not afford to be in his presence any longer.

And yet, how was she to avoid him in his own home?

Eden hoped she would be able to use Verina and Justina as a shield. Once the girls had arrived in the library, relief had filled her. She couldn't help but think how if she had been a member of Polite Society, being unwed and alone in a room as she had been with the duke would have caused her to be ruined. She was a servant, though, albeit an upper one. The rules were far different for those of her ilk.

She doubted His Grace would agree if she requested to be absent from tea each afternoon after the bargain they had struck. Instead, she would do as she planned and behave as she did yesterday, disappearing into the furniture and not contributing to the conversation. The rest of the time, she would be on alert. Make certain she knew where the duke was so that she might avoid those places.

Unfortunately, today's ride was something she was already obligated to. Thank goodness the four young ladies would be with them.

Opening the volume of Blake, her eyes fell to the page, but Eden did not see a word written upon it. Instead, she felt pity for herself growing within her, thinking of all she had lost with her parents' deaths. She had never wanted a minute of pity, knowing it would not change her circumstances, but for a few minutes now, she indulged herself in thinking about if she had made her own come-out years ago.

She would have danced in ballrooms with handsome, titled gentlemen and might have even met the Duke of Millbrooke at some point, sharing a dance. Eventually, she would have settled upon a husband, one Papa approved of, and borne him children. Children she could love with all her heart, watching them grow over the years.

Eden swallowed the painful lump which had formed in her throat. This would be the only time she would ever allow herself to think about the future which had been denied to her by fate. The parties she would have attended. The other girls she might have made friends with. The pretty ballgowns she would have worn. Magical kisses stolen in the moonlight. A wedding ceremony and the night that followed, when she would have been initiated into the practices of lovemaking.

Tears swam in her eyes, the ache real, her youth now lost. She was nothing but an old maid, not even one on the shelf, but a woman who must work to survive. She dug her nails into her palms, pulling herself out of such fantasies and back into reality.

What she must focus on is what was her now. These girls. Her post with Lady Traywick. The countess had taken a huge risk by hiring Eden since she'd had no references. The last several years had been good ones for her. She fully intended to see her obligation to Verina and Justina fulfilled, and then she would move on, finding another family with children for her to teach—and love.

She glanced to Verina, whose pencil flowed across the page, and then to Justina, who frowned slightly as she wrote. Oh, how she loved these two! Eden was fortunate she was a governess and had the opportunity to work with two such lovely young ladies. She hoped she would be as fortunate with the next family she spent time with.

Justina finally put down her pencil and looked expectantly at Eden. She rose and went to Justina's table, taking a seat.

"Is there anything you would like to share with me about what you wrote?" she asked.

"Only that I think Millvale is a very happy place, despite the fact that my uncle recently passed. It is large and beautiful, both the house and the property, and I am so happy to be with my cousins again for an extended length of time."

"You mentioned having seen them once before."

Justina nodded. "I still do not know why, but we were all brought to town a long time ago. For about a week. It was the first and last time I saw any of my cousins. Only Val and Con knew each other from having gone to school together. They have remained the best of friends over the years."

"Con is Viscount Dyer?"

"Yes, that is correct. He is the oldest of Lord and Lady Marley. Then there is Lucy and Dru. And just as Val is the oldest here, he has younger sisters, three instead of two. I am thrilled we will get to know Lia and Tia better, and I hope that at some point we can also spend time with Ariadne. She has already made her come-out and wed a marquess."

"You, too, will make your come-out sooner than you think, Justina. It will be good to have so many of your cousins in town with you when you do. They will make for good company and may even dispense thoughtful advice when it comes time for you to choose a husband."

Eden thought of what the duke had shared with her about bringing his own children to town each spring so that he could spend time with them while also allowing them to get to know their cousins and extended family better.

Would a man who thought so tenderly of children he did not even have yet be the kind to try and seduce her? Then again, a man could love his children and easily break his wedding vows. Papa had told her as much. Her father had never treated Eden as a child, always speaking to her as if she were his equal. Mama would have been aghast at some of the topics they discussed, but Papa had tried to prepare his daughter for Polite Society. He had explained that most men—and a good many women—of the *ton* did not hold their marriage vows sacred as he did. That they engaged in affairs with one another. Papa had hoped she would be able to find one of those rare men who would honor the promises he made to Eden on their wedding day.

She admired how loyal Papa had been to Mama. If anyone would have had an excuse to stray from his marriage vows, it would have been her father. Instead, he was the most faithful husband to his ailing, invalid wife.

Eden wondered if the Duke of Millbrooke would show that kind of devotion to his duchess and then pinched herself for even thinking of him again.

"I will go stop Verina, else she will be writing all day," she told Justina. "Come, we will join her and admire the lovely view."

They moved toward the table by the window, and Verina said, "I am almost finished, Miss Snow. I have so much to write about."

They sat silently and watched Verina complete her thoughts. When she placed her pencil on the table and closed her journal, Eden asked, "Do you have anything you wrote about that you might wish to discuss with us?"

"I am grateful to be here at Millvale," Verina replied. "I see how close Mama is with Aunt Alice, and I want that kind of closeness with my cousins, too."

"Lady Tia and Lady Lia seem to be lovely young ladies," she said. "You cannot always choose the family you have, but you certainly can select the friends you wish to make. When both coincide, it is a blessing. Now, shall we move on to geography?"

"Anything but maths," Justina said, causing them all to chuckle.

Eden went to retrieve the atlas she previously had looked at. For the next hour, they retraced their route from Cumberland to Kent, talking about the topography of the land and the cities they had passed through. Justina also wanted to see where Somerset was because it was where Viscount Dyer and his two sisters lived.

"Perhaps on our way home, we could stop and call upon Uncle Arthur and Aunt Charlotte," Justina said brightly. "It would be wonderful to visit with Lucy and Dru. Con, too."

Verina shook her head. "No, we must wait for an invitation," she told her sister. "You simply cannot drop in on someone out of the blue and expect them to welcome you with open arms. Besides, Lucy is making her come-out this Season. I remember what a pretty girl she was. Most likely, she will receive an offer of marriage, and Aunt Charlotte will be planning a wedding by summer's end."

"I did not think about that," Justina admitted. "And I did hear Val mention that Con spends most of his time in town. I suppose it would only be Dru at Marleyfield if we did go."

Seeing Justina's dejection, Eden said, "But you will both be making your come-outs in few years. You will see much of your cousins while you are in town. It will be a very special time in your life. You will make all kinds of friends and experience the whirl of the London Season. They say there is nothing quite like it in all the world."

While Justina's eyes lit with enthusiasm, Verina looked at her governess with concern.

"I am sorry you missed having your own come-out, Miss Snow. If you had, you would have received a dozen offers of marriages because you are so beautiful and kind. Why, we would never have come to know you."

She swallowed. "Then I will say that I am the lucky one because I have spent these past five years with you girls. Yes, I have taught you as a governess should, but I must admit that I have grown terribly fond of both of you. You have become almost as younger sisters to me. I would not have wished to miss out on the opportunity getting to know the both of you."

Tears filled Verina's eyes. "I cannot imagine you not being a part of our family, Miss Snow. We have seen you every day for years."

Thinking it was never too late to start preparing them about the future, Eden said, "Life changes, Verina. Your own will once you make your come-out. You will find a gentleman to wed, and you will become a part of his family. Justina will do the same."

A fat teared rolled down Verina's cheek. "I really never thought of it that way," she admitted. "Yes, I knew the point of going to the Season was to find a husband, but that means I will go and live with him in his household." She looked to her sister. "That means leaving you behind."

Now Justina grew teary, as well. "I will come to see you, Verina," she promised. Then she grinned. "Of course, you would have to *invite* me because I know not to show up uninvited for an extended visit."

The three of them cackled like hens at Justina's wit.

Eden closed the atlas and returned it to its stand, witnessing the two sisters embrace one another. For a moment, a pang of envy hit her, having no siblings and no true family of her own. She might look upon these girls as her relatives, but in reality, she was no more than a paid servant. They would go on to wed and have children. At the best, they might remember her fondly. At worst, they might not even recall her name, much less mention Eden to one another as the years passed.

She moved toward them and said, "It is time for maths," she proclaimed, hearing both of them groan.

"Must we do maths today?" Justina asked. "I would rather do anything but maths, Miss Snow. Could we please study something else?"

"We could work on our Latin translations," Verina suggested hopefully. "We only did a small portion of them the other day at the inn."

"All right," she said, giving in. "But first thing tomorrow morning will be maths."

Her charges beamed at her as Eden went and retrieved the translation they had worked on together. For the next half-hour, she guided the girls in the translation of a passage describing the Punic Wars.

While she and the girls work on many lessons individually, she found they did a better job and were more engaged when they worked on some activities together.

Once the passage had been translated to her satisfaction, she said, "That will be all for today. Tomorrow we will do history and maths and then see if there is a place where we can continue our music lessons."

Glancing at the grandfather clock in the corner, she said, "You have half an hour to yourselves now before we head down to the stables for our ride."

"I cannot wait to be on horseback," Verina declared. "I almost wish I could have ridden the entire way from the Lake District to Kent, rather than be cooped up in a hot, stuffy carriage."

Justina grinned impishly. "Your backside would have been so sore," she teased. "But I agree. I am already dreading the long journey back to Traywick Manor."

"That will not be for many weeks. Possibly even months," Eden reminded the pair. "Besides, Lady Traywick might wish to break up the trip and have us stay at Lord Traywick's townhouse in London for a few days."

"Oh, that is a marvelous idea, Miss Snow," Verina said. "When the time comes, please suggest doing so to Mama."

"Go," she prodded. "I will clean up here."

After the girls left, Eden finished gathering what they had worked on and placed everything in her satchel. Instead of carting it back to her bedchamber, she set it in a corner of the room, thinking it would remain undisturbed.

Picking up both the Blake and Wordsworth books of poetry, she returned to her bedchamber. She set them on the table next to the bed, recalling how the duke had asked her if she were a romantic because she read these poets. She should have snapped back that governesses did not have the luxury of being romantics, but she was glad she had held her tongue. She must continue to do so around him. She could not afford to be riled and lose her temper, even if he might be teasing.

Or flirting . . .

She supposed Millbrooke flirted as easily as he breathed. That it was something intrinsic to him. Well, let him flirt with all those eligible ladies on the Marriage Mart. Eden Snow would remain unavailable to him. She could not afford to be dismissed from this post. While she did not wish to speak rudely to him ever again, Eden must certainly put him in his place if he tried to start up something unseemly with her.

For a moment, her mind flashed back to Lord Kessley and how he had ruined everything for her. His daughters were so young. She could have spent a dozen or more years in his household before she needed to search for a new position. Of course, with Lady Kessley adding her—instead of blaming her—Eden realized the poor viscountess had most likely had to put up with the infidelities of her husband for years. She should count herself fortunate that she had not wed a *ton* gentleman who was so unfaithful.

Changing into her riding habit, she left her room and knocked on the girls' door. Justina opened it, also wearing her habit.

"Are you ready to leave for the stables?" she asked.

They left their wing of the house and came across Lady Lia and Lady Tia. The five traveled down the stairs to the ground floor, and Lady Tia led them through the kitchens, saying it would be much shorter to cut through them than go out the front door and all the way around the large house. Eden walked several paces behind the four, listening to their conversations. The four were all in high spirits and looking forward to their ride. In truth, she was also ready to be atop a horse again. Her father had helped create a love of animals within her, particularly where horses were concerned.

The stables came in sight, where the Duke of Millbrooke stood, his hands behind his back as he watched them approach.

As they grew closer, she realized his hair was a chestnut color. It had seemed dark brown indoors, but in this afternoon's bright sunshine, the red highlights gleamed brightly. She thought it interesting that each of the three siblings had varying shades of red and thought the color must run in their family's ancestry.

"Are you ready to meet my horses?" he asked, his voice brimming with enthusiasm.

Verina and Justina replied in unison, "Yes, Val."

The duke swept out a hand, motioning for them to enter the stables. All four girls passed him. When Eden started by him, the duke said to her, "I will be relying upon your good judgment, Miss Snow. You know the capabilities and skill level my cousins possess as riders, so you must help me determine which mounts are most suited for them."

"Certainly, Your Grace," she said, feeling her spine stiffen and her chin raise a notch. She caught what she did and tried to relax her posture a bit, not wanting him to know just how much he affected her.

He fell into step beside her. As they entered the barn, he said, "You said you are an excellent rider, Miss Snow. I cannot wait for you to meet the mount I have selected for you."

Chapter Nine

Miss Snow came to a halt. "I do not need a special horse, Your Grace," she said, as haughtily as any duchess might. "Any mount will do. You should spend more time considering those your cousins will ride. They are your chief concern."

Val liked seeing her ruffled a bit. She always seemed to be in such control. He wanted to wrest that control away from her—and see the woman beneath the staid governess.

"Oh, I have also thought of the horses they should ride but as I said, I would appreciate your advice since you know what skills they hold." He paused. "But Andromeda will be for you. I will warn you now. No one has been able to ride her yet except for me, and I prefer to keep to Perseus, my favorite in the stables."

She sniffed. "You are fond of Greek mythology?"

"Do you know of Perseus and Andromeda?" he asked.

"I am familiar with them. That Perseus slayed the Gorgon Medusa, as well as rescued Andromeda from the sea serpent Cetus."

He grinned. "You left out the part where Perseus wed Andromeda."

Miss Snow shrugged. "I suppose she expressed her gratitude toward him by doing so."

"You do not think gratitude a good reason for two people to wed?"

"My opinions on marriage are no concern of yours, Your Grace."

She moved away from him, and Val caught up to her, seeing the girls all waited for them.

Immediately, her demeanor changed. "Oh, look at this roan. What a beauty she is."

The governess lovingly stroked the horse who stuck his head outside his stall, and all Val could think of was having her hands stroke his chest in the same manner. Then she leaned toward the horse and kissed it, causing his manhood to stir.

"That's Sunset," said one of his grooms. "He's even-tempered but a bit spirited."

Miss Snow smiled at the groom, a friendly smile that Val wished she would bestow upon him.

"How apropos. Sunset is various shades of the actual sunset. A clever name."

"I thought Justina might like to ride Sunset," he said.

His cousin moved toward the horse. "Oh, how are you, Sunset?" she cooed, petting the horse. Turning to Val, she asked, "Did you bring the apples?"

He nodded to the groom, who retrieved the basket Val had brought from the house and handed them to the duke. He tossed one to Justina, and she caught it, laughing, then offered it to Sunset.

"Stay here and get to know Sunset better," Miss Snow urged Justina.

"Where is my horse, Val?" asked Verina.

"This way."

He led them down the row, stopping at a stall on the left. Clucking his tongue, Val leaned inside and encouraged the mare to come to him. Verina joined him.

"Verina, meet Glory. She is a sister to Sunset and very pleasant."

"Ah, Glory, my sweet," his cousin crooned.

Val offered her an apple, too, which Verina held out to Glory.

"Look, Miss Snow! She is taking it with no fuss."

"That is good," the governess said. "Go into the stall and brush her some. She will like that."

"Have Val take you to your horse, Miss Snow," Verina encouraged as she opened the stall door.

"Shall we?" he asked, continuing down the row, stopping before a stall. He peered inside. "This is Andromeda."

The governess stepped to the stall, and her shoulder brushed his, causing desire to trickle along his spine.

"It is nice to meet you, Andromeda," she said, her tone smooth as honey. "I hear you are a bit feisty."

She opened the gate and moved inside, closing it behind her, all the while speaking gently to the horse. Andromeda snorted as the governess approached.

Laughing, Miss Snow said, "I will pretend that was a sneeze and not you judging me, my pretty one."

He watched as she worked magic with the horse, talking to it as if they were old friends sharing secrets. He thought how good she would be as a hostess, making her guests feel at ease. And that's when it hit him. He was truly considering Miss Snow as his duchess.

Lord Almighty, what would Mama think? And the *ton*?

Val decided he didn't care for anyone's opinion but his own. Miss Snow would be ideal as his duchess. She would approach things without nonsense and yet be nurturing at the same time. Watching her smooth her hand against Andromeda's flank, a surge of jealousy arose within him.

He wanted her touching him. Cooing to him. He wanted her in his bed, naked, his mouth on hers as he thrust inside her. The thought of him inside her had him growing hard.

"Your Grace?"

Looking up, he sensed the back of his neck heat. "Yes, Miss Snow?"

"I asked if you would hand me an apple."

"Of course."

He retrieved one from the basket he carried. Instead of tossing it to her, he slipped inside the stall and handed it to her, their fingers brushing, heat filling him.

"There you go, love," she told the horse. "That's it. Just for you."

Val signaled the groom to start saddling the horses and said, "Let us wait outside. The horses will be brought to us when they are ready."

He stopped on the way, giving apples to Tia and Lia, and then stopped by Perseus' stall.

"This is for you, courtesy of Miss Snow," he told the horse, who gobbled up the treat.

The five awaited him and their horses outside, and Verina asked, "What will we see today, Val?"

"Millvale is a vast estate, Cousin. We will only ride a small portion of it this afternoon."

"Could you take us out each afternoon and show us a different part of it?" Justina asked.

Before he could reply, Miss Snow said, "His Grace is a very busy man, my lady. Let him show us what he can today, but we cannot ask him to devote every afternoon to us. We shall explore on our own, with Lady Tia and Lady Lia's help, if they are willing to accompany us."

"We would be happy to do so, Miss Snow," Tia said, brimming with enthusiasm. "We have spent all our lives at Millbrooke, so we are very familiar with the estate. We do not need Val at all, to be truthful."

He pretended to stab himself. "Oh, to be so unwanted," he said dramatically, causing the four girls to giggle.

Miss Snow viewed him with disdain.

"Although I might not be able to accompany you each afternoon, I will do so when I can," he told the group. "I enjoy riding, and it will be good to be with my sisters and cousins." He glanced to the governess. "And you, as well, Miss Snow."

She gave him a tight smile.

Grooms led their mounts out, and he tossed each of them into the saddle, saving Miss Snow for last. He clasped her waist firmly and lifted her with ease.

Stepping back, he looked up as she took the reins. "Be careful, Miss Snow. As I mentioned, Andromeda has not wished for anyone to be on her back. Even I have had difficulty with her."

She leaned down and said to the horse, "I cannot understand why His Grace is making up stories about you, Andromeda."

He laughed and went to mount Perseus. "Everyone ready? Then follow me."

Val began cantering away from the stables, keeping at a steady pace, glancing over his shoulder a few times. He knew his sisters were at home in the saddle and quickly saw his cousins were cut from the same cloth. What drew his eyes was how well Miss Snow handled Andromeda. He had not been fibbing. The horse was a handful, and he had not enjoyed riding her. She was too spirited, even agitated at times, and he had wondered if Andromeda might be a good fit for his stables or whether he would have to sell her.

Perhaps she could be a wedding present, he mused, chuckling to himself.

By now, Miss Snow had ridden ahead of the others, joining him. "Something is amusing, Your Grace?"

Airily, he said, "I am amused by life. You ride extremely well."

"Andromeda and I see eye-to-eye on matters," she replied. "But it is taking everything I have to hold her back. I have promised to give the horse her head soon."

"Do so now," he urged. "We are approaching the meadow. Let her run freely."

Without a word, the governess took off. Val reined in Perseus and merely watched as she flew.

"Look at Miss Snow!" Lia proclaimed. "Why, it is if she and Andromeda are one."

He couldn't agree more.

The five of them watched as the horse raced across the meadow, the governess handling her with ease. They reached the far end and his heart almost stopped as she took the fence, jumping it with little effort. Horse and rider disappeared from sight for several seconds, and then they appeared again, once more clearing the fence and galloping back across the meadow.

As she neared them, Miss Snow slowed the horse, until Andromeda returned to a walk.

"You were magnificent, Miss Snow!" declared Tia. "I have never seen a woman handle a horse as you do Andromeda."

She was flushed in the face, happiness in her smile. "Riding a horse of such quality is a thrill," she admitted. "But I will tell you that she is pushing me, even now. I would not advise any of you to climb atop her. She would run away with you, and you would never gain control of her."

Miss Snow looked to him. "Andromeda has some of her restlessness remedied with that merry jaunt, Your Grace. I believe she will behave for a good while now. Shall we begin our tour?"

He looked at her with open admiration. "I would be happy to do so."

For the next two hours, Val led them to various parts of the estate, pride evident in his voice as he told his cousins and their governess about Millvale and its workings.

"We should head back for tea," he finally said. "Our mamas will be wondering where we are."

"Can we race?" Tia asked.

"You four girls can," he agreed, having seen how well Verina and Justina managed their mounts. "I will stay back with Miss Snow for a few minutes, and then the way will be clear for Andromeda."

They paired up, Tia racing against Verina and Lia going up against Justina. He watched, seeing how happy his sisters looked.

"I must thank Aunt Agnes for asking me to allow my cousins to join us in Kent. My sisters have been fighting off the doldrums ever since our father's death and their canceled Season."

"They are lovely young ladies, Your Grace. Although they had to delay their come-outs, they will have a year of maturity on their side. That can only help when the social whirl begins. It is easy for a young girl's head to be turned. Fortunately, you will be there to guide them through the experience."

"I did that for Ariadne. It was the one thing my father trusted me to do, help her find her husband. Con, my cousin, also looked out for her." He chuckled. "Ariadne found Lord Aldridge on her own, however. I claim him as a good friend now. He makes my sister very happy."

"So, it is a love match?" she asked.

"Very much so."

A wistful look crossed her face. "My parents were a love match."

"Mine were not, which is why I am finding it hard to believe Mama is taking her husband's death so hard."

"They may not have been a love match, but they did have four children that bound them together," she reminded him. "No one outside a marriage can truly know what goes on inside one." She sighed. "Though it was easy for me to see just how happy my parents were."

Curious, he said, "You mentioned your mother's riding accident. That she was severely injured."

"Yes. She never left her bed after it. The doctor said there could be no more children. That is why Papa lacked an heir and my spiteful cousin took the title." She sighed. "Accident or not, Papa was staunchly committed to Mama and his vows. They were never apart a single day. He was ever steadfast, dedicated to her happiness."

"Lord Brownley sounds like a remarkable man."

"He was. Mama was just as remarkable in her own way. She never let bitterness overwhelm her, as I would think so many others in her position might. Mama was cheerful. Optimistic. And just as much in love with her husband as he was with her."

"I envy you, being raised in love. Seeing such a shining example of marriage."

"You can be that same kind of man and wonderful role model to your own children, Your Grace. Choose your duchess with care, and the rest will be easy."

With that, she spurred on Andromeda. The horse responded immediately, dashing down the lane. For a minute, Val watched her, the woman and horse as one, a thing of beauty.

Miss Snow was creeping into his heart without knowing it. Soon, she would possess it.

And him.

"Come on, Perseus. Let us have a bit of fun ourselves."

The horse sprang into motion, but they could not catch Andromeda and her rider. He arrived back at the stables, seeing his sisters and cousins moving up the hill, headed toward the house. Miss Snow had dismounted and was stroking Andromeda, resting her brow against the horse.

Quickly, he dismounted, tossing his reins to a groom, and strode toward her.

"Shall we return to the house, Miss Snow? I have worked up quite an appetite."

She seemed to struggle for a moment, and he thought she might try to wriggle out of coming to tea. Then she looked at him, her hazel eyes tinged with a bit of green. He had noticed they tended to go more amber when she was angry, so he was curious as to what the green might mean.

"Go ahead, Your Grace. I will be along shortly."

"I will wait and escort you back to the house," he said, digging in his heels.

They stared at one another, two stubborn souls.

Then she burst out laughing. She patted Andromeda. "I will see you again tomorrow, pretty one. Thank you for a lovely afternoon."

He fell into step beside her, no words necessary. Though he felt there were layers upon layers he wished to explore and learn about her, Val was perfectly content to merely be in her company.

For now, at least.

Chapter Ten

Eden returned to her bedchamber, removing her riding habit and washing. She deliberately kept her mind a blank going through the routine. She dressed again in the gown she had previously worn and headed to the drawing room for tea.

She would not think of the duke.

She repeated that phrase over and over, each step bringing her closer to the drawing room and his presence. She had much to think about regarding him—and yet nothing to think about at all.

When she arrived, Eden saw she was almost the last to do so. Only Lady Traywick and Her Grace had yet to appear. That meant she had a bit of a choice regarding where she sat, and she took a chair that, fortunately, was as far away from Millbrooke as she could get.

"I see the six of us were famished after our long ride," the duke said, causing them all to laugh.

Wanting to seem that she contributed to the conversation at tea, Eden remarked, "Thank you again, Your Grace, for letting us make use of your stables."

"I am happy the horses got the workout they did, especially Andromeda. You are an exceptional rider, Miss Snow, with a true affinity for horses. I hope that you and my cousins will take advantage of the stables on a daily basis."

"Miss Snow won first prize in our village's riding contest three years in a row," Justina bragged.

"And the only reason she has not won more often is because she refuses to enter again," Verina added.

She felt the duke's eyes upon her and met his gaze. Shrugging, she said, "It is only fair to give others a chance at the trophy."

Her employer and the duchess came into the room, the teacarts following behind them. Eden did as she had planned and simply listened to those talking around her. All the while, though, she felt the Duke of Millbrooke staring in her direction.

"How was your ride about Millvale?" Lady Traywick asked the group.

Her daughters responded, telling their mother of the various places they had gone, with the duke's sisters chiming in upon occasion.

Then Lady Tia said, "You should have seen Miss Snow riding Andromeda, Mama."

For the first time, Eden felt the attention of the Duchess of Millbrooke upon her. "You must be quite the rider, Miss Snow. From what Millbrooke tells me, Andromeda is both fickle and feisty. Quite hard to manage."

"Miss Snow did not only manage Andromeda, Mama. She charmed the beast. I did not think it possible."

"I am glad to hear so, Millbrooke. I know you had mentioned you might get rid of the horse if she could not be tamed more."

Without meaning to, Eden made a sound of distress, drawing everyone's attention.

"Have no worries, Miss Snow," the duke assured her. "Now I see all it takes is a very skilled rider to be upon Andromeda's back."

"What will you do with the horse when we leave?" Lady Traywick asked. "If you believe you can find no one to ride her, I will purchase the horse from you, Millbrooke. The horses in our limited stable are far too tame for Miss Snow."

Immediately, she protested. "You cannot buy a horse for me, my lady. It simply is not done."

"I am the Countess of Traywick," her employer replied, the corners of her mouth turning up. "I have found I enjoy being her and asserting a bit of authority every now and then." Her face softened. "I have had to do so ever since I lost my husband, and my son took on his father's title. Fortunately, he has recently come into his majority, but I am certain he would see Andromeda as a good investment."

"I wrote Traywick this morning," the duke mentioned. "I feel remiss for not having done so before. I invited him to come to Millvale once his university term finished."

"That was a lovely gesture," Lady Traywick said, smiling fondly at her nephew. "He will be busy at Traywick Manor this summer, though, followed by a final year of his studies. Extend the invitation to next summer, Millbrooke. Perhaps he might want to come then and see how Millvale is run. He will take on more responsibilities, and your guidance would be a boon to him."

Talk shifted from Andromeda, for which Eden was grateful. She kept silent as the others spoke, skipping from topic to topic, then Justina drew Eden into the conversation.

"Miss Snow, do you remember you were going to inquire about where to hold our music lessons?"

"Thank you for reminding me." She looked to the duchess. "I am seeking a place to conduct pianoforte lessons for Lady Justina and Lady Verina, Your Grace. I see there is an instrument here in the drawing room, but I do not wish to impose and hold the room hostage while we conduct our lessons."

"You may use the drawing room anytime you wish during the day," the duchess replied. "We are not often in it until tea in the afternoons. I prefer my small parlor. My daughters also have other rooms they use. We do have a music room at Millvale, however. It contains a pianoforte and a harp. It would be more than suitable for you to conduct lessons. Perhaps while one of my nieces has her lesson, the other could practice here in the drawing room."

"Then we would be happy to use this music room anytime it is available," she said.

Lady Lia said, "I like to practice after breakfast each morning. It is a lovely way to start my day."

Lady Tia laughed. "And I practice only sporadically. It definitively shows."

"That would work well for us since we do our lessons in the morning in your library," she said. "Thank you for use of both pianofortes, Your Grace."

Tea concluded, and Eden excused herself, returning to her bedchamber. She sat in the chair, opening the book of Wordsworth's poems. The poet had lived in the Lake District near Traywick Manor for a few years, and he had captured the beauty of the land in his poetry. It did not appeal to her today, however. She closed the book and held it in her lap, staring out the window for a good hour, her thoughts drifting aimlessly.

Finally, she stood, placing the volume of poetry on the table next to her. She decided to go and walk the gardens now since she had yet to visit them. Being in nature always brought her comfort. It would be interesting to compare the gardens at Traywick Manor to those at Millvale. This ducal estate was far larger, and she suspected the gardens would hold a larger variety of flowers and plants.

Eden went down the back staircase, designated for servants, and cut through the kitchens, greeting Cook and the scullery maids, who were hard at work as they prepared dinner for the family and staff.

"Going for a walk, Miss Snow?" asked Cook.

"I thought I would see the gardens," she explained. "I have always enjoyed the beauty of nature."

"His Grace's gardens are fine ones," the old woman said. "Enjoy your walk. I'll have a tray for you by the time you return to the house."

"Thank you, Cook."

Eden exited the house and made her way down to the gardens, which looked massive. She entered them and took her time, strolling slowly, studying the different flowers in bloom. She might ask Her Grace for permission to work in them some, something she often did at Traywick Manor. She even arranged fresh flowers she cut into bouquets for various rooms in the household, something which Lady Traywick always complimented her on.

There was a peace here, walking these garden paths. Eden reminded herself when she needed to find solitude, this should be where she retreated.

Left alone both physically and with her own thoughts, she decided she needed to broach the topic of the Duke of Millbrooke.

And try to talk herself out of the growing attraction she felt for him.

VAL WENT TO his study and dealt with some pressing correspondence, continually having to refocus on the task at hand. He decided to go and take a walk to clear his head. He had always done his best thinking when walking. He wished he had Con here, so that he might share his thoughts with his friend. Perhaps he could convince his cousin to abandon the Season for a week and come to visit Millvale.

Withdrawing a fresh piece of parchment, he dashed off a quick letter to Con.

My dear Con —

I know the Season is just getting underway, and I already miss you terribly. You—not the social affairs—which had begun to bore me in recent times.

If you are of a mind and willing to miss a week of the social whirl, would you consider coming to Millvale? I would like to show you some of the changes I have begun making about the property now that it is mine.

To tempt you further, two of our cousins are visiting. Yes, Aunt Agnes asked if she could send for Verina and Justina. They are lovely girls and are proving to be good company for Lia and Tia.

If you are unable to get away at the moment, feel free to visit whenever you can. We have an abundance of guest rooms at Millvale, and it would take but a few minutes to make up one of them for you.

I miss you, Cousin.

Yours,
Val

He wondered if he should sign it in a more formal manner, using his title, but he had never been pretentious with Con. Besides, the ducal seal would be enough to let his friend know who had sent the missive.

Val folded and sealed the note, dribbling wax across it, pressing his signet ring into it. He left his study and coming across a footman, gave it to the servant.

"Have Quigby post this to town tomorrow morning."

"Yes, Your Grace," the footman said as Val walked away.

He left the house, not certain where he might go, and then decided to head to the gardens. He could use a bit of solitude and doubted anyone would be there since dinner started within an hour. Fortunately, his mother had always allowed for a more relaxed seating in the country than in town, and he would not need to change into formal attire for the meal.

Entering the gardens, his thoughts began to drift, knowing he would need to confront the reason he had come here.

Miss Snow.

The pretty governess was dominating far too much of his thoughts. He asked himself why he was interested in her. Was it because she was unattainable? Admittedly, things out of his reach had always presented a challenge to him, and Val was not a man to back down from a challenge. He was drawn to her in an inexplicable way. He had been without a woman for a few months, simply because he'd been too busy in the aftermath of his father's death. That had to be it. He merely missed female companionship, and Miss Snow was of a similar age. He felt comfortable in her company and enjoyed their lively conversations. The fact that he had, for a brief moment, entertained the idea of making her his duchess was absurd. Even if dukes did as they pleased, he could not think of a one whom had wed a lowly governess.

He turned a corner and saw the object of his desire a few paces away. Miss Snow bent, touching a rose, her nose resting against the petals as she inhaled deeply. Because of her position, her gown was molded to her shapely derriere, and all Val wanted to do was squeeze and knead it.

She must have sensed his presence because she wheeled quickly, facing him.

"Are you following me?" she demanded angrily, spots of color staining her cheeks.

"I merely wished to stroll in *my* gardens before dinner, Miss Snow."

More color flooded her face, and he saw she became flustered.

"There. I have gone and done it again, Your Grace. I do not know what is wrong with me. I promise you that I am a kind soul. My mother brought me up to have wonderful manners, but they seem to fly out the window anytime I see you. Please, accept my deepest apologies."

"Apologies accepted. Stay," he urged, seeing she was about to bolt. "Walk with me."

He caught the reluctance in her eyes and knew it was mainly because a duke had ordered her to remain.

Softening his voice, he said, "Stay. Only if you wish to. Not because I am a duke—but because you wish to stay and talk with me."

Obviously, she was torn. Her hazel eyes had gone amber. She nibbled on that plump, bottom lip again, causing him to wish he could do the same.

"I do not wish to seduce you, Miss Snow," he said bluntly, taking her aback.

"I did not say that, Your Grace," she said, her face now flaming.

"But you thought it. Didn't you?"

With a pained expression, she said, "Servants are beholden to their employers. A governess is nothing more than a servant. I will share that I had a previous employer who thought to take advantage of the fact that he held sway over me."

Instantly, anger sizzled within him. "Who?" he demanded. "Who wished to harm you?"

She gently placed her hand on his foreman, soothing him at once. "You are not some white knight charging into battle to protect my honor. It matters not who the gentleman was. Only know that it happened, and because of that, I am more wary than most women in my position."

Her hand fell from his arm, and he longed to catch it, entwining his fingers with hers. After what she had just confided in him, however, that should be the last thing he attempted to do.

"This was before you came to be employed in Aunt Agnes' household?"

Miss Snow nodded. "It was my first post I ever held. I was young and naive, thinking I would be with the family many years. I learned this was a pattern of behavior with this particular viscount, and that I was not the first to leave his household under a dark cloud."

She turned away and began walking, and he fell into step with her.

"Unfortunately, he dismissed me without references when I would not play his games with him. The viscountess felt sorry for me. She told me of a position needing to be filled at Traywick Manor, and I used the last of my meager savings to travel there. For some unknown reason, Lady Traywick hired me, despite the fact I had no references and little experience. I have been at Traywick Manor ever since."

She came to a halt, her gaze meeting his. "So you see, Your Grace, it is not simply a matter of protecting my heart. I must also protect my reputation. It is my livelihood."

"I am sorry if you have felt I have given you undue attention, Miss Snow. You merely are so easy to talk to. I miss Con. We saw each other almost daily over the years, going to school and university together, then sharing rooms in town after our studies had been completed. I adore my sisters, but they are younger and do not have the same life experience as I do. I have never been close to Mama, and she keeps to herself these days, Aunt Agnes her only companion. I did not know Mama's grief would be so strong."

He smiled at her, not flirtatiously, but in a friendly matter. "Now that I am a duke, people treat me differently, even though I am the same man I always have been, merely with a plethora of new duties to fulfill. I suppose I am a bit lonely and have sought your company in friendship."

He saw her softening. "I can be a bit lonely at times myself, Your Grace. Although I am included as a member of the family when I am at Traywick Manor, I know I am not officially a Fulton. And the servants seem to keep their distance from me. So I do have an inkling what you are going through. Perhaps you should ask Viscount Dyer to come and see you."

"You are perceptive, Miss Snow. In fact, I have come from writing a letter to him, asking him to do that very thing. While I hate for him to abandon town and the Season, I could stand to have my closest friend with me for a short while."

He looked at her hopefully. "Might I call you a friend? I know it is most unusual for a duke and a governess to form a friendship, but I would appreciate speaking with you from time to time while you are here at Millvale."

She pondered his words and finally said, "You think it possible for us to be friends?"

"I do. You will be here most likely through the spring and summer months. I would be happy to have someone to share things with. Ask advice of. Even go riding with."

Worrying her bottom lip again, she said, "I suppose we can try. To be frank, I have never had a friend myself. Being an only child was lonely. I spent hours with Mama, talking and reading and playing games. Papa took me about on the estate. We dined as three, taking all our meals together. I rarely even went into the nearest village." She hesitated. "What I am saying is that I am not certain I know *how* to be a friend."

"Other than Con, every other gentleman I know is merely an acquaintance. Not a friend."

Val realized that wasn't quite truthful because he had made a friend in Julian once the marquess had shown interest in Ariadne. He hoped their friendship would grow. For now, though, he understood Miss Snow's loneliness because he felt it weighing heavily upon him now.

"Con and I have been the closest of friends for almost two decades. I think I can teach you how to be one. First, we should be open and truthful with one another. Even if we hold different opinions on a subject, we should be respectful toward one another. And no topic is out of bounds."

She nodded. "I will try to abide by these rules."

Then she smiled brilliantly at him, causing him to suck in a quick breath. He still desired her, but after what she had shared about her former employer, Val would never take advantage of her. Instead, he would try to be her friend—and see where it led them.

He might change his mind about her once he got to know her

better. Most of the women he coupled with he knew very little about and when he did learn more than he wished, he found they lost their appeal to him. Getting to spend time with Miss Snow and learning more about her might be the very thing which might eventually repel him. Then he would be through with his fantasies of her and be able to move on to the Marriage Mart.

But if she proved to be interesting and honorable, he just might need to move from friendship—to romance.

"I agree to do so, as well," he said, returning her smile. "I look forward to knowing more about you and your opinions, Miss Snow."

Chapter Eleven

VAL FINISHED UP his meeting with his steward and returned to his study. His step had been lighter for the past couple of days, things being somewhat settled between him and Miss Snow. She had not shown one sign of being prickly in his presence. In turn, he had been a perfect gentleman, one eager to be in her company.

He took a seat behind his desk and found that Quigby had placed the post atop it. He flipped through until he found one in Con's handwriting and broke the seal.

My dear Millbrooke (Oh, that sounds rather stuffy and formal, doesn't it? I shall try again.)

Your Grace (My, that sounds downright pretentious. Then again, I have never written to a duke before. Perhaps the third time will be a charm.)

Val (That sounds better—but why do I feel guilty calling a duke by his given name? I am looking over my shoulder to see if Mama, who is a stickler for rules, is ready to chastise me thoroughly.)

All joking aside, my dear Val, I must inform you that I cannot leave town at this time. No, it is not because I am sniffing about pretty young things. It is due to my obligations regarding Lucy. You know how protective you were of Ariadne during her come-out Season, and my feelings are the same as far as my sister is con-

cerned. Lucy already has drawn the attention of several gentlemen, but I am most concerned about the Marquess of Huntsberry.

I sense something already between the pair, and I must keep my eyes upon what is unfolding. So, my dear friend and cousin, I will not be able to come visit at Millvale at this point. I hope you will forgive me and that you understand my duty lies in town for now.

Do continue to write to me, though. It was odd, receiving your letter, because I could not recall another time I have ever done so. We have been in each other's company almost daily for years and years. I find myself growing a bit solemn, knowing you are now a duke and will off doing dukely things. I hope we will remain close, no matter what our futures hold.

I will keep you apprised of what is happening during the Season, and you must write to let me know what it is like being an all-powerful duke. Of course, Mama has already been talking about how you will need to come to town next spring and find your duchess.

It seems almost comical to me, the way she talks about things, as if she is in charge of the family now and not you. Then again, that is Mama. I think Lucy is ready to escape Mama's clutches and blossom into the person she has always been meant to be when she weds and leaves Mama's household. Note that I say Mama's and not Papa's. My father may be the Earl of Marley, but the real power in the Alington family is—and always will be—Mama.

I do miss you, Val. Terribly. You are the brother I never had and the friend I will always cherish to my grave. Write to me again.

Constantine Alington,
Viscount Dyer

(See, I know how to close a letter and use my courtesy title as should be done. I fully expect the next letter you send me will mir-

AN UNFORESEEN KISS

ror the same. Love to you, Cousin. Con.)

Val placed the letter on his desk, missing Con more than ever at this moment. His cousin's lighthearted ways had always been entertaining, and he wished he could confide in Con about Miss Snow. He decided he would continue to let the situation between him and the governess slowly unfold. If he thought matters progressed beyond friendship, he would make a trip to town and talk things over with Con. For now, however, he was content to explore the budding friendship between him and Miss Snow.

He decided to go and tell Mama that Con would not be coming. He had casually mentioned to her that he had asked his cousin to visit, and he supposed it would be the decent thing to let her know Con would not be arriving anytime soon. Knowing she and Aunt Agnes spent a lot of time in Mama's morning parlor, he went there now.

As he approached the door and started to knock, he heard peals of laughter coming from the room and paused. He could not recall the last time his mother had laughed so merrily, much less since his father's death and her mourning period had begun.

Waiting for the laughter to die down, he then rapped on the door and opened it. His mother now appeared every inch the Duchess of Millbrooke, haughtiness in her features and posture. He almost questioned if he had actually heard her laughing. On the other hand, Aunt Agnes looked positively guilty, which intrigued him.

As he entered the room, Aunt Agnes rose and said, "I will leave you and your mother, Millbrooke."

When she passed him, Val said, "You do not have to go, Aunt Agnes."

She glanced to his mother and then back at him. "Oh, but I believe I should. You are overdue a long talk with your mama, Millbrooke."

Aunt Agnes departed the room, closing the door behind her, and he went to sit opposite his mother.

"Is something going on, Mama? Something I should know about?"

She looked at him in pity. "To be so intelligent, you wear blinders when you view me, Millbrooke. You always have."

Confusion filled him. "What?"

She sighed. "At least I know my charade has been effective because if anyone asked, you would be the first to say that I have been in deep mourning for His Grace." She paused. "And that simply is not the case."

Confusion turned to intrigue. "What are you telling me, Mama?"

She smiled, not the cold, wintry smile he was used to seeing upon her lips, but a genuine one.

One of joy...

"Frankly, I have been the happiest of my life since Millbrooke was lowered into his grave. You were as close to him as he let anyone get, but he disguised who he was. The world did not know of his cruelties. I am glad the old goat is dead."

Her words stunned him. With concern, he asked, "Did he ... hurt you, Mama?"

Resolve filled her eyes. "I am not one to dwell on the past, Millbrooke. Only know that I been liberated by his death. Oh, I have played the part of the grieving duchess, as is expected of me. I am only sorry that the twins are paying an even greater price than I. If it had been up to me, I would have allowed them to go ahead and make their come-outs, but Polite Society would have skewered me for such behavior."

She smoothed her hair. "I think the girls have already suffered enough. I know you have taken them riding, along with my nieces. Help them to get out more. Take them to the village and let them shop or have a scone and cup of tea. The monthly assembly will be occurring soon. You should escort them to it. I do not want to deny them a little fun, simply because the man who sired them is gone. They had no relationship with him and should not suffer unduly."

"If you think it appropriate for them to attend the assembly, then I would be happy to escort them to it." He hesitated. "Will you and Aunt Agnes attend?"

She laughed merrily. "No. Let them think I am still brokenhearted. When my year of mourning ends, however, I plan to thoroughly enjoy myself in town at the new Season."

Shocked, he asked, "Are you considering marriage again, Mama?"

"Heavens, no, Millbrooke!" she exclaimed, looking aghast at his question. "I have escaped one jailer and have no desire to find a new one." With a mischievous glint in her eye, she added, "It does not mean, however, that I will not take on a lover."

Mortified by their conversation, Val felt the back of his neck go hot. He quickly stood.

"That will be up to you, Mama. I know you will be discreet if you choose to engage in an affair, particularly because I will be trying to arrange good matches for Tia and Lia, as well as pursuing the Marriage Mart myself for my own duchess."

"Oh, I will watch myself," she promised. "I will be a paragon of virtue at each event Polite Society holds. I will do my best to help assist my daughters in finding their husbands. Of course, Ariadne did such a wonderful job on her own. Perhaps she will also become involved and assist her sisters in finding husbands."

"You have surprised me, Mama," he admitted. "And I think you no longer need to tiptoe about the house, looking sorrowful. Our servants have already judged and have their opinions of us. You are the Duchess of Millbrooke. Behave as you wish in your own home."

"Thank you for your advice. I believe after three months have passed in mourning, I might be open to accepting dinner invitations in the neighborhood, but I will not host anyone. Until then, though, I will play my part of the grieving widow if I am in public. Please let your sisters know that they can enjoy themselves a bit. I will not interfere."

"I will do so, Mama. Shall I send Aunt Agnes back to you?"

"Do not feel betrayed by her, Millbrooke. I know you asked her how I fared, and she told you that I was lost. In a way, I was. I wed when I was very young and have never been without the duke telling me what to do and how to think. Agnes was only protecting me, just as you would protect Con."

"Ah, that is the reason I came to see you in the first place," he remembered. "I received a note from Con. He says he cannot come to Millvale at this point. The Season is in its infancy, and Lucy is attracting suitors, one marquess, in particular. Con believes he must stay in town to protect Lucy and her interests."

"I am sorry to hear he cannot come to see you. Perhaps you might go to town and visit with him if you have the need to confide in him."

"I may do so at some point," he shared. "I also need to go in person to visit my other estates at some point. I will not be derelict in my duties."

"You are the duke now, my son," Mama said, tears misting her eyes. "I already knew you would be a better duke than your father."

Val excused himself and left the morning parlor, returning to his study. He took a seat, almost bemused. His mother had certainly convinced everyone in the household—including him—that she was upset by her husband's death. He could see now that she was free and had the opportunity to become a new person, or she might even be the person she always had been and not the one stifled in her marriage by an overbearing husband.

He went to the stables as planned and joined up with his sisters, cousins, and Miss Snow to go riding about the estate again. The girls did not seem to think anything of it when the two of them paired off and rode together, conversing the entire time. Today, he showed them the area where the tenants' cottages lay, and then they followed the stream that separated his property from Lord Arden, his neighbor.

They returned and took tea, where Justina spoke of a history lesson from this morning. It had been about the six wives of King Henry

VIII, and all four young ladies began discussing which wife of the king's they favored.

Trying to draw Miss Snow into the conversation, because she seemed to keep quiet during teatime, he asked, "And which wife is your particular favorite, Miss Snow?"

"It is hard to have a favorite in the midst of such tragedy, Your Grace. Catherine of Aragon, a loyal and faithful wife, was shoved to the side simply because she could not provide her husband with an heir. Anne Boleyn's head was chopped off when false charges were trumped up against her and others close to her. Jane Seymour died in childbirth. Anne of Cleves was put aside merely because of her looks. Catherine Howard was young and immature, saddled with an old man who was most likely impotent. The king had no business wedding such a young, vibrant woman."

She paused, looking pensive. "Perhaps I admire Catherine Parr the most because she did enough to survive, both her husband's reign and the marriage."

Val had never given much thought to the tragic stories of the six wives. "I am glad you are teaching a different view of history to my cousins. While it is important to learn of England's glory and heritage, I suppose it is the people that create that history who should also be studied."

"That is exactly what I try to do, Your Grace. Most heroes in history are but average men. They are just as terrified as anyone else, but they step up in a critical moment and answer a call to greatness. I like for Lady Verina and Lady Justina to delve a little deeper, seeing history from the eyes of those who lived through it, and not simply reel off facts."

Her unique point of view was just another reason that he appreciated Miss Snow so much. He could not think of a single tutor throughout his education who had not focused on large events. In fact, they pretended that every heroic leader in England was a great man in every way. While King Henry VIII may have done things which propelled his country to greatness, the man himself had been terribly flawed.

Tea concluded, and Val went to the library for a bit of quiet time before he joined Miss Snow in the gardens. It had become their habit the past few days to spend time there before they went to their own dinners. He enjoyed their conversations as they strolled through the peaceful gardens. He was beginning to peel a few of her layers away and see more of the woman she was. In turn, he hoped he was giving an unvarnished view of himself, as well.

When he arrived, he entered the gardens, knowing that she would be just beyond the first turn of the path. He found her sitting on a bench and joined her.

"I should have liked to have had a governess such as you," he told her. "One who looks beyond the surface."

"Merely because I taught my charges about one king's wives does not necessarily make me wise or accomplished, Your Grace."

"No, but you are letting them see the humanity of others in history. Yes, Henry is known for beginning the Protestant Church of England, but at what cost? Every life is important, from that of a queen to the lowliest servant."

She pursed her lips in thought and then said, "I do not know of many dukes who would express such an opinion, Your Grace."

He took her fingers and squeezed them gently. "But then again, we have established I am not like most dukes, Miss Snow. And this particular duke is tired of hearing you address him as thus."

She tried to pull her fingers from his, but he held fast, their gazes meeting.

"And how should I address you?"

"When we are alone, as we are now, I would prefer to be Val to you."

Her eyes widened in surprise. "I . . . I do not think I can do so."

He smiled. "I do not think I can do so, *Val*," he emphasized.

She burst out laughing, and he loved the musical sound of it.

"My mother would be appalled, me addressing a duke in such an intimate fashion."

"Your mother is not here. I am. And I am asking—as your friend—if you would do so."

She was silent a few moments and then grinned at him. "Then I suppose you should call me Eden, Val."

Eden . . .

"My parents named me after the Garden of Eden. Mama told me that it was a place in which Adam and Eve had been happy. She likened it to her and Papa's happiness at Brownstone." Pausing, she added wistfully, "But Adam and Eve experienced The Fall and were banished from the Garden of Eden. I suppose I was also destined to be exiled from Brownstone."

He tightened his fingers about hers. "I am sorry your cousin treated you in such an abominable manner, Eden. I am more than happy to punch him in the nose the next time I see Lord Brownley."

His words caused her to laugh again, and Val wanted to always make her laugh.

Not wanting to make her feel as if he had overstepped, he released her fingers and slapped his thighs with his palms.

Rising, he offered his hand to her, saying, "Let us stroll. I have something very interesting to share with you about Mama."

Chapter Twelve

Eden had been at Millvale three weeks now, and the days had flown by.

Mostly because of Val.

She had always thought that her own father was the standard she would use to judge every man by, but the Duke of Millbrooke could almost replace Papa as a measuring stick. He was kind. Compassionate. Intelligent. Interesting. He pushed her to think of things she had never thought about.

And that included becoming his duchess.

Oh, she knew it was fanciful. A silly daydream which could never come to pass. She was destined to spend her life going from house to house, teaching young girls everything from grammar and geography to the manners they would apply when they came out in Polite Society. Val was a duke, one of the highest peers in the land. He would wed a woman of great beauty and impeccable character, and she would come from one of the wealthiest, most established, families in England. He might enjoy spending time with her, but Eden had no family to speak of, barely two farthings to rub together, and worked for her living.

Still, she would fondly remember these days at Millvale for the rest of her life.

She took the girls riding several times a week, and Val joined them when he could. They visited for an hour or so each night before she returned to her room and he went to the dining room for the evening meal. That hour was her favorite part of the day. Val had proven to be insightful and inquisitive. They discussed everything from politics to crops to their youth. Eden had shared more with him than she had another living soul, and she refused to think about the day when Lady Traywick would tell them it was time to return to Cumberland.

They touched one another frequently, comfortable to do so. She would place her hand on his forearm for a moment. He often took her hand, squeezing it as he tried to make a point. Only yesterday, he had plucked a small leaf which had blown into her hair and then smoothed it. She enjoyed his light touch. His citrus scent. The attention he gave her, making her feel as if she were the only person in the world.

She wondered if she should start preparing herself for the day when they would leave and decided she would nest happily in the cocoon she now lived in. Her future, which would prove drab without Val in it, could take care of itself later.

He turned the corner now, a smile on his face which he seemed to reserve only for her. Eden rose, basket and shears in hand.

"What is this?" he asked as he reached her.

"I asked Her Grace if I might create a bouquet for her. I spend a good deal of time in the gardens at Traywick Manor, and I cut and arrange flowers for various rooms. Lady Traywick says I have a gift when it comes to flowers."

"Here, let me take the basket. You can stop as you wish and choose the blooms you want for your bouquet."

As they strolled, he said, "I heard from Tray, Lady Traywick's son."

"I like the young lord," she replied, snipping the stem of two roses and placing the flowers in the basket. "He was ten and six when I arrived, and I thought him like an overgrown pup, brimming with enthusiasm for all around him. He still is exuberant, but he has tempered himself some as he has matured. I think it will be good when his studies are completed and he can be at Traywick Manor more often."

"I had written to him, asking him to come and visit Millvale, especially since his mother and sisters are here. He told me that he was committed to a few projects on his estate this summer and would prefer to see them through instead of leaving everything for his steward to do."

"He is a good young man. Dedicated to the land. He assumed his title when he was very young. The steward has shared with me that Lord Traywick met with him for the first time when he was but ten years of age and that he is quick to learn."

"I was sorry about the carriage accident which killed Uncle George and Lucius. Tray was Hadrian back then." Val chuckled. "He hated his name more than most did. And there did not seem to be a good nickname for him. Aunt Agnes said that he asked to be called Tray, and she honored his request."

"I think it a nice bit of family history that all you cousins were given such unusual names."

"Your name is also unique," he said. "I have yet to meet another Eden. I even looked up the meaning of your name in an old book I found in the library."

"What did it say?"

"That Eden was Hebrew in origin and meant *place of pleasure*."

"Well, I did tell you that Mama named me after the garden where the first people God created dwelled."

His gaze seemed suddenly intent, and Eden grew warm under it. She turned away, moving to snip some primroses and then hyacinths. Though their conversation had ceased, she still enjoyed his company immensely.

When the basket was almost full, she told him, "I must arrange them before we return. There is a gardening shed with tools and a table. I can put the arrangement together there."

She led Val to the shed, and he opened the door. The small building had two windows, but she told him to leave the door open for more light. Quickly, her fingers got busy, snipping stems as she placed the various flowers into a vase she had brought to the shed earlier. Eden pulled out a rose and moved it to another place, fussing a bit more, then stepping back to admire her work.

Val rewarded her with a smile. "You could always find work as a florist in town if you ever tire of being a governess. This bouquet is so creative, Eden."

She flushed with the compliment. "Thank you. It is something I enjoy doing. I have tried to get the girls interested in it, but neither seem to have the patience it takes to arrange flowers."

He had set the basket down as she worked and picked it up again, along with the large vase. "This will grace our dinner table this evening." Pausing, he added, "I wish you would agree to dine with us."

"No, I like the current arrangement we have settled upon. I actually enjoy a bit of time to myself each evening. And it is not only dinner. I know you all go to the drawing room after."

"Yes. Tonight, Verina and Justina are to play for us, some pieces you have been working on with them. They also will sing a duet together." He hesitated. "Would you care to come hear them perform?"

He looked at her pleadingly, and Eden could not refuse him. "I would be happy to do so."

"Then dine with us, as well. That way, you will already be with us and not have to be sent for when the girls play and sing for us."

"Just this once," she told him, an ache in her chest. She did not want to become accustomed to dining at his table with the rest of his family.

Because it would hurt too much when she left Millvale.

"I shall take this into the house," he said, and they left the shed, returning to the house.

They entered the kitchens, and Cook and two of the scullery maids fawned over her for creating such a beautiful arrangement.

"Cook, Miss Snow is joining us for dinner," Val said, repeating the same to Mrs. Quigby, who entered the kitchens. "And have this arrangement placed on the table for this evening's meal, Mrs. Quigby."

"Yes, Your Grace."

"I should go and change," Eden said. "Since I am dining with the family." She glanced down. "My gown is a bit stained and wet from putting together the bouquet."

"I will see you soon, Miss Snow," he said formally, his lips twitching in amusement. "Come to the drawing room. We shall go in to dine from there."

Eden returned to her room and removed the gown she wore. She draped it over a chair so it could dry. Usually, she wore an apron when she put floral arrangements together, but she had not thought to do so. She only hoped she could remove the stains upon her gown. She hadn't many to her name, and it would be a great loss if even one were taken from her rotation.

She donned a gown of midnight blue. It was the nicest she owned and would be suitable for her dinner with the others. Eden made her way down to the drawing room, finding the duchess and Lady Traywick already present.

Feeling the need to explain her presence, she said, "His Grace requested that I come to dinner this evening because my charges will be performing after dinner."

"Did he now?" Her Grace said. "And do you sing or play, Miss Snow?"

"I do, Your Grace. But tonight is for Lady Verina and Lady Justina to shine. Perhaps I might play for you another time."

"You always have a quick answer, Miss Snow," the duchess observed.

"I think it shows just how intelligent Miss Snow is," Lady Traywick said. "She has been a wonderful influence for my daughters. And here they are now."

Justina and Verina entered, their cousins in tow. They seemed pleased to see Eden present, and she told them she was eager to hear them entertain after dinner.

"You are dining with us?" Justina asked. "Oh, I am so glad to hear that, Miss Snow. You always liven up a conversation."

"You are saying we are dull, Justina?" the duchess asked.

"No, of course not, Aunt Alice," the girl replied. "I just enjoy Miss Snow's presence."

"As do I," Val said, joining them. "Miss Snow is wise and knowledgeable. She is pleasant to be around."

He took a glass from a tray Quigby brought around and nodded to Eden to do the same. She did so and talk turned to an assembly to be held in three days in the village. She had heard Lady Lia and Lady Tia discussing it and was a bit surprised their mother had granted them permission to attend.

"I hope Verina and Justina can also go," Lia said, looking at her aunt with a pleading expression.

"Do they allow girls as young as my daughter to attend?" Lady Traywick asked.

"Oh, yes," Tia said enthusiastically. "Lia and I have gone since we turned ten and four. Everyone that age or older is welcome."

"May we go, Mama?" Verina asked excitedly.

Lady Traywick hesitated, and Val said, "Let them come, Aunt Agnes. I will be there to chaperone them. In fact, perhaps Miss Snow would also like to attend. Four girls might be a little much for me to keep up with. If she will agree to split the burden with me, you might be more comfortable." His gaze met hers. "What do you say, Miss Snow?"

"She says yes," Justina answered. "Miss Snow loves to dance. She goes to the assemblies at Kidsgrove, which is the village closest to Traywick Manor. I hear that everyone wants to dance with her because she is so graceful."

"Well, Miss Snow does sit a horse and ride well. Dancing is also very athletic." He smiled. "I hope this means you will accompany us."

Eden felt a bit lightheaded, thinking she might actually have a chance to dance with him.

"I would be happy to chaperone the young ladies with you, Your Grace."

"And dance," Verina insisted. "You must, Miss Snow."

"Only if I am asked," she said. "And only if the four of you also are engaged for a set. Otherwise, I take my chaperoning duties seriously. I will not leave any of you alone."

Quigby called them in to dinner. Val escorted his mother, and Eden found herself walking with Lady Traywick.

"My girls think of you as family, Miss Snow. Thank you for agreeing to go with them to this assembly."

"Dancing is something we practice regularly, my lady. It will be not only easier but more enjoyable for them to do so with a partner and music being played instead of me humming to them."

"Are you enjoying your time at Millvale?"

"Yes, my lady. I do believe it has been good for your daughters to travel a bit, and they have been good company to their cousins. The bonds of friendship are growing between the four of them. Lady Lia and Lady Tia will certainly look out for their cousins when they do come to town for their come-out Seasons."

"And what of you, Miss Snow? Will you come to town with us?"

"I would like to come with Lady Justina when Lady Verina makes her come-out. I think it would be good for the younger sister to see the older one make her preparations. Being in town would also give us a wonderful opportunity in regard to our studies." She paused. "But once Lady Justina is set to make her come-out, I will no longer be needed, my lady. I should move on to another household."

"I know Verina will welcome your advice when she decides to wed. Justina will be the same. I hope you will consider staying with us at least through Justina's first Season before you leave us."

"I am touched by your offer, Lady Traywick. Of course, I am happy to stay with the girls as long as I am wanted."

They reached the dining room, and Eden received numerous compliments on the arrangement sitting upon the table. Supper was wonderful, consisting of a white soup, a delicate cod, and roasted chicken with fresh vegetables. The wine was particularly good, and Eden enjoyed two glasses of it. Her head felt a bit light as dinner ended since she was not used to partaking often, and she moved carefully back to the drawing room.

Taking a place on a settee near the piano, she tried to contain her excitement when Val came to sit next to her. The scent of citrus filled the air, making her slightly dizzy.

The others gathered about, and Verina played first for them, two selections from Bach, her favorite composer. Justina played next, one selection by Mozart and two more from Haydn. Then the girls sang their duet, with Verina accompanying them on the pianoforte.

Once they finished, everyone applauded, with Val being the loudest.

"You both were a delight," he told his cousins. "Your lessons with Miss Snow, as well as your dedication to practicing, have paid off. Keep practicing those pieces so they become second nature to you. You will be asked to play often when you enter Polite Society, especially while you are looking for your husbands."

He looked to his sister. "Tia, you might learn something from your cousins' strong work ethic when it comes to practicing the pianoforte."

"Are you afraid you will be stuck with me for the rest of your life because I play in such a mediocre fashion, Val?" she teased.

Everyone laughed, and he said, "I would be happy to always keep you at Millvale with me, but you deserve a family of your own—and another man to harangue besides your loving brother."

More laughter followed, and then the duchess rose. "It was a wonderful evening, but I am ready to retire."

"I will go with you," Lady Traywick said. "I am a bit sleepy myself."

They left the drawing room, and the four young ladies started talking about a number they might sing together.

"Will you work on the harmonies with us, Miss Snow?" Lady Lia asked.

"I would be happy to once you decide on a song."

"Let us look through our music," Lady Lia said. "We can make our selection, and Miss Snow can play it for us tomorrow."

"She is good about helping us blend our voices," Verina said.

"Then we can practice together tomorrow," Eden said. "Meet in the music room at noon. I will see our studies are completed by then, Goodnight to you all."

Val rose. "I will see you girls at breakfast. May I walk you out, Miss Snow?"

"Certainly, Your Grace."

They left the drawing room, and he asked, "Would you care to go to the library? I know Justina has said that you excel at chess. Perhaps we could play a game or two."

She blinked sleepily. "I am not at my best tonight. Two glasses of wine have made me sluggish."

"Then come to the library anyway," he urged. "I will find you a boring book to help you drop off even faster."

She giggled, something she hadn't done in ages, and he chuckled.

"All right," she agreed. "Just for a few minutes."

They arrived at the library, and Eden took a seat, trying to stifle a yawn. She closed her eyes to rest them for just a minute, until Val brought her a book.

And tumbled into sleep.

Chapter Thirteen

Val had hoped Eden would agree to a chess match. They had yet to play one another, but he thought she would be an accomplished player. Besides, it would mean more time spent in her company. The more he was around the spunky governess, the more he enjoyed himself. He knew that she, too, liked the time spent in his company.

He only hoped she would be willing to go beyond friendship, especially before Aunt Agnes bundled everyone up and took them back to the northwest of England.

Since Eden was too tired to play against him this evening, he would spend a few quiet moments with her before sending her off to bed. He pulled a book by Thomas Gray from the shelf, another poet, since she seemed to fancy them. He turned and saw her eyes closed, not knowing if she had fallen asleep or not. Remaining where he was, he studied her a moment, something he never had a chance to do.

He liked what she had been doing with her hair recently. Justina, who chattered away about whatever came into her head, had shared with Val that Miss Snow helped her and Verina dress their hair each morning and how she had encouraged the governess to try something new. What he wished he could do with her tresses was free them from the pins which secured them. His fingers itched to run through those honeyed locks.

Returning to the settee, Val settled in, slipping an arm about Eden.

In sleep, she nestled against him, her cheek resting against his chest, her lashes long. He rested his chin against the top of her head, inhaling her essence. He already knew the soap she used had no floral scent, as so many women used. Then again, he understood her financial circumstances and knew she had to pinch her pennies, even when it came to the kind of soap she could afford. More than anything, he longed to take care of Eden. It seemed she worried about everything. All he wanted to do was see her at ease. Enjoying life. Not having to think about how she would make it through tomorrow.

She stirred, her arm reaching for him, slipping about his waist as she snuggled closer to him. He felt his cock stir and ordered it to be still. The last thing Eden needed was to awaken to a bulge in his pants and a pained expression upon his face. Val willed himself to think of mundane things. Bills to pay. A fence to mend. Instead, his thoughts turned to her name and its meaning.

Place of pleasure . . .

Yes, he could see how perfect her name was for her because every place he could touch would be one of pleasure for him. His mouth on hers. His tongue sliding down to her breasts, teasing the nipples with his teeth. Moving lower to her sex, bringing her to orgasm. Thrusting inside her in a dance of love.

Val shuddered, his yearning for this woman greater than anything he had ever known. And yet he was content to merely hold her as she slept. Not rush her. Show her he thought more of her than a woman to rut with. That he valued her as a person. It suddenly struck him how he would never do this for any other woman of his acquaintance. How he respected and admired Eden beyond measure.

That was when he finally listened to what his heart had been whispering all along.

He loved her . . .

Val had seen the miracle of love. Ariadne and Julian had tumbled into love, and for all his doubts of love's existence, he had been proven wrong as he watched them. Their love had only grown stronger with

Penelope's birth. He had decided he would be interested in making a love match for himself, being with a woman he liked as much as he loved. Fortunately, his financial position would allow him to freely make his choice and not have to wed a woman merely for the dowry she would bring with her. Eden had nothing other than herself.

And that would be plenty for him.

He didn't want to hasten things between them because of her past experiences. They were steadily building a friendship, and he hoped it would be the foundation for a lasting love in their future. At the same time, he was afraid of losing her if he did not act soon. The days were rushing by, and before he knew it, Eden would be returning to Cumberland with his aunt and cousins. He found himself at a standstill. Afraid to act. Afraid not to act. And he knew Eden would never be the first to make any kind of move. She had stuck in her head that she was only a governess, someone who would never be suitable for any titled gentleman, much less a duke.

Wanting to be closer to her physically, Val took the chance of lifting her. She mumbled in her sleep as he set her on his lap, but her eyes remained closed. He cradled her to him, feeling the rise and fall as she breathed, her warmth filling him. It wasn't merely a tangible warmth. It was something which filled a hole in his soul, nurturing his spirit. In a short time, this woman had become everything to him. He could see coming home from the fields and walking straight into her arms. Sharing everything about his day with her. Laughing together over something their children did or said.

Eden Snow was a woman he could build a life with. Not any life, but a satisfying one.

He brushed his lips softly against her hair, wishing they could caress her mouth. Telling himself it would happen in due time, he closed his own eyes. With Eden in his arms, he fell asleep, thinking this is how every night could be once they were wed.

EDEN WAS HAVING the loveliest dream and began to awaken from it. When she did, it dissipated like a fog quickly lifting, leaving her with no memory of what she had dreamed, only that it had brought sweet contentment to her.

Warmth blanketed her, and she refused to open her eyes, burrowing deeper into her pillow. No. Wait. Pillows were never this hard.

Slowly, she opened her eyes. The first thing she was aware of was Val's scent, that mixture of citrus and male essence which was all him. It enveloped her—as did the man himself. She closed her eyes again, trying to get her bearings, realizing she sat in his lap and his arms were about her, keeping her safe.

The library. Yes. They had gone there. To get a book. She had been so drowsy and supposed she had fallen asleep. He had graciously not awakened her, instead scooping her up and keeping her safe. She became more aware of him. The hardness of his muscled chest. The even harder lump resting against her bottom. The thought of what that was caused heat to ripple through her.

She had never felt desire in such a pure, physical sense. What she wanted was for him to awaken. To kiss her. To breathe new life into her.

To make love to her.

Eden bit her lip, tamping down the whimper which threatened to escape. How could she want something so badly, knowing it was impossible for her to have? Val deserved the best of everything. He had proven to her what a good man he was. He was thoughtful toward his tenants and family. What he didn't know, he put his mind to and learned quickly. Most of all, he had given her the gift of true friendship, not ever attempting to take advantage of her.

At this point, she almost wished he would. Just one kiss. That was all she needed from him. But if either of them acted upon it, the kiss would change everything. If she kissed him, he would be horrified. She was so far beneath him, and all the trust he had put in her would dissolve in an instant. Yet if he kissed her, she would feel he violated the spirit of the friendship which they had established.

She told herself she couldn't have it both ways. She couldn't kiss Val and remain friends with him. If she did initiate a kiss between them, things would grow uncomfortable, so uncomfortable that it would be hard for her to remain at Millvale. Eden must think of her future, which was at stake. No kiss was worth risking what she had built over the past five years. If they kissed, she would lose everything in an instant because she could not be around him and not want to constantly kiss him. They would not be able to spend time alone together anymore because the dynamics between them would have changed so abruptly.

As much as she wished to remain nestled against him, Eden had to leave. Now. If anyone caught them together, it would be over for her. While it was nothing for a duke to dally with a servant, her reputation could not withstand a hint of scandal. Reluctantly, she took two fingers and gently clasped his wrist, moving his arm away from her body. He was snoring lightly, and she hoped he was deep enough in sleep to not miss her.

Gently, she pushed away from him. How she managed to get to her feet, she had no idea, only that Val slumbered on. His sensual lips were slightly parted, and without thinking, she bent, pressing her own lips to his for the briefest of moments. Then she stepped back, seeing the lazy smile that crossed his lips, turning the corners upward slightly.

She dare not stay any longer. Already, it was late, and she worried a servant would catch her in the corridor. Eden crept across the room and slipped out the door, closing it behind her. With watchful eyes, she made her way back to her bedchamber. The bedclothes had been turned back for her by a maid, and a candle still burned at the bedside table. Quickly, she undressed, slipping into her night rail and blowing out the candle before she crawled beneath the covers.

Sleep did not come. Eden knew it wouldn't. Not when she still could smell the duke's scent upon her skin. Feel her cheek resting against his chest. Warmth spread through her, as well as an ache, one of loneliness and heartbreak. That is what happened now as her heart tore in two. Eden had gone and done the very thing which was forbidden.

She had fallen in love with the Duke of Millbrooke.

And there was no going back.

Her future stretched before her, empty and bleak. She silently chastised herself for being such a fool. He was the kind of man her parents would have loved. Val would have been considerate and caring toward her mother, and he would have had much in common with her father. But her parents were gone, as were her dreams of marriage and having children. She, who had prided herself on her good judgment and prudence, had fallen hopelessly in love with a man who was as unattainable as the king himself.

The first thing she would do would be to put a stop to their nightly discussions. They had grown incredibly close, sharing their opinions and opening up about their childhoods. That hour before dinner each night had been a magical time, but it must come to an end. The same thing with riding. If Val planned to ride out with his sisters and nieces, Eden would make an excuse and return to the house. She knew she could not get out of the daily teatime, but she could limit these other activities.

Then she recalled the Willowshire assembly occurring two nights from now. She had agreed to help chaperone the four young ladies. Her Grace and Lady Traywick might change their minds about letting all their girls attend if Eden did not accompany them. She would do so.

But she would not dance with the duke.

Even if he asked her to do so, she would refuse. In fact, she would refuse anyone who asked her to dance. That way, he could see it was not him being punished. She would merely say she was more comfortable by sticking to her chaperoning duties. Dancing had no part of her evening.

After the assembly, she would keep to herself. Val would press her, wondering why she wished to end their friendship. As honest as she had been with him about everything, she could never reveal she had fallen in love with him. After all, she did have a bit of pride. Eden would have to come up with a good way to word how she wished to extricate herself from their friendship. She would think on it—and trust when the time came, the words would, too.

She lay sleepless for hours, tossing and turning, feeling Val's arms about her. It caused hot tears to fall, and she tried to banish all thoughts of him. Finally, she gave into them, fantasies of him kissing her. Touching her to soothe the ache between her legs. Holding her close, as if he would never choose to let her go.

Only then did sleep come.

Chapter Fourteen

Val awoke. Immediately, he realized Eden was no longer with him in the library. She couldn't have been gone for long, however, because his skin was still warmed by her body, and her scent clung to him.

He was upset that he had fallen asleep, wondering what she had thought when she awoke, cradled in his lap. He had wanted to assure her that all was well. That nothing had changed between them. He could not deny, though, that his feelings grew stronger for her each day. At some point, he would have to tell her that he loved her.

Frustrated, he raked his fingers through his hair, knowing there was nothing he could do now. Should he bring it up with her when he saw her tomorrow? Or should he let sleeping dogs lie? He would hope the right answer came to him and that Eden would not do what he feared most and shut him out.

He left the library and returned to his rooms, the bed seeming far too large and empty for his liking. Ariadne had confided to him once that she and Julian spent their nights together. He had never heard of such a thing with a married couple but had been intrigued by the idea of holding his wife in his arms the entire night. Now that he had found the right woman, he was eager to have the same kind of marriage his sister did with Julian.

Val tumbled in bed, refusing to shed his clothes because if he could not have Eden beside him, at least her scent provided him the memory of her.

When he awoke hours later, he stripped off his clothes and washed before ringing for Fisham. The valet was his usual, cheerful self, chatting away about everything from the weather to the new housemaid Mrs. Quigby had hired.

He went down to breakfast and took generously from the buffet laid out. The newspapers and post awaited him on the table. He flipped through the post first. The only thing needing his immediate attention was a note from Mr. Clarke. The vicar asked Val to stop by at his convenience, which could only mean one thing. The church needed a new roof. With him being the highest-ranking peer in the parish, he would be expected to fund a large portion of it if not pay for the roof in its entirety.

Once he finished his breakfast, he decided to deal with Mr. Clarke first. Going to the stables, he had Perseus saddled so he might ride into Willowshire. He called at the parsonage and was greeted by Mrs. Clarke.

"Oh, Your Grace, do come in. Might I get you a cup of tea?"

"No, thank you, Mrs. Clarke. I have come straight from breakfast to see your husband. He sent me a note, requesting that we meet."

"Then let me fetch him. He is in his study, hard at work writing Sunday's sermon."

The couple returned, both taking a seat opposite him.

"I would like to get right down to business, Your Grace," the vicar said. "No sense wasting your time or mine. This is something I had addressed previously with His Grace, and he showed no interest."

Annoyance filled Val, knowing that his father had had more than adequate funds and could have given Mr. Clarke any amount that he requested.

"How much do you need?" he asked brusquely. "For the new roof."

The clergyman looked startled. "Oh, no, Your Grace. We are not in need of anything." He smiled benignly. "At least at the moment. I reserve the right in the future to come to you if we do find ourselves in need."

"Then what is it?"

"While I know Her Grace is still in mourning and it would not be possible to do so this summer, I would like to toss out the idea to you for an event for next summer. For a fete to be held at Millvale."

"What would this involve?" he asked, intrigued by the idea.

"It is something which is held at my brother's parish in Surrey. Mrs. Clarke and I have visited when it has gone on. It is a day for the community to come together and have a bit of fun. There are games for the children and contests and competitions for adults."

"Bobbing for apples for the children, for example, Your Grace, and archery and pistol shooting for the adults," added Mrs. Clarke. "They also have numerous booths where people can sell their wares. For instance, a knitter might sell everything from a dish cloth to scarves."

"And a small portion of the monies raised for these games and entry fees to competitions would go to the church," Mr. Clarke added. "All we ask is that Millvale might host such an event. His Grace—your father—showed no interest in doing so, but I believe it would be good for the community, as well as the pocketbook of our parish." The vicar smiled. "You never know when a new roof might be needed."

He looked to Mrs. Clarke. "What about food?" Val asked. "Would Millvale need to provide this?"

"That is not necessary, Your Grace. At my brother-in-law's church, they designate booths for food and drink to be sold. The local inn and tavern did a lively business, selling meat pies and ale. Your tenants might wish to do so, selling items from their gardens, for example. It would be a lovely way for them to also be involved."

"This is an excellent idea. When would you suggest holding it?"

"Decent weather would be important, so summer is the best time. Kent is at its loveliest then. My brother's parish holds their event on the day of summer solstice, but naturally, since you are agreeable to hosting, it would be up to you when you wished to do so."

Val didn't like the association of the pagan solstice coupled with the church, and so he suggested, "Perhaps we could hold it the last Saturday in June each summer. I do not see why we could not start the event this year. Yes, Her Grace is in mourning, but this would be something I would host as the new duke." He paused. "And once I wed, my duchess and I would be responsible for organizing the fete."

The couple gave him gleeful smiles, with the clergyman saying, "It would be wonderful if we could start this year, Your Grace. Might I announce it in church on Sunday? And since the monthly assembly is tomorrow night, we could also bring it up there. Word will spread quickly."

"That is acceptable to me. Just to be clear, who would be responsible for creating the games and contests?"

"That usually falls to the host," Mrs. Clarke said. "If you would like, we can put this off for a year, until your mother is up to planning and hosting such a large event."

He had seen the excitement in their eyes and knew this would be an excellent way for him to put his own mark on the dukedom he had inherited.

"No, my family will plan everything, with input from Her Grace. Announce away, Mr. Clarke. Once we have some of the planning underway, we will need to meet with you and Mrs. Clarke again and see what progress has been made. Shall we say next Friday morning, a week from today?"

The vicar agreed to the time, and Val rode back to Millvale, knowing exactly who he wanted organizing this fete.

Eden—because he fully intended to make her his duchess.

He would wait and take it up with her during their conversation in the gardens tonight. She was so efficient, he knew she would be ideal to manage such a large affair with ease. It would help to get Lia and

Tia involved, as well. And his cousins. All four could assist Eden, and it would give them something to look forward to.

When the appointed time came, he returned to the stables. He had not had the opportunity to ride yesterday with his family and looked forward to doing so this afternoon.

He saw the four girls making their way toward him as the horses were being brought out. Eden was missing, however. He wondered if she had been detained, and his concern grew. The girls hurried to the horses the grooms led out, their usual apples in hand.

"Where is Miss Snow?" he asked casually.

Verina told him, "Miss Snow had some work to do and told us to go without her today."

Val cursed under his breath, knowing she was avoiding him after last night.

He mounted Perseus and asked, "Where would you care to ride today?"

For the next hour, he rode the estate with the girls but was miserable. Every second of the ride, he missed Eden's presence. She had a way of bringing others together so effortlessly, not to mention she had become his whole world. Without a doubt, he loved her and wanted to spend the rest of his life with her.

Perhaps that was what he should tell her this evening. No more holding back. Whether she was ready to hear his declaration or not, Val needed to let Eden know how much he cared for her.

They returned from their ride, and he went to freshen up, washing and changing his clothes. He went to the drawing room, dismayed that Eden was not already present. She ducked into the room just before his mother began pouring out, avoiding meeting his gaze.

As usual, she was quiet during tea. She would speak if addressed, but she never initiated any conversation. Knowing her as he now did, he understood she would think it not the place of a governess to speak unless spoken to.

When tea ended, Eden said to Justina, "If you are free now, my lady, I think we need to work a bit more on the piece you wish to play for everyone."

Justina nodded. "You are right, Miss Snow. I am finding the fingering challenging. Bach's inventions are complicated. Would you help me work through it?"

"Of course. Let us go to the music room and do so."

Val did not want to follow them. He had hoped for an opportunity to speak to Eden after tea. Since that was now impossible, he returned to his study and buried himself in work. He left it to go out to the gardens, eager for their daily time alone together. That hour was the best part of his day. Declaring his feelings to her must be done at once, else he might go mad.

He entered the gardens and strode down the path, heading to their usual rendezvous. Eden was not there. He sat on the bench, waiting for her, his frustration growing by the minute.

Had he missed her? Had she arrived before him and gone deeper into the gardens, losing track of time?

He rose and hurried down the path, looking everywhere, but Eden was nowhere to be found. Panic surged through him, and he tried tamping it down. Perhaps the music lesson with Justina had taken longer than planned. He returned to the house, rushing to the music room, only to find it empty.

"The library," he said aloud.

Oftentimes after tea, she went there to prepare the next day's lessons. He strode there now, hoping he would find her. Throwing open the door, Val spied her sitting at a table, pencil in hand, not acknowledging his presence.

Slamming the door got her attention, she looked up and frowned, only as a governess could do.

He moved toward her, demanding, "Where were you? I worried something had happened to you. I searched the gardens, only to find you here."

Something was wrong. Her face was expressionless. He had grown accustomed to how she lit up when she caught sight of him.

Calming himself, he asked quietly, "What is troubling you, Eden? Are you upset about something?"

She rose, unconsciously licking her lips, stoking the fire burning within him. Val wanted nothing more than to capture her in his arms and kiss the life out of her.

"I have assessed our friendship and found that the time for it must come to an end."

Her words stabbed him in the heart. "Why?"

"I do not owe you any explanation, Your Grace," she said formally, and he realized she was no longer addressing him as Val.

Taking a step toward her, he begged, "Eden. Please. Do not do this."

She snatched the diary she had been writing in, holding it protectively to her, as if wishing to create a barrier between them.

"If you hold any value to the friendship we have had the last several weeks, you will respect my wishes."

"Is this about last night? I—"

"I do not wish to speak about last night, Your Grace. In fact, I do not wish to speak to you at all. Goodnight."

He stood helplessly, watching her go, knowing if he tried to stop her—touch her—she would totally shut him out. If he declared his love for her now, she would not believe him and think it was some ploy.

As Eden walked out the door, Val felt as if she had walked out of his life.

Chapter Fifteen

The hardest thing Eden had done was to walk away from Val in the library yesterday.

Especially because she loved him.

But it was because she did so that she knew she had to pull away. Their friendship had grown with the time they had spent alone, and nothing could come of it. Governesses didn't belong in the world dukes inhabited, and she was fooling herself to think she did. The more she was in his company, the more she craved time with him, and it had already caused her to fall in love with him. She had once told him that she must guard her heart. Well, she had certainly done a poor job of doing so, because it was breaking in two.

She had determined she must end all private contact between them now, even though she would be at Millvale until the end of the summer. Eden saw no sense in continuing to spend time with Val. It gave her false hope, and she was a practical woman who must depend upon herself to earn her living. The sooner she broke ties with him, painful as it might be, the better it would be for her own heart.

Of course, she would miss their conversations dreadfully and believed he would, as well. His sisters and cousins were several years younger than he was, and while they were family, they had little in common. Being of a similar age, and having spent many years in her father's company so that she understood the responsibilities of a titled gentleman, Val had been able to confide in her, especially about what he wished to do at Millvale. He had listened thoughtfully to her suggestions and even implemented a few. But he needed to find friends of his own social standing in the neighborhood.

That was one reason she had encouraged him to ask his cousin to come to Millvale. Val trusted Lord Dyer implicitly, and Eden sensed the viscount would always be there for Val, for decades to come. Unfortunately, his cousin was tied in with the Season, helping his sister navigate the waters as she made her come-out. When Val had told her that his friend could not come for a visit now, she nudged him into the idea of going to town himself. Perhaps with their parting of ways, he would do so. Let him be hurt she had abruptly ended their friendly outings. He would recover and move on.

She would miss him terribly, but she could no longer be around him and keep silent about her love for him. That would be a secret which she took to her grave.

Changing from her riding habit, she washed her face with cool water from the basin. She was proud of how she had handled today. Her attention had been solely focused on her charges this morning as they had worked on grammar, French, and did a bit of dancing in preparation for tomorrow night's assembly. She had taken them riding, along with their cousins, and fortunately, Val did not join them. Eden would see him at tea now, but she doubted they would interact much, if at all.

Once she was in the drawing room, she took a seat, encouraging Verina to sit with her. Val came in at the last minute. No, His Grace. She must not ever think of him as Val. It was too intimate.

After the duchess had poured out, he cleared his throat, drawing everyone's attention.

"I have something to share that will affect all you, some more than others."

"What is it, Val?" Lady Tia asked impatiently. "Tomorrow night's assembly?"

"It has nothing to do with the assembly."

"Oh, I cannot wait to dance at it," Justina said, steering the conversation back to the assembly and ignoring that the duke had something to share. "I have just the gown to wear."

"Is it the pale blue one?" her sister asked.

"I like that one," Lady Lia said. "I am going to wear a soft pink."

The four girls took over the conversation, and Eden couldn't help but smile. She caught the duke looking at her and said, "Give them a few minutes before you try for their attention again. They are so looking forward to the assembly."

"I would think they would possess better manners," he said, rudeness in his tone, which caused her cheeks to grow hot. Justina had been the one to change the topic, and Millbrooke's words implied that Eden was not doing her job properly in teaching her charge good manners.

"Girls," she said firmly. "His Grace wanted to share something."

But Lady Tia asked, "What will you wear tomorrow night, Miss Snow? We are of a similar size, so I am happy to loan you something if you would like."

Wishing she could vanquish the blush spilling across her cheeks, Eden said, "That is most gracious of you, Lady Tia, but I will wear something from my own wardrobe. Besides, I will not be dancing. I will be chaperoning, so it really does not matter what I don."

"No, Miss Snow," Justina said, frowning. "You love to dance. You dance at our village assemblies."

"My role is a bit different here, my lady," she said. "I attend the assemblies at Kidsgrove, but you are not with me when I do so."

Verina looked to her mother. "Mama, tell Miss Snow she must dance."

Lady Traywick's gaze fell upon Eden. "I see no reason why, if all the girls have been engaged for a set, that you and Millbrooke might not dance."

"Oh, Val dances superbly," Lia bragged. "You would do well together."

"We will not be dancing together," she insisted. "It is not appropriate for a governess to dance with a duke."

"But you've have danced with an earl before," Verina reminded her. "And both viscounts who have attended have also danced with you, Miss Snow."

"I will dance only if you four girls have suitable partners. Which reminds me, you must bring any partner to meet either His Grace or me before you will be granted permission to dance with him."

"Yes, Miss Snow," she heard in unison.

"Very well. Enough talk of the assembly." Turning her attention back to the duke, Eden said, "You have their attention now, Your Grace."

"Thank you," he said, looking directly at her. Then he gazed about the group. "I met with Mr. and Mrs. Clarke. They are eager to start a new tradition which would raise funds for the church."

"Oh, is this the fete?" Her Grace asked. "They were keen to have it, but His Grace was not in favor of doing so."

"What activities take place at fete?" Justina asked. "I have never been to one."

"An outdoor entertainment," the duchess shared. "It seems our current vicar's brother does something similar at the parish where he serves."

"Yes, exactly," the duke said. "They want me to host the event here at Millvale. There are to be booths which sell food and drink. Stalls for people to sell their wares. Games for children to play, with prizes to be awarded. And contests of skills for adults. Riding. Shooting. Archery. That sort of thing."

"That is quite a bit to organize," Lady Traywick said. "When do they suggest this occur?"

"It is planned for the last Saturday in June."

"*This* June?" Her Grace asked.

"Yes, Mama."

She shook her head. "I am not ready to plan something so elaborate, Millbrooke, much less in so little time."

"I know that. That is why I am asking Miss Snow to do so. She is extremely organized and efficient. She could involve all the girls in helping her. It would be good experience for them to learn how to plan a large affair."

The duke turned to her. "Would you be willing to take on this project, Miss Snow?"

"In all honesty, I am not certain I am capable of it, Your Grace," she said, thinking it wholly inappropriate for her to take on such a task, one which should belong to the lady of the house.

"Nonsense," Lady Traywick said. "You would do a marvelous job, Miss Snow. And Millbrooke is right. This would be excellent experience for my daughters and nieces to gain under your watchful eye."

Eden wanted to refuse, but her employer was looking hopefully at her.

"Then I would be happy to do so, my lady. I am afraid I might have to put aside some of the girls' lessons, though, in order to finish everything on time."

"No maths!" declared Justina. "Oh, I am all for helping plan this fete if we can eliminate maths."

"Maths is involved in everything we do in life," she said primly. "We will have to figure out the number of booths. Create the games to play with the children and make certain they have adult supervision in playing them. Decide upon what prizes the children will be awarded. And then there are the contests for adults. We will need judges. Scoring sheets. Prizes for the adult competitions, as well."

"Agnes and I can help with some of this," the duchess volunteered. "The planning. Not the actual working of a booth or competition." She looked at her son. "Millbrooke, you will need to work with Miss

Snow in regard to the prizes. They should be small but tasteful."

He smiled. "I can do so, Mama. We can finish tea and then meet about them."

"All of us should meet, the girls included," Eden insisted, not wanting to be alone with him for any reason. "We have much to plan. Deciding upon the actual prizes can wait. Let us begin our initial planning, Your Grace. I will inform you when we can meet at a later time regarding the prizes."

He smiled and breezily said, "Oh, I would love to sit in as you formulate your plans, Miss Snow. I promise to be like a fly on the wall and merely listen."

Drat . . .

Smiling graciously, even though she was now boiling inside, she said, "Of course, you are welcomed to do so, Your Grace. I only hope you will not become bored during the tedious planning."

"I doubt I will be bored," he replied. "We have so much to talk about."

They finished their tea, everyone talking about how delicious the raspberry scones were, but they had tasted like dust in her mouth.

"Shall we go to the library?" the duke asked.

The thought of being in the library again with him, even though others were present, had Eden flustered. All she could think about was waking in his strong arms. How the scent of his cologne lingered on her skin. How she tingled, her softness against his hard, muscular chest.

"That is a good idea," Lia said. "We could sit at the tables to write, and there is plenty of room for all of us."

All four girls came quickly to their feet and left the drawing room, leaving her to walk there with the duke.

When they reached the corridor, he said, "We have things to talk about, Eden."

"Miss Snow," she snapped. "And we have nothing to discuss, Your

Grace. I hope you will sit quietly and not interrupt as we toss about ideas for your fete."

He chuckled. "I see you are putting me in my place and ordering me about, as usual."

Mortified, she could only apologize. "I regret my hasty words, Your Grace. Naturally, your opinion is of value. Feel free to give it."

"Oh, I will, Eden. You can count on that."

She rushed ahead of him, her skirts swishing, his laughter ringing in her ears. She told herself to take deep breaths to calm her racing heart and reminded herself that four young ladies would be present. He would not dare bring anything up in their presence that was inappropriate.

Or would he?

Suddenly, she felt she couldn't trust him, but she had no choice.

She reached the library and saw Justina and Verina had already gone to where she kept their school things, bringing out parchment and pencils.

"I can take notes. My handwriting is neat," Verina said.

"Mine, as well," Lady Lia shared.

"Then you two should sit at the table and write down whatever we talk about," Justina said, sitting on a nearby settee, where Tia joined her.

Eden took a seat at the table with Verina and Lia. She hid her dismay when Millbrooke joined them. He was too large, taking up so much room. It made her feel as if she were suffocating. She kept silent, though. These four young ladies were all intelligent, and she did not want them to pick up on any strife she felt being in the duke's presence.

"All right. Let us talk about the games for the children first," she began.

They discussed various types of games, simpler ones for the younger children, deciding that they might put an age limit on those who could participate in them.

"No child over seven years of age," Verina said, writing down the suggestion.

Within half an hour, they had a list of six games for younger children and five for older ones. They spent another half hour discussing where to hold the games and decided they should all be in the same area, so parents could more easily keep up with their children. Some of the games would require them making items to be used in play, while others, such as the bobbing for apples, would merely need barrels of apples to be collected and brought to the area, along with water.

"We can talk of prizes later," she said. "While children enjoy prizes, simply playing a game will be fun for most of them. Let us discuss the contests for adults now. I will be honest. With so many children running about, I am not in favor of any contest involving pistols."

"I agree," the duke said. "But archery could be more confined and in an area away from the children's games. The targets more obvious, even to children. I believe archery to be less dangerous."

"Should we have divisions?" Justina asked. "Men and women. Even children?"

They debated the topic for a while and finally decided to hold separate contests for men and women. No children would be allowed to compete in this first year.

"Set a cap then, regarding age," Millbrooke suggested. "Perhaps four and ten?"

They agreed and Eden said, "A riding contest was another suggestion His Grace made."

"We could model the riding contests on the ones in our village, Miss Snow," Verina said eagerly. "We are familiar with them."

"Why don't you explain it to the others?" she suggested.

Both Verina and Justina took turns sharing the various contests. They decided to limit it to two this first time, with the possibility of adding new riding competitions in years to come. One would be a timed course where jumps were required. Another would be a race, and they discussed the distance riders should go.

"The meadow would be ideal for the horse racing," Lia pointed out. "We could have three or four riders at a time, with the winner moving on to the next round. I think men and women could compete against one another."

"I agree," Eden said. "At Kidsgrove, which is near Traywick Manor, I competed against men and women in the same contest. A horse is the great equalizer between the genders."

The duke spoke up. "The same would be true for the skills course."

"I agree," Tia said. "Why, I think Miss Snow could beat anyone, as long as you allow her to ride Andromeda, Val."

"Oh, I would not be competing," she said quickly.

"Why not?" demanded the duke.

"I am not from here. It should be for locals only. Besides, I will be monitoring all the booths. Making certain the many volunteers make it to their stations. Showing the judges to their posts. I simply will not have time to compete."

"Miss Snow is right, Val," Lady Lia said. "I know usually those tasks would fall to Mama, but she will not want to participate so heavily this first time while she is in mourning." She brightened. "And by next summer, you might even have found a bride. She can be the one who takes on the planning of the fete."

Quigby appeared. "Dinner is served, Your Grace."

"Thank you," the duke said. "In the meantime, Miss Snow, please draw up the number of judges you might need for the various contests. We will need to start asking some of my neighbors to participate. The older ones who still have their wits about them, but ones who would not wish to compete in archery or riding."

"Yes, Your Grace," she said demurely, her gaze lowered.

"Come along then," he told the girls. "Off we go to dinner." Then turning back to her, he said, "I will go over your lists after tea tomorrow. Better yet, before tea. The girls will not wish to ride tomorrow, with the assembly beginning at seven o'clock. They will want to fuss over their attire and hair. We shall meet at two o'clock. That will give us two hours before tea begins."

"I doubt we will need that long to—"

"This will be the first fete I host, Miss Snow. I want everything to run like clockwork. I will see you in the library at two o'clock. Please, be prompt."

She bowed her head, waiting for him to leave the room. Eden wanted to say that she was not his employee. She should not have to be doing his bidding or work on something on such a large scale for him. But she did want him to succeed. He wanted to be a good duke and leave his mark behind. This fete could become a community tradition which would occur for decades to come. Starting off on the right foot would be imperative.

Eden would do what she could in order to make the fete a huge success—and she would do her best to keep her contact with Millbrooke to a minimum.

Chapter Sixteen

She had survived.

Eden had presented her neat list to the Duke of Millbrooke. In fact, several lists. Verina and Justina had been unable to concentrate on their lessons, so she had sent for Lady Lia and Lady Tia to join them. Together, the five of them had talked for several hours, honing their suggestions, while she made meticulous notes. As she finished, Verina would make a copy of her notes so that they would have more than one set to use as a reference.

They had completed everything they could, from the types of games and contests to the rules to the number of entrants for each. It also listed the number of judges needed for each. They had created separate lists for booth ideas, and the girls were eager to accompany her into Willowshire. They would go to some of the various business and offer them the chance to sponsor a booth first before opening it up to individuals.

Lady Tia had likened it to a fair she and her sisters had gone to several years ago, saying the fair had booths that sold everything from jewelry to hats to sewing supplies and ribbons. She liked how the girls were coming up with such creative ideas and how they wanted to follow through. Lady Lia said that after they contacted the businesses, she and her twin would go and speak to each of Millvale's tenants and give them a chance to sell vegetables from their gardens to manning a booth of their own.

The duke had mentioned to them yesterday afternoon when planning had been underway that an announcement would be made at church come Sunday morning, so most of the residents in the area would be made aware of the fete to be held. The clergyman would also mention it at tonight's assembly. Knowing how quickly news could spread, especially at an assembly, Eden would be surprised if most of Willowshire had not heard of the Millvale fete by the time church was held on Sunday morning.

She had watched as the duke read through each of the prepared lists, asking her several questions which she easily answered. He asked that copies be made, and she proudly told him he could have the lists in his hands because copies had already been drawn up. Everything between them had been formal and dignified. She had worried he would bring up the incident in the library, but he had not. If he had, Eden didn't know what she would have done.

He had mentioned that he hoped Con could come to the fete, and she hoped his cousin would make time to do so, even if he only came for the day.

When the duke's questions had run out, Eden excused herself. He reminded her that he would see her at tea, which would be a heavier meal than usual since no dinner would be served at Millvale this evening. The assembly started at seven o'clock, and the girls were adamant about being there from beginning to end.

At tea, she hadn't needed to utter a word because all the younger ladies talked about was the assembly. They finally began sharing some of what had been planned for the fete with the duchess and countess, and both women approved of the activities. The only fly in the ointment had been when Millbrooke had mentioned an upcoming meeting with the local clergyman and his wife for the next Friday morning. He said he would require her presence at the meeting because she was the one actively involved in the planning of the fete.

Though reluctant to go with him and mentioning the lessons

which would be missed if she did so, he suggested the girls could ride in the morning after they returned and then do their academic work that afternoon. She had agreed, not wishing to seem peevish or difficult in front of Lady Traywick.

Now, she stood in her room, slipping on a dowdy gown. While she had been brought up in the country and had never had to dress as smartly as one did for town, she knew nothing in her wardrobe flattered her or was even remotely fashionable. The gowns she wore were several years old and plainly designed. Eden told herself that it didn't matter. That she was going to look after the four young ladies. She wasn't expecting to dance herself. She knew no one in Willowshire, so she doubted anyone might ask her to dance.

Unless the duke did.

Her mouth grew dry thinking of that. Her body tingled in anticipation, and she briskly walked about the room, trying to get over the odd sensation that came whenever she thought about Val. No, Millbrooke. He could never be Val to her again. She only hoped that he would draw the attention of others and be too busy to even think of asking her to dance.

Because if he did, she would not have the willpower to say no to him.

At least she could do something special with her hair. Eden spent a long time brushing it out and then piled it high atop her head. She also took out a gold locket which had belonged to her mother and fastened it about her neck. It was the only jewelry she possessed, and she had never had an occasion to wear it since her mother's death. She only wished she had a pair of earrings or delicate slippers to help dress up her appearance more.

"Ah, if wishes were horses, beggars would ride," she said aloud to herself, quoting the old Scottish proverb her father used upon occasion. Eden needed to look on the best side of tonight. She would be getting out with the girls. Hearing music. Watching the dancing. All that in itself would be quite exciting.

She knocked on the connecting door and entered, asking if Verina or Justina needed any help. Bessie, the maid who had accompanied them from Traywick Manor and had cared for the girls, finished smoothing Verina's gown.

"They are ready except for their hair, Miss Snow," the maid said. "You have a knack for doing so which I lack."

Justina sat at the dressing table. "Do me first, Miss Snow. What do you think?"

They had endlessly talked of hairstyles since learning of the monthly assembly, and Eden had visualized what she thought would suit each of her charges. She now dressed Justina's hair and then Verina's, seeing both girls were pleased.

"Thank you so much, Miss Snow," Verina said. "We are beautiful, thanks to you."

"I look older," Justina said. "Don't you think I look older?"

"You both look lovely," she complimented. "And before you know it, you *will* look older. You will be a matron with graying hair and a houseful of children and wonder where the time went."

They laughed at her words, and Verina said, "If you are not a companion to Mama, Miss Snow, you must come and teach my children. All five of them."

"Five?" she asked.

"At least," Verina said. "I want five or six."

"Then I want seven or eight," Justina retorted, trying to outdo her sister.

"Husbands first, then you may negotiate the number of children," she said, her heart light.

They went to the foyer, where the Duke of Millbrooke paced. Lady Lia and Lady Tia were already there. She deliberately kept her eyes off his tall frame and tailored clothes, focusing on his sisters instead.

"You will break a good number of hearts next Season," Eden predicted.

"I hope I do not," Lady Lia said worriedly.

"I hope I break many," Lady Tia countered. "I cannot wait to do our Season. It will be so much fun."

She decided Lady Lia would be the first to wed between them, and Lady Tia would take her time and enjoy a few Seasons before she grew serious about marriage.

"The carriage is waiting," the duke said.

They went outside, Millbrooke handing up each of them. She came last, as she should, and he frowned.

"Is something wrong, Your Grace?"

"You are beautiful, Eden," he said softly. "I only wished you had a gown which would allow you to shine."

A lump formed in her throat. "Thank you," she said softly, accepting his compliment without disparaging him.

When she climbed in, she saw Lady Lia, Lady Tia, and Justina sat on one of the cushions, while Verina had taken a spot opposite them, against the window. She wished the girl would sit in the center so that Verina could act as a buffer between her and the duke, but she did not know how to ask Verina to move without drawing attention. Eden took the spot by the other window, leaving the duke to sit between them. As he did, she caught the whiff of his cologne, which caused a great yearning to ripple through her. His entire left side pressed against her right, and her body welcomed the heat, even as her mind warred against the pleasure she felt touching him.

They arrived in the village at the assembly room, and Verina and Justina were more excited than she had ever seen them. Their party of six entered the rooms, and she saw a group of musicians tuning their instruments. The room was large but already crowded, and she knew at some point, she would need to drink some punch and get some fresh air, not particularly liking large crowds.

Immediately, others made their way toward them. After all, a duke always drew attention wherever he went. Soon, the girls were asking for permission to dance and introducing her and Millbrooke to their prospective partners. She approved of the partners for the first set. None of them were what Eden would consider too mature.

Fortunately, the duke was swept away from where she stood by a viscount's sister. Now, she could relax and take a seat and enjoy watching the girls dance.

"Miss Snow? It is Miss Snow, isn't it?"

She turned and found a gentleman who looked to be in his early to mid-thirties, fair-haired and blue-eyed. He was just under six feet and had the nicest smile.

"Yes, I am Miss Snow, governess to Lady Verina and Lady Justina Fulton."

"I hope you do not think me too forward in introducing myself to you. Country rules are more relaxed. I am Lord Arden."

Eden had heard his name before. "Oh, you own the property which abuts Millvale."

"Yes, that is correct. Might I ask you to dance this first set with me, Miss Snow? I know you were charged to look after His Grace's sisters and nieces, but it seems they all will be dancing."

Suddenly, Eden wanted to dance very much.

"Yes, my lord. I would be happy to partner with you."

Lord Arden led her onto the dance floor, and soon the fiddles were playing and she was twirling, happy to have been asked to dance. The set went on for a good twenty minutes, and she found herself out of breath by the time it ended.

"Shall I fetch some punch for you, Miss Snow?" Lord Arden asked as he escorted her off the dance floor.

"I could certainly use a cup," she replied. "Yes, my lord. Please do so."

He returned her to where he had claimed her, and the others

joined her. All four girls radiated happiness. New partners showed up, and she was introduced to all of them. Lord Arden joined their group and whispered in her ear a thing or two about who was requesting a dance. Eden gave her approval and then sipped on her punch as the girls went to talk to others from the village before the second set began.

"The punch is quite good," Lord Arden remarked. "And you are a wonderful dancer, Miss Snow."

"Thank you, my lord. You are, as well."

"I try my best. I dance with my girls every night before they go to bed."

"Oh, you have daughters?" She looked about. "Is Lady Arden here with them?"

Sadness crossed his face. "Lady Arden died giving birth to our younger girl, who recently turned five. My older daughter is eight. Obviously, they are too young to attend the village assemblies."

"I am sorry for your loss, my lord. My own parents have been gone almost six years now, and not a day goes by when I do not mourn their absence from my life."

"My wife was a good woman," he said. "And an excellent mother. I only wish my girls could remember her. I had a painting done of Lady Arden shortly after we wed. I take the girls to look at it every day and tell them stories about her." He sighed. "She is simply a pretty lady in a picture to them."

"Keep doing what you are doing, my lord," Eden encouraged. "One day, they will be old enough to understand, as well as remember the stories you tell them. In fact, I think they will be eager to hear more from you."

"I hope so. But I feel it is time I move on. The girls need a mother—and I need an heir."

He looked at her intently, and it took her aback.

Was this gentleman considering her for that role? Goodness, they had only met. And yet she liked him already, quite a bit. He seemed like a good father, and that meant a lot in her eyes. She was reading things into the situation, though, which simply were not there.

"It looks as if the music is ready to start again." Lord Arden looked at her hopefully. "Would you care to take to the dance floor again, Miss Snow?"

"Yes, my lord. I would."

Once more, Eden thoroughly enjoyed her time dancing with this gentleman. Perhaps he needed a governess for his own girls, and that was why he was getting to know her a bit. She would have to refuse, of course, because she still had three years left at Traywick Manor.

Lord Arden returned her again, and one by one, the girls joined her. Others appeared, and she was introduced to different people in the village, but Lord Arden remained by her side. When the girls went out for a third time, after receiving Eden's approval, Lord Arden smiled.

"I would ask you to dance again, Miss Snow, but that would keep you from meeting others."

Suddenly, the Duke of Millbrooke was at her elbow.

"Miss Snow promised me this set, Arden. If you will excuse us."

He placed her hand atop his sleeve and guided her to the center of the room, where a square was forming.

"I did not promise you anything," she hissed.

"If I had not stepped in, Arden would have danced with you a third time."

"No, he had just told me that he would not be asking me again."

For a moment, the duke had no reply. Then he said, "You owe me a dance. After all, we are old friends."

Before Eden could reply, the music began again.

Chapter Seventeen

SHE WAS DANCING with a duke.

Eden watched Val dancing across from her. For a large man, his movements were graceful. Then again, she would have expected nothing less from a handsome duke. She did not want to enjoy the dance, but she couldn't help herself.

And knowing this would be the only time they would dance together, she threw herself into it with abandon.

For the next twenty minutes of the set, Eden lived in a fantasy, one much better than anything she had ever conjured in her mind. When she and Val came together, their movements were as one. She felt attractive. Powerful. Desirable. And she was having the time of her life.

But all good things finally come to an end, and so must this dance. As he escorted her from the floor, she noticed the musicians setting down their instruments, and one said they were taking a respite for half an hour, directing those in attendance to the next room, where punch and light refreshments were being served.

While Eden had been light on her feet the entire time she danced, her knees now grew weak. She stiffened them—and her spine—and immediately began playing mother hen, rounding up and ushering the young ladies in her care to the adjacent room. The duke did not follow. Someone had called his name and drawn him aside, for which she was grateful.

"I am having ever so much fun," Lady Tia declared to them.

"I am, too," her twin said softly, a smile on her face. "I am grateful Mama let us come tonight."

"I think these musicians are wonderful," Verina said. "Dancing to music is better than you humming along, Miss Snow."

"I am glad to have danced every dance," Justina said. "It makes me eager for my own come-out."

She looked at these four young women, and for a moment, a bit of envy filled her. They were on the cusp of a new chapter in their lives, while her story would play out the same, over and over, as she went from household to household over the next several decades. She would have to hope that some family would think enough of her, or take pity on her, to give her a small cottage where she could retire, because she would never earn enough money on her own to be able to do so.

"I am in need of the retiring room," she told them. "Go and get yourselves something to eat. I will join you in a few minutes."

What Eden needed was fresh air. So many people had entered the refreshment room, and she was beginning to feel suffocated. She slipped out the front door and went to the side of the building, where she had spied a courtyard when they had arrived.

Being outside with a bit of a breeze helped, and she strolled the length of the courtyard twice, admiring the fountain in its center. She trusted by now that the duke had joined the girls because she still needed a few minutes to herself before she returned inside.

Then the air about her changed, feeling charged, and she caught the scent of citrus. Turning, she saw Val standing in front of her.

"Why did you follow me?" she asked harshly. "Can I not have a moment to myself?"

She turned away and began walking quickly, sensing that he followed her. When she reached the end of the courtyard, she wheeled again and said, "Go away, Your Grace."

"What happened to speaking to me in an amiable fashion?" he asked, his emerald eyes boring into her.

"Rudeness should be treated with rudeness," she said crisply in her best governess voice. "You were extremely rude to Lord Arden. I told you he was leaving me and planned to dance with another."

He took a step closer to her, their bodies almost touching. Her back was to the wall of the building, giving her no avenue of escape.

"Are you upset that I danced with Lord Arden?" she asked, her tone acrid. "It is not as if anyone else had asked me to dance with them. To be truthful, I believe he felt sorry for me standing there all alone." She wet her lips. "I thought it extremely kind of him to ask me to partner with him. He's a widower, you know."

"I do know," he said huskily. "And Arden is not known for dancing much at assemblies. He needs an heir, Eden."

His words hung in the air, heat radiating from him.

She swallowed nervously. "That has nothing to do with me." The words had sounded right in her head but came out weak and ineffectual.

Suddenly, Val placed his palms against the building, caging her. "You will not become Lady Arden," he commanded, as if he owned her.

Her heart was beating wildly. "I have no desire . . . to become Lady Arden."

"Good," he said softly, his head dipping.

Then his lips were pressing against hers. Firm lips—and yet so soft in their touch.

Eden had not expected this kiss. It was an unforeseen kiss and took her totally by surprise.

The duke continued brushing his lips softly against hers, bringing about a huge yearning within her. Her scalp tingled. Her heart slammed against her ribs. Her fingers itched, wanting to run through his thick, burnished locks. Then he nibbled on her bottom lip, causing her to gasp. The kiss became firmer. Demanding more of her. Without meaning to, her fingers went to the lapels of his coat, tightening on them, pulling him closer to her.

Their bodies now pressed together as their lips did, and a low growl came from him. The sound caused her nipples to pucker, feeling so sensitive.

His hand clasped her nape, holding her in place as the kiss heated up. It was a series of kisses, their lips parting and then coming back together, causing her belly to flutter and the place between her legs to ache in a way it never had before.

When he broke the kiss, she tried to tell him they must stop, but his tongue began running slowly back and forth across her bottom lip, sending fevered chills through her. Then the tip of his tongue ran along the seam of her mouth, and she gasped, opening her mouth to protest his actions.

It was all the invitation he needed, and his tongue swept inside her mouth. Tasting her. Teasing her. She had known a kiss was an intimate gesture, but this intimacy went even further than she could have imagined. Hesitantly, she allowed her own tongue to brush against his, and a growl sounded from him. Soon, their tongues were at war, attacking and retreating, then lazily exploring one another.

She could have done this all night, but a sudden clarity filled her, clearing the haze of desire which had lulled her. Eden realized they were kissing in a public place. Someone could come along at any moment.

And her reputation would be in tatters.

Not so the duke's. Oh, it would be known that he had dallied with some governess, her name quickly forgotten by the gossips as he moved on to another conquest. For her, though, she would be dismissed, yet again, without references. This time, there would be no Lady Kessley to assist her in finding a new post. She doubted she would be able to find any opening for a governess.

Anger filled her, and she pushed against his chest, hard, breaking the kiss.

He didn't budge and merely looked down at her, smiling, which further infuriated her.

"Move, Your Grace. Now," she commanded.

"You certainly enjoy ordering me about, Eden."

Tears swam in her eyes. He would see them as a sign of weakness, but she knew they were ones of rage.

"I do not want to kiss you," she said firmly, pushing against him again, which did absolutely no good.

"You weren't protesting before," he said, a devil-may-care look in his eyes.

"I thought you were a good man. A gentleman. But you are like all other men. You use a woman and then discard her."

He frowned deeply. "No, Eden. Your words offend me. I—"

"If you have any decency within you and feel anything for the friendship we once had, please, Val, let me go," she begged.

Tears spilled down her cheeks, and his hands fell away. He stepped back two paces.

"I apologize, Eden. I did not mean to—"

"It does not matter what you meant," she said bitterly. "Your actions spoke loudly enough. Do not attempt to ever do something like this again, Your Grace. Else I will be gone the next morning—and you will have to explain to Lady Traywick why her governess was so frightened that she had to flee Millvale."

Eden fled the courtyard, thankful no one else had thought to come out for air. She rushed to the retiring room and hid behind one of the curtains, willing herself not to shed any more tears. Finally calm, she went and washed her hands and face, a servant handing her a cloth to dry herself. She had no mirror in which to inspect herself and only hoped she could return to the assembly room without questions being asked of her.

She rejoined the girls, who stood with cups of punch, a few other young ladies talking with them.

Lady Lia looked at her with concern. "Are you all right, Miss Snow?"

The lie quickly came to her. "I stepped outside to get a breath of fresh air. The wind blew something into my eye. I have been trying to get it out—and shed a few tears before it was removed. I must look a sight."

"I hope you will be all right," Verina said. "Do you need us to leave, Miss Snow?"

"Why, of course not," she said cheerfully. "After all, we are all enjoying the dancing, and my eye is fine now."

"We are!" Justina assured her.

The duke joined them, his face unreadable. "How has this evening gone for you all?"

The four bombarded him, telling him about how much fun they had had and how they could not wait to attend another assembly next month.

"I am so grateful that Mama allowed us to come," Lady Tia said. "I thought she would hold us to mourning for the entire year."

"Mama understands that you do not have much to mourn about," Millbrooke explained. "While it would have been unseemly of you to make your come-outs, she knows things are more relaxed in the country. Mama believes it fine that you go a few places and enjoy yourselves."

People began moving back to the large room where the dancing had been held earlier, and Eden downed a cup of punch for fortification. Once more, she approved of partners who wished to dance with the young ladies she chaperoned. She did this alone because the duke had abandoned the five of them. He moved to the far end of the room and never rejoined them the remainder of the evening.

She did not lack for partners, however. She danced a set with a shopkeeper from the village. Another with the local doctor. A different set with a blacksmith, who was lighter on his feet than any of her previous partners. When she told him so, he laughed loudly and said, "You have been my favorite partner of the night, Miss Snow. It was a pleasure dancing with you."

When the night ended, she and the girls returned to the ducal carriage. Millbrooke joined them, and Eden made certain that she was not sitting next to him, getting into the carriage first. Verina and Justina followed her and sat on the cushion next to her.

Unfortunately, that meant she sat opposite the duke. She could not meet his gaze and turned hers out the window the entire journey back to Millvale.

When they arrived, she was the last to exit the carriage. The duke himself handed her down, holding her hand a moment longer than he should have, forcing her to meet his gaze.

"I am sorry, Eden," he said quietly. "I meant no harm. I only wished to—"

She turned away, pulling her hand from his and hurrying into the house, not wanting to hear excuses from him. She climbed the stairs behind the four girls, holding in her tears until she reached her own bedchamber. Then it was if a flood began, and she wept silently, more than she had when Lord Kessley had dismissed her into an uncertain future.

This time was more painful than that particular incident. Because she actually loved Val. She had given in, enjoying his kisses when she could have easily stopped him. Eden was as much to blame—if not more so—and that made her cry all the harder.

She climbed into bed, sobbing into her pillow, not knowing if she could make it another day at Millvale, having to see him.

Chapter Eighteen

HE HAD BEEN *an utter clot.*

Val silently berated himself as he followed the others into the house. The girls still chattered about the assembly, Eden following them. He paused in the foyer, wanting to put some space between them.

In her sweet naivety, she had misunderstood his behavior this evening, thinking him arrogant and a boor—when he was merely jealous of the attention Arden had paid to her. He had wanted to kiss her. Whisper words of love to her. Yet everything had gone to the devil in mere seconds, and he was as distant from her now as he ever had been.

He felt so lonely. So isolated. In a short amount of time, Eden had not only become the woman he loved, but she was also his best friend. He wanted to talk over his problems, but he had no one to listen to him at Millvale. Suddenly, the urge to talk with Mama swept through him. True, they had never been close, but if he were to make amends with Eden and bring her into the family as his duchess, Val would need to speak to his mother about it. Knowing she liked to stay up late and read, he made his way toward her rooms.

He decided to enter without knocking, crossing through the small siting room designated for the duchess. Then he knocked gently on the door leading to her bedchamber, not wishing to wake her if she were sleeping.

"Come," she called, and he pushed open the door, seeing she was in her dressing gown, sitting in a chair by the window, a book opened in her lap.

"Millbrooke. Do come closer." She closed the book and placed it on the table, indicating for him to take the seat opposite her. "What brings you to me so late?"

He sat, raking his hands through his hair in frustration.

Before he could form a sentence, Mama said, "It is Miss Snow, isn't it?"

Startled, he asked, "How did you know?"

"We may not be close, but I gave birth to you. I know you better than you may know yourself after having watched you all these years. Are you planning to offer for her?"

"I may have ruined my chance of doing so," he admitted.

"Tell me," she urged. "You are my son—and a duke. Any woman would be thrilled to accept you as their husband."

"I have been drawn to her from the first," he began. "Yes, at first, it was because of her beauty, but beneath that lies a beautiful soul. She is caring. Compassionate. Intelligent. Supportive. We used to spend an hour together every day in the gardens."

"I know," she said. "I have seen you both go there." Her gaze intent on him, she asked, "Are you in love with her?"

Val nodded. "Hopelessly. And I have yet to tell her that."

"Then why not do so?" she encouraged.

"You would approve if I did so? Ask a governess to wed a duke?"

"My approval is not needed in this matter, Val," she said, addressing him for the first time by his given name since he had claimed his father's title. "What matters most is that you care for her. Now, do I believe Miss Snow would make for a good duchess? I do. From what I have seen of her, she not only carries herself with grace, but she has a quiet authority about her. Agnes told me that Miss Snow is the daughter of Viscount Brownley, so it is not as if she is someone with unknown bloodlines."

"I do love her, Mama. And I made an arse of myself tonight."

He told her how he had seethed with jealousy, watching Eden dancing with Lord Arden. How he had interrupted them and claimed her for a set.

"She was not happy with me," he confided. "She dressed me down as if I were a schoolboy. Said that I was rude. I wanted to tell her this evening of my feelings for her, but my ill-mannered behavior made that impossible. I fear she will never give me a chance."

Val left out the part about them kissing, too embarrassed to provide that detail to his mother.

"I envy you," Mama said. "First Ariadne, and now you. You have both found love. The road to love is not an easy one, my son. I am not one of those fortunate enough to ever have experienced it. But if Miss Snow is meant for you, it will come to pass." She hesitated and then said, "I think you need to give her two things you may be reluctant to give. Time—and distance."

"What do you mean?"

"There is a line from a poem I once read which stayed with me. *Absence doth sharpen love.* Perhaps if you are not so readily available, Miss Snow would come to realize just how much she misses you. You have mentioned previously about visiting the other estates you have inherited. This might be the time to do so."

"But I could be gone a month or longer, Mama," Val protested. "I would miss all that time with Eden."

"If she is keeping you at arm's length now, you would not be spending time with her anyway. I know you have ended your daily conversations in the garden. You have no other time to be alone with her. Why not do your duty and go see your properties? Make certain they are in good working order. It will give your Miss Snow time to think. Time to miss you."

He could see her reasoning held water. At this point, Eden wanted absolutely nothing to do with him. He would get nowhere if he kept pushing her—and would most likely push her even further away if he continued along the same course.

"You are right, Mama. Your advice is sound. I will leave in the morning." He thought a moment. "Of course, there is the fete coming up in June."

"Haven't you already put the majority of the planning in the capable hands of your future duchess?" she asked, smiling.

"I will leave a note for her, telling her to continue with the preparations. That I will return by the day of the fete."

He stood, leaning over and brushing a kiss against her cheek. "Thank you. And I give you permission to talk this over with Aunt Agnes."

She chuckled. "Oh, Agnes and I have already talked this to death," she revealed. "The girls may not have noticed, but Agnes and I both have. In fact, she is the one who first noted the spark between the two of you. You may not recall, but Agnes and George were a love match."

"I was not aware of that. I remember how jovial Uncle George was. It is even more tragic to think she lost him so early."

"Agnes will never wed again. George was the love of her life. Go, Millbrooke. Write your letter to Miss Snow. I will check on her every now and then as to the plans. The fete will come off as promised. It will be something good for the area. Goodnight, my darling boy."

"Goodnight, Mama."

Val left her to go to his study. Removing fresh parchment, he paused, not knowing how to begin. If he opened the letter using Eden, she might be so angry that she might not read it. Also, if someone else saw it, they would question him addressing a governess in so familiar a fashion. She was so concerned about her reputation that he knew he could not begin the letter that way.

Simply saying Miss Snow seemed so cold, though. So sterile. He wanted somehow to convey his feelings for her without saying it outright. Val finally decided upon how to address her and dipped his pen into the ink.

My dear Miss Snow —

I have been remiss in not visiting the other estates which I inherited upon my father's death. I did want to make certain that I first settled in at Millvale since this is my country seat. Now that I am comfortable with the workings of the estate, I can trust my steward to continue with plans we have made together, allowing me the freedom to travel to my other properties throughout England.

This will mean you will shoulder the bulk of planning for the fete. For that, I am sorry. We both know, however, that you are incredibly efficient. You will have the help of my sisters and cousins, and Mama has assured me she would check with you on a regular basis to ensure things are going as planned. You will also be granted use of my carriage, as I know you will be calling upon many people in order to secure judges for our various contests and booths to fill the lawn.

I have four estates to visit, along with the time traveling between them. I will be gone for several weeks, but I promise you I will be home in time to take my hosting duties seriously regarding the fete and greet the guests to Millvale.

I would say if you had any questions to take them to Her Grace, but you are both bright and creative, and I know you will come to whatever solution is needed all on your own. Thank you for taking on this task, along with your governessing duties. I remain in your debt.

Millbrooke

Val read through the letter three times, seeing nothing needed to be added. He let the ink dry before sealing it and scrawling her name across the front. Taking the letter to the library, he left it on one of the tables, knowing she was always the first to appear in the room in order to ready lessons for Verina and Justina. She would find it tomorrow morning—after he was gone.

He retired to his bedchamber, Fisham assisting him from his clothes. He informed the valet they would leave after breakfast tomorrow morning, traveling about England to visit his various properties.

"I will have everything packed and ready for you, Your Grace," Fisham assured him. "Do you have an idea how long we might be gone from Millvale?"

"It will depend upon what I find at each estate and how long I must stay at that particular one," he replied. "I do plan for us to be back in time for the fete, however."

"Well, you should, Your Grace. You're hosting it. It would be a bit odd for you not to attend."

"Have I told you how much I appreciate your honesty, Fisham?"

The valet gave him a toothy grin. "You have, Your Grace, but I appreciate hearing it, all the same."

Surprisingly, Val dropped off to sleep quickly. When he awoke, Fisham was already in his bedchamber, quietly packing his things. The valet helped Val to shave and dress, and he went downstairs to breakfast. He was the last to arrive and glad all four girls were present so that he might say his goodbyes to them at the same time.

Taking a sip of coffee to fortify himself, he said, "I will be leaving this morning."

Immediately, they began peppering him with questions, and he held up a hand to silence them.

"It is time for me to go to my other estates. I have gotten my feet wet studying everything at Millvale, but it is important to me to have an active hand in my other properties."

"But what about the fete?" Tia asked. "You could be traveling and miss it."

"I am leaving the planning of it in Miss Snow's capable hands. She will need a good deal of assistance, though, from the four of you. Do not let the entire burden rest upon her shoulders."

"We are glad to help Miss Snow," Lia told him. "You will have nothing to worry about. Between Miss Snow and the four of us, the fete will be a tremendous success."

"People were so excited to hear of it last night," Verina shared.

"And they are already hoping it will become an annual tradition," Justina added.

"Then that makes it doubly important that the first one held come off flawlessly." He gazed about the table. "I am counting on all of you."

"We will not let you down, Val," Lia assured him.

He finished his breakfast and asked that the second carriage be readied for him before summoning the Quigbys, telling them of his plans to be absent from Millvale for the next several weeks.

"You are not taking the ducal carriage with you, Your Grace?" asked the butler, clearly puzzled.

"No, the other carriage is smaller and faster. It will get me to where I am going with no problems. Besides, I wish to leave the regular carriage so that Her Grace and my family may move in comfort about the countryside. A lot of planning will need to occur regarding the fete, and I want the two of you to understand that Miss Snow has full authority in my absence."

Mrs. Quigby's hand flew to her mouth in surprise.

"If Miss Snow has need of the carriage, it is to be available to her. My sisters and nieces will most likely be accompanying her on the various errands she will be running. Do you have any questions?" he asked, his tone brokering no response was necessary.

Fisham came through the front door. "Your trunk has been loaded into the carriage, Your Grace. We are ready when you are."

"Then this is goodbye," Val said, following Fisham out the door.

Beside the carriage stood one of the grooms, a favorite of his. He had asked Fisham to send for the groom and now moved toward him.

"Rollo, in my absence, you will serve as coachman for my family. Look after them."

The groom's eyes lit with surprise, and he beamed at Val. "Certainly, Your Grace. Thank you for having the confidence in me."

Fisham climbed up next to the coachman, while Val entered the vehicle. He used his cane to rap on the roof, and the carriage began its journey.

He glanced back at the house, hoping he was doing the right thing in separating from Eden.

And when he returned to Millvale, he would tell her of his love—and ask her to be his duchess.

Chapter Nineteen

Eden went to the library for the day's lessons. She had slept little after last night, lying in bed, reliving Val's kisses, torturing herself. She kept telling herself that he was like Lord Kessley, but she knew she was lying to herself.

Could he have kissed her the way he did and *not* have true feelings for her? Not that she thought he loved her, but he might actually be developing some sentiment for her. She doubted anything could ever come of it, with him a duke and her a governess, but the more she thought about it, the more Eden decided she had been too abrupt with him. She had made up her mind to apologize. If he were half the man she thought him to be, he would gracefully accept. Perhaps they could even return to being friends.

Or more.

The thought of being in his arms again, sharing magical kisses, made her throw caution to the wind. She might not be acceptable as his duchess, but she would humble herself and hope they might enjoy a quick romance before she departed with Lady Traywick for Cumberland.

When she arrived, the first thing Eden noticed was something lying on the table. Thinking it odd because she always put everything up and out of sight, she went to see what it was. When she saw her name written across it in a bold hand, she knew only one person could have left this for her.

With trepidation, she broke the seal and read the contents. Once. Twice. Her throat swelled with emotion—because he was gone. Without a word, Val had left Millvale.

And her.

Had she driven him away? She had been short with him last night, castigating him for his behavior regarding Lord Arden. Why on earth had she taken it upon herself to rebuke a duke? A governess might need to reprimand those in her care every now and then, but no one had appointed her Millvale's keeper. He was a bloody duke—and dukes did whatever they wanted.

Even kiss foolish governesses.

She swallowed, clearing her throat, trying to rid herself of all emotion. She could not afford to have Verina and Justina see her so upset. They might already be suspicious after last night, when she lied about getting something in her eye. She could not fool them with the same story again.

"He will be gone for several weeks," she said aloud, knowing not having to face him every day during tea or rides with the girls would actually be to her advantage. It would help her to get over these foolish feelings she had for him. She wouldn't call it love ever again. What she had felt for Millbrooke was a passing fancy. An infatuation. Not love. They had spent time having some lovely conversations, but that was it. He had kissed her, but those kisses had meant nothing to him. He was a man who asserted his power wherever he went. He had kissed her because he wanted to do so. Perhaps he found her somewhat attractive, possibly because Lord Arden had been so attentive to her.

Wait. Had he been *jealous* that she had danced with Lord Arden? She had been so busy at the assembly that she had not noticed who Val had danced with. Yes, she had put an end to their friendship and private time together, which he had been upset about, but was it possible he had harbored feelings for her? If he did, no wonder he appeared and rudely claimed a dance. Eden then recalled that he had said she would not become Lady Arden. His words had surprised her. Even embarrassed her. She had quickly replied that she had no interest in being Lady Arden.

And that was when he had kissed her.

Had she misjudged his intentions toward her? Even if he did care for her, nothing could be done about their feelings. She was a governess and would be leaving when summer came to an end. He needed to view the young ladies on the Marriage Mart and find a suitable one to be his wife. No matter what either—or both—might feel, she was not an appropriate choice. He would choose a bride amongst the cream of Polite Society.

Glumly, Eden realized that was most likely why he had vacated Millvale so swiftly. Val realized they shared feelings for one another. Being in close proximity would only lead to heartbreak. He deliberately had gone away. True, he had mentioned to her on more than one occasion that he needed to visit his other holdings. In an attempt to put distance between them, he had gone to do so. She must respect his decision and do her best to keep her mind on the many tasks at hand.

First, she would continue to do the best job possible in educating Verina and Justina. The girls were her chief priority. Second, she must organize this fete to be successful. It would take hours and hours devoted to it, but she was willing to do so. Regardless of what her head said, her heart wanted the best for Val. This was something important to him, a practice which might become an annual tradition. She would do everything in her power to make it a triumph. It would be her gift to him since she apparently had made a mess of everything.

The next week was a busy one. After speaking with Lady Traywick, in the Duchess of Millvale's presence, the three agreed that lessons could be suspended for the next month or so while they worked on the fete. The duchess proved quite kind, giving Eden several suggestions, which she eagerly took.

Knowing she had full use of the ducal carriage also helped since she had many people to see in the area. Much to her surprise, Her Grace asked if she could accompany Eden on a few of her visits.

"Just enough to get things off to a pleasant start," the duchess had said.

They had visited a few titled gentlemen in the area. Most of Polite Society was in town for the Season, but a few, such as Lord Arden, had remained behind. Of those who had, she and the duchess called upon them all, asking them to be judges in various competitions. Lady Traywick had suggested they add food to the list of competitive entries, and Eden and the duchess came up with several categories for food to be judged, from pies to jams.

The visit with Lord Arden proved the most difficult for her. The widower had invited the pair to the nursery, where she had met his two daughters. Clearly, the girls idolized their father, and he was quite good with them. Lord Arden agreed to judge one of the horse competitions and when given a preference, he asked if he might judge sweets, confessing that he had a sweet tooth.

When they left, he had held her hand a moment longer than acceptable, and she had gently withdrawn it. She did not want to hurt him, but it was important that she make things clear to him. "I hope you will find a wife, my lord. I can see how dedicated you are to your girls, just as I am dedicated to teaching Lady Verina and Lady Justina Fulton."

Apparently, he had received her message, saying, "I hope I will find a woman who will not mind already having a readymade family and still be willing to add to it."

"I wish you the best of luck in that endeavor, Lord Arden," Eden had replied.

Once upon a time, she would have leapt at the chance to become the wife of a titled gentleman. It would not have been fair to Lord Arden, however, to wed him—when her heart would always belong to another.

By the time Friday arrived and she was to meet with the vicar and his wife, Eden was thrilled by the progress made in a week's time. Unexpectedly, Her Grace asked to accompany her to the vicarage as she waited in the foyer for the carriage to be readied.

"Are you certain you wish to go out again, Your Grace?" she asked. "I know you have been in mourning for the late duke. You have already helped me so much this week as it is."

The older woman smiled. "I find that it feels good to be out and about, Miss Snow. While I will decline any social invitations on a matter of principle, I would like to see what the Clarkes think about our plans so far. That is, if you are willing for me to accompany you to the rectory."

"I would be most happy if you did so," she replied. "Frankly, I was a bit worried how they would react when I showed up without His Grace." She sucked in a quick breath. "Oh. That is the reason you have asked to come with me today."

The duchess shrugged. "It does not ever hurt to have a duchess on your side. I will make certain they know this fete is in your hands. The rest will be easy because you are doing such a remarkable job."

They rode into the village and exited the ducal carriage. Mrs. Clarke fussed over them, fetching tea and cakes for them before she went to find her husband. He seemed almost cowed by the duchess' presence, and Eden was grateful for it. She had a suspicion Mr. Clarke would not have accepted all her ideas so easily if she had not had Her Grace there for support.

By the time they left, Mr. and Mrs. Clarke were ecstatic at the progress being made, and they had agreed to the percentage that would go directly to the church from what was earned at the booths and registration fees for the competitions.

Once in the carriage, Her Grace said, "There, that was not so bad after all, was it, Miss Snow?"

She couldn't help but chuckle. "Only because you came along, Your Grace. I would have experienced a difficult time without your presence. Or that of His Grace's."

"Ah, yes. I received a letter from Millbrooke yesterday. He has arrived in Oxfordshire and found much to his liking. He wrote that he would plan to stay there for a few days before moving on to his next property."

"It is good he is taking the time to tour all the estates he inherited," she said, glad to have gleaned even a small kernel about where Val was.

"My son may appear lighthearted, but beneath his exterior is a serious man dedicated to being the best duke he can be."

"I understand that, Your Grace. That is why I wish to do everything I can to see this fete meet with success."

Nodding, the duchess said, "It no doubt will be. You have only been at things a week, and look how much you have already accomplished."

"It is nothing."

"Do not underestimate yourself," the older woman insisted. "I know you have had assistance from the girls, but you are the one calling on people, convincing them to have booths or enter the different contests. You are designing games for the children to play, old and young alike. Do not sell yourself short, Miss Snow. If this fete is a success, it will be because of the tremendous effort you are putting into this project."

"Thank you," she said, in awe of this woman. "It is nice to be acknowledged for my efforts."

"Be certain that when Millbrooke returns to Millvale, he will hear directly from me just how much of yourself you have put into planning this fete."

"That is not necessary, Your Grace."

The duchess frowned sternly at her. "*I* say it is necessary. I do not give praise lightly, Miss Snow. Accept what you get."

"Yes, Your Grace," she said, lowering her gaze. She had never thought to have such a champion in her corner.

By the end of the second week, Eden had commitments from thirty people who wished to man a booth, selling everything from embroidered handkerchiefs to dolls to jewelry and boots. Slots were filling quickly for the different food competitions. They almost had every shift covered for the children's games, and both horse competitions were now filled, with Eden even creating a waiting list in case someone dropped out at the last minute and a replacement would be given a chance to compete.

She fell into bed, exhausted, but in a good way. Her days were filled with activities regarding the fete. It was the nights which gave her trouble. Anytime she closed her eyes, she saw Val's image. She continued to regret her harsh words to him and hoped that he would be willing to accept her apology when he returned to Millvale. She wanted him to be proud of the work she had done on the fete.

Eden lulled herself to sleep, reliving Val's kisses, finally falling asleep on her tearstained pillow.

Chapter Twenty

Eden bid the Clarkes goodbye and left the parsonage to return to the ducal carriage. She had been giving the couple an update regarding the progress made on the fete this past week. As she moved toward the vehicle, a post chaise came into sight and slowed next to the carriage. The door opened, and a man bounded from it, his valise in hand. He spoke briefly to the driver and then turned, greeting her coachman.

"When were you promoted, Rollo?" he asked as she reached the vehicle, causing his attention to turn to her.

He was about six feet and lean, with an aquiline nose. Eden had a good idea who he might be, thanks to his familiarity with Rollo.

Approaching her, he looked about. "Hmm. The ducal carriage without its duke. And who might you be?"

"I am Miss Snow, Lord Dyer," she said crisply. "Governess to Lady Verina and Lady Justina Fulton."

He brightened. "Millbrooke told me that our cousins had joined Aunt Alice and Aunt Agnes at Millvale. Obviously, you have heard of me, Miss Snow, since you were easily able to identify me, just as I recognized Millbrooke's coach and ducal seal."

"His Grace has spoken of you on several occasions," she said.

"Well, is he in the carriage?"

"No, my lord. His Grace is away at one of his other country properties."

"Drat. I knew I should have written to let him know that I was coming, but he told me to come down whenever I had the chance. Might I request a ride to Millvale with you then?"

"Of course, my lord."

The footman opened the door, and Viscount Dyer handed her up, following her and setting his valise on the floor by his foot.

As the carriage started up, he asked, "And how does it come to pass that a governess uses the ducal carriage to run her errands?"

She caught the teasing light in his eyes. "Because I am on business for His Grace." She couldn't help but like this genial man, and added, "The fete will be occurring the last Saturday in June. His Grace is thinking it will become an annual tradition held at Millvale. While in his absence, I have been tasked to plan this first fete."

Viscount Dyer whistled low, studying her a moment. "Millbrooke left the planning of this . . . to you. I find that most astounding, Miss Snow."

"Actually, it is a series of lessons which I am helping teach his cousins, and I am even including his sisters in this complicated planning. I am certain you know of your uncle's passing. Her Grace has been in mourning. The duke knew Her Grace would not be up to seeing to the many details in regard to the fete, and he wished for his sisters and cousins to be exposed to something such as this. Since I am known for my organizational skills, I have been put in charge of the preparations. The young ladies are assisting me in various aspects of it. It will be good for them to have this experience, especially because one day they will be managing their own households. Who knows? They may even wish to do something similar for their own husband's family."

"What does this fete consist of?" he asked, his curiosity obvious.

Eden spent a few minutes explaining to him about the various stalls which would sell food, drink, and wares, along with games provided for the children and competitions for the adults.

She concluded, saying, "A healthy portion of the profits will go to the church, hence my meeting with Mr. and Mrs. Clarke today where we encountered one another."

"You sound most efficient, Miss Snow. My cousin must place great trust in you to have you heading up such an effort during his absence. When might he be returning to Millvale?"

"His Grace did not share that information with me, my lord, only that he would arrive in time for the fete. Whether that is the day before it is held or two weeks prior, I cannot speculate. Not only is he the host, but His Grace is also scheduled to be a judge for the horse competition."

The viscount laughed. "He would have to be a judge. If not, he would sweep everything. Millbrooke is a superb horseman."

A part of her had wanted to be able to enter the competition—and win—simply because she wanted to show off her horsemanship skills to Val. However, Eden thought it inappropriate to do so since she had helped to organize the entire affair and had voiced that in the beginning.

"I suppose I will stay a day or so to make Aunt Alice and Aunt Agnes happy. It will be good to see my cousins, particularly Justina and Verina. I only met them once many years ago and have no idea what they even look like now."

"They will be delighted that you have come to Millvale, my lord."

The carriage slowed, and she realized they had already reached Millvale. Lord Dyer exited the carriage first, handing her down, and then claimed his valise. They entered the foyer, and Quigby appeared, looking startled to find her in Lord Dyer's company.

"Viscount Dyer, we had no idea you would be visiting with us," the butler said, looking slightly flustered.

"His Grace extended an open invitation to me, Quigby, and I was only free now to come to visit him." He gave the butler a wry smile. "I suppose I should have written first to make certain he was in residence."

Eden slipped away while the two men were talking, sorry that Lord Dyer had not been able to come sooner. She went to the library, where she found all four girls working on a map for the horse course.

Joining them, she said, "Your cousin, Lord Dyer, has arrived."

"Con is here?" Lady Tia cried. "Oh, we must go and see him."

Lady Lia, ever a calming presence, said, "Wait just a moment. Let us show Miss Snow what we are thinking about regarding the horse competition."

Quickly, Lady Lia explained the course they had created, with the other three chiming in.

"This has been thoughtfully planned," she praised. "I am to meet with the head groom tomorrow and walk the area where the competition is to be held. I will take this map with me, and we will determine if it is viable. Thank you for all your hard work on it."

"It is almost teatime," Verina said. "We should go straight there and visit with Cousin Con."

She followed the four to the drawing room, where Lord Dyer was talking with his two aunts. As the girls entered, he hurried to greet each of them with a kiss and a hug.

"It is so exciting to see you after so long," Justina told him. "Val will be upset that he missed you."

He smiled at her. "It means that I will get to spend more time with you four beauties. I can see Val any time. What is one duke when I can visit with all of you?"

Eden thought the viscount charming and knew he must be one of the biggest flirts in the *ton*.

"Come and have a seat," Her Grace instructed, and they all moved across the drawing room to do so as two teacarts were rolled in.

While the two older women poured out for them, Lord Dyer said, "I have some good news to share with you. Lucy is wed."

Immediately, they began bombarding him with questions, and he laughed. "I will tell you all that I know. My sister met the Marquess of

Huntsberry before the Season even began. I suspected they had feelings for one another, and my assumption proved correct. They are now wed, and they—"

"That was sudden," Lady Tia said. "The Season has barely begun. Did they need a special license?"

Eden suspected the quick marriage had been a necessary one. That the couple had been caught in a compromising position and chose to wed swiftly to lessen the gossip.

"Huntsberry did purchase one," he told them. "I believe they did not wish to put off the ceremony."

"It sounds as if it is a love match to me," Lady Traywick declared. "I felt the same way the moment I met Lord Traywick. I would have wed him that very night if it had been possible."

Verina smiled, taking her mother's hand and squeezing it. "It is wonderful that you and Papa were a love match, Mama. I hope Justina and I will be as fortunate as you when we make our own come-outs."

"And when will that be?" Lord Dyer asked. "There are so many cousins, I have lost track of your ages."

"Lia and Tia will make their delayed come-outs next year, and I will do so the following year," Verina shared. "Two years after I do so, it will be Justina's turn." She smiled at Eden. "Miss Snow will remain with us until then. We are hoping she might even become a companion to Mama after we are wed and gone from Traywick Manor."

Eden had not mentioned this to her employer and carefully watched Lady Traywick's reaction.

"I had never considered having a companion, but Miss Snow would be a lovely one." She smiled warmly at Eden. "We do not have to make any decision about that at this point since Miss Snow will be with us another three years."

Justina spoke up. "Mama, what if Miss Snow and I came to town when Verina makes her come-out?" I know I cannot attend any of the events, but it would be nice to see what my sister experiences and help me understand better what might be in store for me. I know Miss Snow would have ideas for all kinds of lessons since London is so rich in history."

"Why, that is an excellent idea, Justina," the countess said. "In fact, Miss Snow and I discussed something of this earlier. Yes, I do believe we can do so." She glanced to Eden. "If that would be acceptable with you, Miss Snow."

"I would be happy to accompany you and the girls to town, my lady. Lady Justina is correct in that there would be a plethora of history opened to us by being in town. The girls are so close, and I think it would do Lady Verina good to have her sister in town with her to talk over her prospects."

"Well, that is settled," Lady Traywick said.

Talk then turned to the fete, and the girls eagerly told their cousin about the course they had been designing.

"Miss Snow is going to meet with our head groom tomorrow and show him our obstacle map," Lady Tia said.

"I would be interested in going with you, Miss Snow," the viscount said. "I am a lifelong rider and have entered horse competitions myself. I might be able to offer some advice."

"Your advice would be valuable, my lord," she said. "I am to meet with the head groom and Rollo at the stables at ten o'clock tomorrow morning if you are free to do so."

"I will see you then, Miss Snow."

The next morning, Eden went down to the stables, the map in hand. Lord Dyer was already present, and she joined the three men.

Miller, the head groom, took them to a small office inside the stables, and she opened the map, lying it flat on top of the desk. The trio studied it while she pointed out the various features.

"And you say my cousins created this entire design?" Lord Dyer asked.

"Yes, my lord. They have been actively involved in every aspect of the fete's planning. I know they used their math skills, going out and measuring the meadow and then working to place the various obstacles."

"Let's go out and see how it might work," Miller suggested.

They decided to walk instead of riding, and Lord Dyer fell into step beside Eden.

"You seem almost a part of the family, Miss Snow."

"I hope you were not offended by my presence at tea yesterday afternoon, my lord. It is just that Lady Traywick is gone for several months to the Season, leaving the girls to my care. They insisted that we take tea and meals together in their mother's absence. When Lady Traywick returned to Cumberland, she saw no need to change the arrangement."

He frowned. "Then why were you not at dinner last night?"

She felt heat enter her cheeks. "We are not at Traywick Manor, my lord. My presence is not required at the Millvale table."

"Did Millbrooke or my aunt prevent you from sitting with them?"

"No, my lord. Quite the opposite. His Grace was perfectly willing to have me join them." She hesitated. "I am not of the world of Polite Society, however. It is one thing to eat with my charges when their mother is absent, but quite another to be at a ducal estate. They are guests, while I am only a servant."

"You seem familiar with Polite Society, Miss Snow, even though you are a governess. Might I ask who your parents are?"

"Lord and Lady Brownley," she replied, tears springing to her eyes at the thought of her parents. "They are no longer with us."

"Oh!" he said sharply. "I did not know your parents, but I have met the current viscount and his wife." He shook his head. "Forgive me for being judgmental, Miss Snow, but they are bad news. It is best you have no association with them and their fast reputations."

"What you say does not surprise me, my lord. Once my father was gone and my cousin came to claim his title and estate, he held all kinds of wild parties at Brownstone before I left."

"I am sorry you were exposed to him and his crowd of friends."

"I was living in the dower house with Mama at that time, so I was able to avoid them."

"Were you there long with her?" he asked, sympathy in his eyes and sincerity in his voice.

"She passed a few months after my father did. She was quite ill. That is when I left Brownstone."

"It sounds as though you have been through a difficult time. It seems you are happy now, though, with Aunt Agnes and my cousins. I can see a true warmth between all of you."

"I look upon Lady Traywick as an angel, my lord. I feel she saved me. It has been a delight teaching Lady Verina and Lady Justina. They are bright, sweet girls."

They reached the meadow where the competition would be held, and all four of them studied the map. They took turns pacing off where the different jumps and turns would need to occur, and Eden made notes in the journal she had brought along with her. They made one adjustment which Lord Dyer suggested.

"Now that things are settled, I will speak to the carpenter about helping to build the fences. We will also need holes dug in which to place the poles and flags to show where the turns should occur."

"I know where we can purchase the poles," Rollo said. "I'm not sure about the flags, though."

"I can have the girls sew handkerchiefs. We can then attach those to the poles to serve as flags," Eden suggested. She then thanked the two grooms, saying, "This was a most productive morning, gentlemen. Thank you for your help."

"Everyone is looking forward to this fete, Miss Snow," Miller said. "I have heard you are doing a fine job in putting it together. His Grace will be impressed."

They returned to the stables, and Viscount Dyer asked her, "Are you up for a ride, Miss Snow? Or I suppose I should ask if you ride."

Rollo laughed. "Miss Snow rides like the wind, my lord. Why, she could outrun you, especially on Andromeda."

The viscount looked startled. "*You* ride Andromeda? Why, Millbrooke has told me he was close to selling her since no one but him could control her, and he prefers riding Perseus." Smiling, he said, "Saddle Perseus and Andromeda for us. I am eager to see Miss Snow on horseback."

She rode with him for over an hour, racing when he wished to do so and jumping fences when he dared her.

They returned to the stables, and the viscount shook his head. "You are the best female rider I have ever seen, Miss Snow. I do believe you might be an even better rider than Millbrooke himself."

"I have always enjoyed riding," she shared. "Both my parents thought it important that I learn how to control a horse."

Eden presented Andromeda with an apple which Rollo handed her, and the horse nibbled daintily until it was gone. Lord Dyer accompanied her back to the house.

Before they parted, he said, "I am glad I came to Millvale and was able to make your acquaintance, Miss Snow. I hope we see more of one another in the future."

"I am only sorry that you missed seeing His Grace. Perhaps he might stop in town before he returns to Millvale, and you can visit with him there."

"I will be returning to town tomorrow, so I suppose this is goodbye."

He took her hand and gallantly kissed her fingers. "Until we meet again, Miss Snow."

Chapter Twenty-One

Val had arrived in town late last night and gone straight to the ducal townhouse. He planned to be in town only for a few hours this morning and hoped to see Con before he left. In fact, speaking to his closest friend was the only reason he had come to London.

He had missed Eden more than he thought possible. He had written to her once, not expecting any kind of reply, merely making contact with her so she would know he was thinking of her. Of course, he did not let anything he felt for her be expressed in his letter and simply discussed the fete, saying he hoped all the planning was going well and reminding her if she had any problems to go to his mother.

He had written Mama three times in the six weeks he had been gone, never mentioning Eden to her. He told her of where he was and the state of affairs, including some of the changes which he had recommended a few of his stewards make. Overall, he had been pleased with how each property was being run. Someday, he hoped to visit them all again, Eden with him.

If she would agree to wed him.

Had she hankered for him as he had her? Or had the planning of the fete and her governessing duties kept her so busy that she hadn't a moment to devote to missing him? Val supposed he would discover the lay of the land once he returned to Millvale. For now, he wanted to see Con and talk things over with him.

Fisham shaved and dressed him, and he decided to walk to the rooms he had once shared with his cousin. Those had been good times for the both of them, but now he looked to his future. Many people were counting on him, and Val was not going to let any of them down.

He rapped on the door loudly. It was only ten o'clock. In the country, he would have been up for hours, but this was the city during the Season. If Con had attended one of the nightly *ton* affairs the previous evening, he might not have arrived until dawn and would still be sleeping. Since they only had a woman who came in twice a week to clean up after them, he knew there would be no servant to answer the door. He knocked again, harder, and could hear a voice call out, causing him to stop.

After a few moments, the door swung open. Con appeared sleepy-eyed, his hair sticking up, wearing nothing but his banyan.

"I suppose you had a late night," he said, sweeping past his cousin and sitting in what had been his favorite chair.

Con closed the door and took a seat opposite Val. "Not as late as usual. It was a card party. I was home a little after one." He stroked his unshaven jaw. "You look as if you have been up a while. When did you reach town?"

"Late last night. I wanted to stop and see you before heading back to Millvale. I do not have time to stay longer and visit with Uncle Arthur or Aunt Charlotte or meet all Lucy's suitors and recommend which one she should focus on."

His cousin chuckled. "That will not be necessary. My sister wed early last month."

"Lucy is already married?" He paused, his mind jumping to the worst conclusion. "Please, no. I hope she was not compromised."

"She was—and she wasn't," Con said mysteriously. "Do you recall Lord Eaton or Lord Humley?"

"Only that Eaton has a terrible reputation, and Humley is one of his toadies." Val gasped. "Tell me my cousin is not wife to either of them."

"Relax, Val. Lucy is now the Marchioness of Huntsberry. I will not go into the sordid details, but Eaton cooked up a scheme to ruin Lucy merely for the fun of it, and Humley went along, as usual. Judson—Lord Huntsberry—came upon them and ruined their evil doings. Unfortunately, in comforting Lucy, it led to a kiss. Or several. I did not ask. I did tell you Huntsberry had been sniffing about her, and it was obvious to me the two had feelings for one another."

Con raked a hand through his wild hair. "Unfortunately, Lady Billingsley found them together."

"The young widow who is a vicious gossip?" he asked.

"The very one. Apparently she had made a play for the marquess, and Huntsberry had turned her down. She was out for revenge and ready to spread malicious lies about Lucy and him. Judson offered for Lucy, and they wed quickly and quietly by special license."

"Are they happy?"

His friend guffawed. "Sickeningly so. They are madly in love and quite affectionate with one another. Of course, Mama is thrilled that her daughter wed a wealthy marquess. That was what was most important to her. Lucy was looking for love, however, and was fortunate to have found it."

"Where is Huntsberry's country seat?" Val asked.

"Huntsworth is in Surrey. Ironically, it is adjacent to Aldridge Manor, so Lucy and Ariadne are neighbors."

"I cannot believe Ariadne did not write to tell me of this. My sister has always been good at correspondence." He shrugged. "Then again, I have been away from Millvale almost seven weeks. I may find more than one letter from her waiting for me when I return to Kent."

"I went to see you."

"You did? When?" He wanted to ask if Con had met Eden, but Val thought he would hear about Con's visit first.

"Once Lucy was taken care of, I thought I would slip away for a few days and see you and what you were up to at Millvale. After all, you had told me I had an open invitation and could visit at any time."

"I regret not being there to greet you," he apologized. "I thought it was time to tour my other properties and see how they fared. I had already gotten a good grasp on Millvale and did not want to be remiss with my other holdings and the tenants living on those estates."

Val took a deep breath. "I also needed to get away for personal reasons."

"You mean you had to leave Miss Snow."

"You met her? What did you think of her?"

Con said, "I am not certain I have ever met a more capable woman—and you know Mama sets the standard for capable women."

He laughed. "Yes, Aunt Charlotte has always been a force of nature."

"Mama thinks she would have been a better duke than your father," his cousin confided.

"Most likely, she would have. But back to Miss Snow. You truly liked her?"

"I did."

His cousin explained how they had met. "She is most impressive, Val. You look at her and think she is merely a beautiful woman, but much is going on inside her head. She has planned this fete of yours with confidence and creativity, leaving no stone unturned."

"I am in love with her," he blurted out, feeling his nape go hot. "No one else will do. I even told Mama how I felt before I left Millvale, and she had no objections."

Con rose and placed a hand on Val's shoulder. "Then my advice to you? Follow your heart, Val. Miss Snow is worth ten times what the young lady who is diamond of the first water this Season is. She may be a governess, but her father was a viscount. Her life may have been difficult in recent years, but she would make for an excellent duchess."

He looked at his cousin, asking, "How much time did you spend with Eden? You seem to know a great deal about her."

Laughing, Con said, "I raced against her. She and Andromeda were as one. I have never seen a more magnificent rider. Not even you."

"She *is* magnificent. In every way possible," he agreed.

"Then why are you still here?" his friend teased. "If I were in love with Miss Snow and had yet to tell her, I would now be on my way to Millvale. In fact, if you do not leave town in the next half-hour, I just might have to ride to Kent myself and offer for her."

Even though he knew Con was teasing, jealousy poured through Val.

"Stay away from her," he warned. "Eden is mine."

"Then go claim her," his cousin encouraged. "And I hope you will invite me to your wedding. I suppose you will need to return to town for a special license because I believe you will be in a hurry to wed."

"What a brilliant idea!" Val proclaimed. "Why waste time with another trip back to town—when I can purchase it while I am here. Get dressed, Con. And shave, as well. We are off to Doctors' Commons in order to see the Archbishop of Canterbury."

"Won't we need an appointment?"

Val grinned. "In case you have forgotten, dear cousin, I am a duke. Dukes do not need appointments. I will breeze into the offices. Offer my card and smile. We will leave minutes later with the special license—and then I will hurry to Millvale and pour out my heart to Eden."

"Not to put a damper on things, but are you certain she will have you?"

Determination filled him. "She will have me, Con. Our fates are joined together. I can love no other but Eden."

"Then give me an hour to ready myself."

"Half an hour. No more," he declared. "I need that special license in hand today before I leave town for Millvale."

They arrived at Doctors' Commons an hour and a half later. When he announced to the clerk who he was and that he needed to see the archbishop in order to obtain a special license, the clerk shook his head.

"I am sorry, Your Grace. His Grace is not in town at the moment."

An expletive escaped his lips.

"But do not fear, Your Grace," the clerk said cheerfully. "A representative has been authorized to issue a special license in His Grace's absence. Wait here a moment. I will tell him you are here."

The clerk returned momentarily, leading them to an office. Con stood by his side in support as Val spoke to the representative. The man had obviously been told it was a duke seeking the license, because Val was quickly assured that his request would be granted. They waited for about twenty minutes while the documents were drawn up, and he left Doctors' Commons with the folded license resting in his inside pocket, next to his heart.

He dropped off Con at his rooms and said, "You will hear from me soon. In fact, you should return with me. The wedding will be in the next few days."

"That is *if* Miss Snow says yes to you," his cousin reminded.

"She will, Con. She has to," he said fervently. "I cannot imagine life without her."

"Then give me time to pack. I do not have a valet as you do."

"I will go home and collect Fisham and my things, and then we will be back for you. Be ready."

"You certainly have become tyrannical since you have become a duke. Ordering me about," Con teased. "Then again, something tells me that Miss Snow will be the one telling *you* what do."

Val laughed boisterously. "You know, I believe you to be absolutely right."

Chapter Twenty-Two

EDEN MOVED BRISKLY, watching as the stalls were being erected. She consulted her notes as she went, checking with each vendor, making certain they were setting up in the right place. She'd had the girls assign the places for the vendors, telling them to mix things up, not wanting food next to food or handkerchiefs next to handkerchiefs. The four had done an excellent job, leading to variety down each row.

"Miss Snow!" called Verina. "Would you please come and check on the children's games now?"

"I will be there in five minutes," she promised, wanting to walk the last row.

As she moved down the way, a few women gave her samples of the food they would be selling tomorrow.

"Oh, those scones are heavenly," she told one. "And these sweets will have people lining up at your booth," she complimented another.

Everything seemed to be falling into place—except for the fact that the Duke of Millbrooke had yet to make an appearance.

He had written to her once, a brief note, encouraging her to speak with his mother if she ran afoul of anything. While not everything had gone smoothly, Eden knew she had done an excellent job in putting the fete together. Yes, the duchess had helped her in recruiting the judges, but for the most part, she and the four young ladies had done the bulk of the work.

She could already tell, however, that Mr. Clarke would take credit for much of what had been done. The clergyman had been strutting about all afternoon like a peacock as booths had been assembled and the obstacles for the riding course were being set up for her to test it a final time. He kept saying how delighted he was that everything he and Mrs. Clarke had planned had come out so well. Eden was only glad Lady Tia was not around to hear him. Of the four, she was the one who would confront the vicar—if not bash him in the nose. Eden enjoyed being around all the girls, but Lady Tia was definitely the most entertaining of the lot.

Satisfied that everyone was in the right place, she walked down to where the games were being set up. It had taken hours to create some of these games, as well as come up with the small prizes to be awarded. Lia and Verina had worked out the volunteer schedule for adults to take turns supervising these games, and she had accompanied the pair as they called upon various residents in the community, asking them to take a turn for an hour, watching over the children and administering the games. Because they were young, pretty, and the sisters and nieces of the local duke, not a person had turned them down.

Eden went to each station, seeing how the games would be set up, and even having the girls test out things when possible. Children would be doing everything from an egg toss to racing with a partner, their legs tied together, so that they would have to work as a team to reach the finish line.

She gathered the four young ladies. "I cannot tell you how proud I am of you. It is your hard work which will pay off tomorrow when the community comes calling at Millvale."

"Where on earth is Val?" Lady Tia complained. "He should be here."

"He promised he would be home in time for the fete," Lady Lia assured her twin. "Have faith that he will."

Eden wasn't as certain as Lady Lia.

Rollo appeared. "Miss Snow, Miller has Andromeda saddled for you. He's waiting for you to run the course a final time."

"Excuse me," she told the girls, accompanying the groom back to the large meadow.

"There you are, Miss Snow," the head groom said. "Rollo, toss Miss Snow into the saddle now."

Rollo assisted her and once she was settled, he handed her the reins. "I'll climb onto the judge's platform and time you from there."

The course consisted of several different fences of diverse heights, as well as a couple of ditches of varying sizes which they had dug and filled with water. All those would need to be jumped, as well as the competing riders making turns around the poles. Competitors would be timed, and while a point would be awarded for each clean jump, one would be deducted for missed ones.

She went to the start position and looked to Rollo, who declared, "Go!"

Off Eden went, making each turn with precision, jumping each obstacle with ease. She crossed the finish line, to the applause of a few of the workers who had stopped to watch her.

"A perfect ride, Miss Snow," said Miller. "I am only sorry you refuse to enter the course or the race tomorrow."

"I want everything to be aboveboard, Mr. Miller," she told the head groom. "How would it look if I won—when I had prior knowledge of the course and had been able to practice on it?"

"Then at least enter the race," he urged. "No one could beat you and Andromeda. It is a straight shot, so no one has an advantage over another."

"No, we must let some local win so that he—or she—might defend the title next year. Remember, I will be back in Cumberland." She swallowed, trying not to think of leaving Millvale, which had begun to feel like home to her.

"I understand," Miller said. "You have done something good for

Millvale and the surrounding area in planning this fete, Miss Snow. I hope His Grace will appreciate your efforts."

She smiled at the groom and dismounted, handing off the reins to him and collecting her journal and pencil which she had left with Rollo.

The duchess and Lady Traywick approached her, and Her Grace said, "I have never seen anyone ride as you do, Miss Snow."

"Oh, Andromeda makes me look better than I am. She is the true talent."

"You must have ridden from a young age," Lady Traywick commented.

"I did. My father was an excellent rider. Both he and my mother encouraged me to do so."

"I do not recall your parents, Miss Snow," the duchess said. "They were Lord and Lady Brownley, Agnes? Is that what you told me?"

"Yes," Lady Traywick said.

"I doubt you would have met them, Your Grace. My parents did not attend the Season after their marriage," Eden explained. "Mama was increasing with me the Season after they wed, and so they stayed at Brownstone Manor." She paused. "Then after birthing me, she was in a riding accident and never left her bed. Papa refused to go to town without her, and so they remained in the country."

"Such devotion," Lady Traywick said. "It reminds me of my late husband."

Wanting to change the subject, Eden asked, "Will either of you come to the fete tomorrow?"

"I think it important that I make an appearance," the duchess said. "I do not plan to stay long, but it will be good to see everyone gathered. You have outdone yourself, my dear. You must plan the fete every year."

"No, that will be something His Grace's wife will need to do," she said, gently correcting the duchess. "But I will leave all my diagrams, lists, and maps for the future duchess in case she might find them useful. Lady Lia and Lady Tia will also be able to share what they know."

"They will be gone next year at the Season, making their come-outs," Her Grace replied. "It may just be Millbrooke who leaves town and comes down for the day to watch the games and competitions."

Her belly tightened, thinking of Val bringing his betrothed with him to Millvale to take part in the fun and games.

"If you will excuse me," she said, hurrying away before tears could spill.

Eden returned to the house, yearning filling her. She scolded herself for letting her thoughts turn to Val. After all her efforts on his behalf, he most likely would not even be here tomorrow to see how the fete turned out. Anger filled her, and she decided she must hold onto it.

Or else she might die of a broken heart.

EDEN RETIRED EARLY, exhausted from the long day. Sleep, however, did not come. She finally got out of bed and went to sit in the chair by the window, her feet curled under her, a slight breeze coming in through the window. Darkness surrounded her as she looked out at Millvale. From her view, she could see silhouettes of the temporary wooden stalls which had been erected. Pride washed through her at all she had accomplished during the past several weeks.

After tomorrow's fete, though, life would go back to normal. It would be time to pick up her lessons with Justina and Verina. They would return to the routine of their studies in the morning, followed by music lessons, riding, and afternoon tea. She wondered how she would be able to sit in the same room with Val and not crumble. Eden told herself she was strong, though. She had lost both parents and her childhood home and had taken up governessing for a living and been successful at it these past five years. She would continue to prepare her charges for their come-outs.

A light tapping sounded. She froze, listening. It wasn't coming from the door which joined her room with that of the girls. It was at her bedchamber's door. She quickly rose, tossing on her dressing gown, belting it as she crossed the room. Opening the door, she found her heart in her throat.

Val was on the other side.

He looked taller and more handsome than she remembered. His hair was windblown, and he seemed out of breath.

"Eden," he softly. "Eden."

She could only stand there, dumbfounded. Then she realized she was in her nightclothes.

"Oh!" She started closing the door, knowing how inappropriate the situation was.

He firmly planted his foot so that she could not shut it all the way.

"Your Grace," she whispered. "You cannot be here."

"Come to me," he begged. "Come to the library. I will wait for you there. We must talk, Eden. It is important."

Without waiting for her reply, he strode off. Eden even stepped into the corridor, watching him move quickly down the long hallway. She couldn't do what he asked.

And yet Eden found herself closing the door, shedding her dressing gown and night rail, donning her clothes and stockings and shoes, heading to the library. As she reached it and slipped inside, the clock in the room chimed midnight.

Val waited for her, looking hopeful and unsure at the same time, confusing her to no end. She closed the door, not wanting anyone to know they were here together, and marched across the room, pausing in front of him.

"What on earth do you have to say to me?" she asked. "Why

would you think—"

She never finished her sentence, much less the thought, because suddenly she was in his arms, his mouth on hers, his kiss urgent and desperate. Eden didn't want any part of this.

And yet she was helpless to refuse.

Her arms went about him, and he crushed her to him, his mouth ravaging hers. She clung to him, relishing his scent. His warmth. His strength.

He kissed her, over and over. Between each kiss, he said, "I am sorry. I missed you."

Tears sprang to her eyes. She was able to say, "I missed you, too," and then he was kissing her again, as if he were a man dying of thirst and she the source of water to fill him. He urged her to open to him, and his tongue swept inside her mouth. Tasting. Taking. Giving. Her breasts grew heavy. The place between her legs pulsed violently. Eden heard herself whimper.

Val broke the kiss. "I am never letting you go. Never."

The daze she was in abruptly ended. "No," she said, pushing him away. "I cannot keep doing this, Val. You have hurt me too much and too often."

He cradled her face in his large hands. "I never will again, Eden. I promise."

The tenderness in his eyes made her grow faint. She felt the room growing dark. Her knees buckled, and he caught her, sweeping her into his arms and carrying her to the settee. He sat, her in his lap, giving her soft kisses. Tears began falling down her cheeks.

"No," she murmured. "I cannot."

"I botched things badly between us the first time. That is why I left Millvale. I thought you needed time away from me. Time to think. Mama agreed with me."

"What?" she cried. "What did you tell Her Grace?"

He grinned at her. "That I love you. That I wished to wed you."

Dumbfounded, Eden could only stare at him as if he'd grown a second head.

He kissed her again. "Mama is the one who thought you could use time to think without me hovering about. I knew you were unhappy with me, Eden. I was not certain of the cause, but she encouraged me to leave Millvale and check on my other estates. That way, I would not constantly be underfoot, upsetting you."

Val looked at her hopefully. "Did you truly miss me? I was a terrible mess without you. I thought about you every waking moment and dreamt of you each night."

She shook her head. "I think I must have fallen asleep in the chair and am dreaming."

He kissed her again. Hard. Demanding. The kiss took on a life of its own, and it went on for some minutes before he ended it.

"This is not a dream. I am flesh and blood, here with you, loving you." He swallowed. "Hoping you will love me in return."

"I . . . I . . ." Her head could not even form words, much less her bruised lips.

"Oh, I forgot!" He shifted her a bit, reaching inside his coat, withdrawing something. "This will convince you."

Eden accepted what he handed her, not sure of anything. She opened it. Began reading it. Stopped. And looked at him.

"Is this what I think it is?"

"Yes, love. It is a special license. We can wed as soon as we wish. Anywhere. At any time. I stopped in town this morning and spoke to Con. I told him of my feelings for you. My cousin is almost as ardent an admirer of you as I am." Val brushed his knuckles against her cheek. "He told me to follow my heart. It will always lead me to you."

Another soft kiss followed. Then he said, "I dragged him to Doctors' Commons so that I might purchase the special license for us. Then Con came with me." He frowned. "At least as far as we could. An axel broke on the carriage. It was taking forever to repair it. I rented a horse and rode it as far as I could before changing out again. And again." He cupped her face. "All I wanted was to get home. To you."

She still couldn't quite believe what she was hearing. "You wish to wed me?"

He chuckled, kissing the tip of her nose. "I would not have gone to such trouble unless I wanted to spend the rest of my life with you, love."

Love. He'd called her love. Eden's gaze met his, and she saw that he truly meant it.

"Yes," she said softly.

His thumbs caressed her cheeks. "Yes, what?"

Her voice firmer, she said, "Yes. I will marry you, Val."

"When?" he pressed.

For the first time, she smiled. "I suppose you would want Con to witness our union. How long will it take him to reach Millvale?"

He beamed at her. "He should be here sometime tomorrow."

She pushed her fingers into his thick hair, loving the feel of the silky locks. "Well, the fete is tomorrow. Perhaps the day after?"

"No. We have been apart far too long. I refuse to wait. Why not wed during the fete? Everyone will be there. Family. Friends. Neighbors."

"Do you truly wish for a wedding outdoors, with hundreds of people?" she asked.

"I think it the perfect time to make you my duchess, love."

Val kissed her again. "Then we will do as you ask. But first, the contests must be completed. After all, you are a judge in one of the riding events."

He kissed her, laughing. "All right. But once that last contest takes place, there is no escaping me, Eden." He gazed at her tenderly. "My betrothed."

Love for this man poured through her.

"Tomorrow night, we will celebrate as man and wife. You do not know how much I have wanted to make love to you."

A bit of uneasiness filled her. "I hope I will not disappoint you. I know nothing of it, Val."

He grinned. "I know enough for the both of us. And something tells me you are going to be an excellent pupil and take to every lesson I give you."

They spent another hour simply kissing. Finally, her betrothed stood and placed her on her feet.

"Let me escort you to your bedchamber."

They walked, fingers entwined, stopping at her door.

"Not a word to anyone," he told her. "I want things to be a surprise."

"You will have to inform Mr. Clarke. He will need to be present in order to perform the ceremony."

"Clarke would let the cat out of the bag, Eden. That man could not keep a secret to save his own soul."

She thought a moment. "He has been underfoot, wanting to claim credit for much of what has already been done. The riding events are the last two things scheduled tomorrow afternoon. I guarantee that he will be near the judge's platform, wanting to take part in the awarding of the prizes."

"Then I will make certain that after *I* hand out the prizes, I tell everyone we are to wed, and he is to perform the ceremony immediately."

"Oh, what about Her Grace and Lady Traywick? They told me they will come to the fete for a short time tomorrow morning. They must be there to see the ceremony."

"Then I will tell Mama that I wish for her to award the final prize of the day. Naturally, Aunt Agnes will be with her. Will that do?"

"That will do," she said, standing on tiptoe and pressing a kiss to his lips. "Tomorrow."

"Tomorrow," he echoed.

Eden floated back into her bedchamber, falling atop the bedclothes. She loved—and was loved in return.

"Mama, Papa, if you are watching, know how very happy I am," she whispered as she fell asleep.

Chapter Twenty-Three

VAL AWOKE, FEELING on top of the world. It would be hard not to shout from the rafters that Eden had agreed to become his wife. Still, he liked not only the element of a surprise wedding ceremony—but also the fact it was a secret the two of them held. He only hoped that Con could get the axel repaired and reach Millvale in time to be at the wedding.

Since he had no Fisham to ready him for the day, having left the valet behind when he rode home, he shaved himself carefully, not wishing to appear with nicks upon his cheeks. He rang for hot water, wishing to have a bath after yesterday's long ride.

As he sat soaking in the large bathing tub, his thoughts centered upon Eden. Contentment washed over him.

And love . . .

He dried off and dressed, going to his mother's rooms, being admitted by her maid. A look of happiness appeared upon her face, and she dismissed the servant.

"Millbrooke," she said, holding her hands out to him.

He walked to her and took them, kissing her on each cheek. "Mama."

"How are your estates?" she asked, indicating for him to take a chair, while she did the same.

"Everything is in excellent working order," he shared. "I had no idea how I would find the properties, but they are all fruitful and in the hands of excellent stewards. How are things here at Millvale?"

"If you are asking about Miss Snow—and the fete—I would say she has been in her element planning this event. It has also been excellent training for your sisters and my nieces. They have played an active part in putting this celebration together. It will do them well when they plan things for their own households. I believe they will be extremely confident when they do so because of this experience."

"I know the fete begins this morning, and I hope you and Aunt Agnes will come for a while."

"I thought to go when it first opened. It may not be so crowded then."

He winced inwardly, knowing he needed her there at the end of the day. "I think it a good idea you make an appearance then, Mama, but I would have you come to the closing, as well. Everyone is looking forward to the two riding events, which will end the fete, and it would be lovely if you were there to present the prizes alongside me."

She looked pleased and said, "If you insist, I will be happy to turn out later in the afternoon."

"I will send word to you when those contests are beginning. You and Aunt Agnes can leave the house as soon as you receive my message."

He rose, and she did the same.

"I am glad you were able to make it home in time for the fete, Millbrooke. Miss Snow has done an incredible job, pulling off the impossible. You must make certain to give her ample praise."

Grinning sheepishly, he said, "I plan to do so, Mama. By the way, Con will be arriving at some point. I stopped in town for a quick visit with him, and he was eager to attend the fete. We had trouble with the carriage. An axel broke. Knowing I must be back for today, I rode the rest of the way home, while Con stayed with the carriage to see to its repair. Hopefully, it will be ready sometime this morning, and Con will be here by noon or early afternoon. If you would, have a room made up for him."

"It will be good to see my nephew. Agnes will be thrilled as well." She paused. "Did you know Constantine came to Millvale while you were away?"

Val decided to play ignorant. "No, he did not mention that to me. I am sorry I missed him. At least the rest of you got to enjoy his company. I will see you at the fete, Mama."

He left her rooms, thinking that she would need to vacate them soon so that Eden might have them. Then again, he planned to keep his duchess with him, so perhaps Mama might not need to move right away.

In the breakfast room, he saw all four girls were finishing up their meal. They all greeted him with enthusiasm, four voices talking at once.

He embraced each of them, saying, "One at a time, please. My head is already aching by trying to listen to everyone at once and decipher what you are saying."

Tia took the lead. "It is about time you got home, Val," his sister scolded. "You are the one who wished for this fete to occur on Millvale lands. It would have been awkward if the host had not made an appearance."

"You cannot imagine the amount of effort which has gone into planning something of this nature," Lia said. "While all four of us have worked extremely hard on your behalf, you owe a great deal of thanks to Miss Snow."

"I knew by leaving things in Miss Snow's competent hands that everything would prove to be successful. I will make certain to seek her out and sing her praises to the rooftops."

"Well, we must get going," Justina told him. "We all have stations in order to organize our volunteers. We are glad you are home, Val."

Verina echoed the same. "We are very glad to have you back, Cousin."

The four left him in peace, and he helped himself to the breakfast buffet, the footman pouring him a cup of strong coffee. He sat almost smugly, holding his secret to himself, thinking tomorrow he would awaken with his Eden in his arms as they started their first full day together as man and wife.

He took time to go to his study and quickly looked over the correspondence he had received. Three letters had come from Ariadne, and he read through them quickly, thinking he would reply to her tomorrow. Nothing else was so terribly important that he must deal with it immediately. Instead, he walked down to the stables to let Miller know that his carriage would arrive sometime later today.

"One more thing, Miller. I assume you will be attending the fete."

"Yes, Your Grace," the head groom said with enthusiasm. "Her Grace has given leave for all the servants to attend."

"Might I ask a favor from you?"

"Certainly, Your Grace. What might I help you with?"

"I would like Andromeda to be saddled and brought to wherever the horse events will be held. I plan to include Miss Snow as a participant."

The groom shook his head sadly. "I have encouraged Miss Snow to do that very thing. She will not budge. She claims she would have an unfair advantage since she has ridden the course several times. She also mentioned it should be a local who wins so that the winner can defend his title next summer."

He recalled before he left that she had not wished to compete. That was just like Eden, thinking of others before herself.

"What about the actual race itself, the one without obstacles? She would have no advantage over anyone else regarding it." He grinned. "Other than the fact she would be riding Andromeda, of course."

Miller's grin matched his own. "I think if you signed up Miss Snow for the race and I stood nearby with Andromeda ready to run, it would be extremely hard for her to disappoint a duke."

"Then it is settled. Please have Andromeda brought wherever the race will be run. I will make certain Miss Snow competes."

He caught sight of Rollo. "Walk with me," he told the groom. "I wish to hear something about these two horse competitions."

As the two men headed toward the group of stalls in the distance, Rollo told him about the design of the course and how riders would have to jump fences of different heights and clear trenches which had been dug.

"And the races for speed?" he asked.

"It will depend upon the number of riders who have registered for the event, Your Grace," the groom explained. "Miss Snow has it planned so that groups of four will race against one another. The winner of each round then competes in a group of two, with the winner of those contests finally meeting in the end."

Rollo smiled at him. "I heard what you told Miller, Your Grace. There is no way Miss Snow will *not* win."

"Do you think others might be upset if she did?" he asked. "Would it reflect poorly upon Millvale for the organizer of the contest to be the victor?"

"Everyone enjoys a good race, especially seeing a horse such as Andromeda running several times. I don't think anyone could be upset with that horse winning. It would not matter who was on her back."

"Then I will make certain Miss Snow competes."

Val spent a few hours walking amongst the different stalls, greeting tenants and villagers alike. He saw a few of his neighbors, knowing that most of the gentry currently were in town at the Season. This fete was not for titled gentlemen and their families, however. He wanted it to be for the people of Millvale and others who lived nearby. He decided he would keep the date as the final Saturday in June. He and Eden could attend the Season for a good two months or so before they returned to Millvale for the fete. He would help her in organizing it before they left for town, so that all would be in place when they returned.

He was astounded at the size of it all, though. There were triple the number of booths that he would have thought would be there. He found the jeweler's stall, realizing he had no ring to give Eden.

"Might you have any type of ring with you today?"

"I have a few, Your Grace. What might you be looking for?"

He leaned in and quietly said, "A wedding band."

The jeweler's eyes widened. "I only have two with me, Your Grace. Both are very simple. Of course, I can have it engraved inside if you wish to purchase it."

He suspected that Eden would not like anything too fancy. A simple, gold band would be to her liking.

"May I see them?" he asked.

The jeweler removed one and handed it to him. Val inspected it and then the other.

Handing one back, he said, "I prefer this one. Might I keep it and pay you tomorrow?"

"Certainly, Your Grace," the jeweler said, grinning from ear to ear. "And I will keep quiet about this."

"See that you do." Then he softly said, "But if you stay until the end of the fete, you may be a witness to the ceremony."

Val took the ring and slipped it inside the pocket which held the special license. He could not believe in but a few more hours, he would be a married man. He would not miss his carefree bachelor days one whit. He was in love with the most wonderful woman in the world and could not wait to make her officially his.

He finally came across Eden at the games being held for children. He heard the squeals and laughter and watched her, seeing how much she enjoyed herself. She would make for an excellent mother. He had spoken to her of Ariadne's idea to bring children to town for the Season. Val realized he would not need to go to many social events, just enough to show off his gorgeous duchess. What he did look forward to was spending time with his family. His siblings. His cousins. His niece and extended family, as well all the babes who would make their arrivals as more of his cousins wed.

He decided he would have to take Eden on a trip very soon, so that she could meet Penelope, Ariadne, and Julian. Lucy and Huntsberry, as well, since they resided nearby.

Approaching Eden, he asked, "How has everything gone so far?"

"The children are so happy. Have you been through the section where all the stalls are?"

"I have, and I only purchased one thing."

"What was that?" she asked.

"I will show you later. For now, I am starving. Would you like to accompany me to one of the food stalls?"

"I am famished myself. That sounds heavenly."

They stopped and purchased several meat pies and two tankards of ale. He led her to a large oak tree, and they wound up sitting on the ground. Eden rested her back against the trunk, while he sat in front of her.

"You haven't changed your mind, have you?" he asked.

"No." Concern filled her eyes. "Have you?"

"Not at all," he declared.

"There you are!" a voice called, and Val looked up, seeing Con coming toward them.

His cousin took a seat on the ground with them. "The axel is fixed. Your carriage and team are safely back at Millvale. And good day to you, Miss Snow. It is good to see you again."

"I am delighted to see you again, Lord Dyer. It is so nice that you were able to come to the fete."

Con pointed to Val. "My cousin insisted that I come. He said it would be a most interesting time."

"You obviously know more than you are saying, my lord," Eden said. "You know, don't you?"

"Know what?" Con asked innocently.

"Do not act a simpleton with me, Lord Dyer," Eden teased. "Val told me that you accompanied him to Doctors' Commons yesterday to purchase the special license."

"Thank goodness," Con said, looking relieved. "I did not know how much longer I could keep up the farce. I was not certain if Val had spoken to you yet. I suppose by that silly grin on his face that you have accepted his offer of marriage."

"I did, but no one knows. Except for you."

"If you can keep a secret for a few more hours, we are to wed at the end of the fete," he told his cousin.

"You devil! Aunt Alice will be shocked—but pleasantly surprised." Con glanced to Eden. "And Aunt Agnes will need to start looking for a new governess for her daughters, I suppose."

"I will help her do so," Eden said.

Con sniffed. "Those meat pies look quite tasty. I think I will go purchase a few for myself."

"I will leave you gentlemen together," Eden said. "I must walk about some more to see that everything is going well."

Val quickly came to his feet and assisted Eden to hers. "Will you be at the horse events?" he asked casually.

"Yes, they are the last two competitions to be held. The obstacle course will come first, followed by the race. Then both winners will report to the judges' dais and be awarded their prizes."

"Then I will see you there," he said cheerfully.

The moment she was out of earshot, Con turned to him. "I know you too well, Cousin. You are up to something."

"I am glad that Eden is so busy because she would probably have guessed something was afoot herself. Thankfully, she is too distracted by seeing to the fete."

Briefly, he told his cousin about entering his betrothed in the horse race, explaining why she had not done so herself.

"She may be too angry with you to wed you," Con remarked. "But seeing her on Andromeda as I did, I know Miss Snow is destined to win."

"She has worked too diligently and deserves the recognition. I will stay with you while you finish eating, and then we can walk around a bit."

The time passed quickly, and soon others began gathering to observe the first of the two horse competitions. Val asked Con to return to the house and escort his mother and aunt so they would not miss out on anything.

"And not a word about the ceremony," he cautioned.

"Trust me. My lips are sealed."

After some minutes, he saw Miller arrive and met the groom, asking that he step out of sight so that Eden would not see Andromeda.

When Eden joined him several minutes later and said, "You should take your place on the dais with the other judges. I will also be there announcing each contestant." Then she smiled. "Your Grace. Lady Traywick. I was not expecting to see either of you."

"We did come earlier this morning," Lady Traywick said. "We were most curious about the competitions for the adults, though."

"I know we already missed the archery contest. I spoke to Lord Arden and learned that he won it," the duchess said.

"He did," Eden said. "His daughters were cheering him on. There is room for you on the platform if you wish to observe the contest from there. The height will give you an advantage in watching it."

"Thank you, Miss Snow," Her Grace said. "We will take your advice."

The four of them went to the stairs, Val handing all three women up, and then he joined them atop the platform. The crowd had grown quite large by that time. He saw Con, his sisters, and two cousins together. Con nodded at him, and Val returned the nod.

Eden explained the rules of the competition, how contestants would be timed and then gain or lose points, based upon the number of successful jumps and whether or not they accrued penalties on the course.

It took three-quarters of an hour for a winner to be determined, and the crowd cheered loudly as Rollo was proclaimed the winner.

Eden said, "You must wait for your prize, Rollo. It will be awarded at the same time the winner of the race receives his—or hers," she said, causing the crowd to chuckle.

"If you will head toward the meadow," she told those gathered. "The first race will commence in ten minutes.

Val walked her to the meadow, glancing over his shoulder to see that Miller followed at a discreet distance. On the way, she explained to him how the groups would race until the final two contestants would face off, showing him her lists of racers when he asked.

He pointed to the last group of four. "I only see three names in this last grouping. It seems it would give those racers an advantage. A one in three instead of a one in four chance."

She shrugged. "It could not be helped. It is as fair as I can make it."

"Whatever the outcome, you have done a superb job in planning today," he complimented. "I promise that I will not abandon you next year. I plan to be by your side every step of the way, down to planning the smallest detail."

"It will be much easier, having done so once. I will have all my notes to refer to." She smiled saucily. "Perhaps I should have *you* plan the fete next year. Then I could help you in the following years."

"I would kiss that wicked smile off your face if I could," he declared. "But that would give away too much." He paused, looking at her heatedly. "Be ready to kiss me for hours, Eden Snow. And then be prepared for me to kiss every inch of your lovely body."

"I will hold you to that, Your Grace," she said pertly.

They reached the area where the starting line was and parted, Eden busy gathering up the first group of racers.

Val watched her, thinking of the night ahead.

Chapter Twenty-Four

Eden was glad Lady Lia had suggested they all wear their riding habits today. The fuller skirts had given her greater range of movement, as well as allowing her to move quickly about. The only regret she had was the habit would also serve as her wedding gown. She told herself not to worry about it. That Val would not focus on what she wore. He would see the love she had for him shining in her eyes, and everything else would fade from view.

She collected the first group of competitors and lined them up, telling them to wait for her command. Glancing across the field, she looked to Rollo, who gave her a thumbs up. The groom would not be entering the racing event and had agreed to serve as a judge at the finish line in case there was a close call to be made. At first, she had thought to put someone of high rank in the community at the end, but if two competitors were close, she did not want to sow seeds of discord in the community. Better to let a man familiar with horses—and in the duke's employ—make the call, with no hard feelings.

Seeing the riders were ready, Eden quieted the crowd and then signaled that the race was on. The four men on horseback tore across the meadow, but the local doctor pulled ahead within seconds, easily winning victory. She made a note on her list that he would move on to the next round and then gathered the second set of four riders. The crowd had cheered the first racers on, and now they grew even louder, clapping, whistling, and stomping.

Again, Eden indicated for the race to begin, and those gathered shouted loudly for their favorite in the contest. This time, the winner proved to be one of Lord Arden's grooms. As the riders turned and galloped back toward the crowd, she saw his two daughters jumping up and down with joy. She thought Lord Arden a decent man, and she hoped the widower would find a wife.

The third group in the competition was the closest race yet, but a shopkeeper edged out the others, claiming victory. Now, only one race was left to run.

Suddenly, someone plucked her lists from her hands, and she turned to scold them, finding Val on the other end of the pages.

"You are racing next," he said firmly.

"I did not even enter," she protested.

His eyes gleamed. "I entered you—and Andromeda is waiting."

She looked over his shoulder, seeing Miller had the horse in hand. If she argued with Val now, she would seem churlish, and it might put a damper on the day for all those in attendance.

"All right," she said good-naturedly, heading to the horse, secretly excited she had been given a chance to race against a field of all men.

When she reached Andromeda, Eden stroked the horse's neck and said quietly, so that only the horse could hear, "They are challenging us, Girl. All males in this race. Let us show them that it is not only men who can be filled with mettle."

Kissing the horse's nose, she allowed Miller to toss her into the saddle.

He handed her the reins. "Ride like bloody hell, Miss Snow. We're all cheering you on."

A warm glow filled her. "Thank you, Miller."

Eden guided the horse to where the other three men were lining up.

"What's this?" one cried. "A woman in the competition?"

She gazed at him steadily. "A woman who plans to leave you far behind."

Val had taken over and shouted, "Racers, get ready."

She wound up on the inside, a competitor on each side of her. Eden patted Andromeda's neck. Then, hands on the reins, she heard Val's cry and took off. The horse had always had speed, but as Eden rode, she could tell Andromeda was making an extra effort. Leaning low into the horse, she focused on outrunning her competitors.

Moments later, she crossed the finish line as the victor.

The crowd went wild, and the applause and cheers were almost deafening. Eden turned her horse and trotted back to the start, giving Andromeda a few well-deserved love pats.

When she arrived, those still seated atop their horses and moving on in the competition all tipped their hats to her, and she felt good about having earned their respect. It was definitely a man's world, but she felt as if her small victory had been one for all the women in the crowd.

She remained on Andromeda, letting Val gather the two winners from the first two races. As they went head-to-head, the doctor easily pulled in front, coasting to victory over Lord Arden's groom. Then she and the shopkeeper trotted to the start mark.

"May the best man—or woman—win," he told her, grinning.

The horse he rode was fast, but Andromeda was on fire, giving Eden the victory. She cantered back, and Val announced a five-minute respite, in order to give Andromeda a few minutes of rest, as the physician's horse had received.

She looked about, seeing Justina waving at her. She returned the wave and thought how happy she was in this moment. Even if she did not win the final race of the day, she believed she had found a home at Millvale.

And the love of a wonderful man.

Before she moved to the start line, none other than the Duchess of Millbrooke came up to her.

"I expect you to win this race, Miss Snow," Her Grace said. Then she motioned for Eden to lean down and softly said, "I would make Andromeda a wedding present, but the horse will be yours soon anyway. I must find something else special for you. In the meantime, know that you have my full support."

Tears sprang to her eyes. "Thank you, Your Grace."

Val motioned for her to take her position, and she guided Andromeda so that her horse and the doctor's were alongside one another. She readied herself and took off, knowing this was the ride of her life. For half the race, she sensed they were neck-and-neck, but gradually, Eden pulled away. She crossed the finish line moments before the doctor did, her heart pounding, the blood rushing in her ears.

"You ride superbly, Miss Snow," her final competitor complimented. "I am not ashamed at all to have lost to a woman—and her splendid horse."

"You were a hard competitor to beat, Doctor." She offered her hand, and they shook before cantering back to the beginning.

Everywhere she looked, Eden saw smiling faces. Then Val was capturing her waist, bringing her down from Andromeda, and kissing her.

In front of everyone.

She could hear the noise die down around them as he ended the kiss. Looking out, she saw some people smiling, while others appeared confused.

His voice ringing loudly, Val said, "Thank you all for attending the first annual fete at Millvale. It was organized by my betrothed, Miss Eden Snow. We will award the prizes now for the two horse competitions." He pulled out the special license he'd been carrying in his pocket. "And then if Mr. Clarke is willing, we will hold our wedding ceremony immediately after. I hope you will all stay and act as witnesses to our union."

Cheers erupted as he pulled her into his arms again for a lingering kiss.

When he broke it, she said, "You certainly know how to put on a fete, Your Grace."

Smiling, he told her, "I could not have done it without you, Miss Snow. In fact, I do not wish to do anything unless you are by my side."

They led the entire crowd back to the dais. He assisted her in mounting it and then helped his mother up to join them. As everyone gathered around, Val motioned for Rollo to mount the steps.

"Mama?" he said, handing her the five guineas which had been designated as the prize for the obstacle course winner.

The duchess accepted them. "This will be the only time I present the prizes. It will be the role of the Duchess of Millbrooke to do so each year in the future." She smiled at Eden.

Her Grace thanked everyone for coming, and then she told those gathered that the fete would not have taken place without the efforts and patience exercised by her future daughter-in-law. Eden knew her soon-to-be mother-in-law did so to show her support for the marriage. Then the duchess gave Rollo the coins, and the groom held up both arms in victory, smiling as the crowd applauded.

The duchess looked out. "Mr. Clarke? Where are you? Get up here at once!"

The clergyman weaved through the crowd, a stunned look still on his face. Val presented him with the special license, and he agreed to officiate at the impromptu ceremony.

Just before he began, Val said to her, "You did not receive your prize, love."

She gazed at him, tears misting her eyes. "My prize is *you*. You are everything I could ever want."

They repeated their vows, and her groom pulled out a ring. Holding it up, he said, "I told you I would show you what I bought."

She felt a warmth rush through her. "It is perfect."

"I know. Simple and elegant—just like the woman who will wear it."

Val repeated the words the vicar said, slipping the ring onto her finger. After another few minutes, Mr. Clarke announced they were husband and wife.

Her new husband gave Eden a lingering kiss as those in attendance cheered him on. Everything that had happened to her—the good and the bad—had led to this moment, when she committed herself body, heart, and soul to Val Worthington, the Duke of Millbrooke.

They were going to have a wonderful life together.

MUCH TO EDEN'S surprise, Val mounted Andromeda. The usually frisky horse must have been tired after the three races she had run because she gave him not a hint of trouble. He crooked his finger, and Eden came to him. Her husband leaned down and lifted her up and onto his lap, riding back to the house. A footman hurried outside to greet them.

Val lowered Eden to the ground and dismounted. Handing the reins to the footman, he said, "Walk Andromeda back to the stables. Do not attempt to ride her."

"Oh, no, Your Grace," the servant said, wide-eyed. "I've heard she's a handful."

"Wait until a groom appears to rub her down. Then you may return to the house."

"Yes, Your Grace."

The footman led Andromeda away, and Val entwined their fingers together, guiding her inside the house and to the kitchens. There, he asked Cook and two scullery maids to heat water for a bath and have it brought up as soon as the other servants returned to the house. Then he escorted Eden up the stairs to his ducal rooms.

As they entered the first one, he told her, "This is a small study. I use it more as a reading room."

He showed her his dressing room and bathing chamber, saying,

"These connect to the rooms designated for the duchess. I will be asking Mama to leave them so that you might occupy them." He squeezed her fingers and led her back to his bedchamber. "I hope, though, that you will only use your rooms for dressing and when you need a bit of quiet time, away from everyone else. Because I want you to spend your nights with me."

Her gaze shifted to the large, four-poster bed. "Well, you certainly have plenty of room for me in it."

Laughing, he embraced her and then kissed her for a long moment.

"You will always say what is on your mind, won't you?" he asked.

"Only to you," she promised. "As a duchess, I suppose I shall have to curb my tongue and tone with others."

He framed her face with his hands. "Honesty always between us, right?"

"Yes, Val. Always."

They indulged in a long session of delicious kissing until a knock sounded on his door. Breaking apart as if they had been caught, they both laughed. He went to the door and opened it, and a long line of servants carrying buckets of water came in and went to the bathing chamber. She knew it would take a good deal of water to fill the bathing tub, the largest she had ever seen.

When the last servant left, Val locked the door. "I want no interruptions."

He led her through his dressing room, saying, "Your rooms mirror mine, with the shared bathing chamber in the middle." Looking at her hopefully, he added, "The tub is rather large. I thought we might bathe the sweat of the day from us together."

An erotic picture formed in her mind, and Eden felt her face grow hot. He grinned.

"I see you are thinking of naughty things, Your Grace."

For a moment, she didn't realize he had spoken to her. Then it struck her that yes, she was a duchess, and that was how others would always address her.

"I know nothing, Val," she admitted. "The marital bed was not something Mama ever spoke to me about. And heaven forbid Papa say anything about the intimacies between a man and a woman."

He took her in his arms. "I know enough for the both of us. Whatever we choose to do, we must both be comfortable with it. If at any time you do not like something, simply tell me."

Eden stroked his cheek. "I have a feeling I will like everything we do together."

"Then let us start."

He undressed her slowly, kissing her as each garment left her body. When she stood bare before him, she felt no shame. No hesitation. The admiration she saw in his eyes made her feel worshipped.

"You are a vision from heaven," he said, awe in his voice.

He wrapped his arms about her, holding her to him., nuzzling her neck. Then he stepped back and quickly shed his own clothes, only asking for her assistance in removing his Hessians. The boots were molded to his muscular thighs, and Eden had to straddle his leg and pull with all her might.

"I must say, I do enjoy the view from here," he told her, causing them both to laugh.

Val climbed into the tub and held out his arms. She joined him, placing her back against his chest, reveling in the deep, warm water. He wrapped his arms about her, and Eden felt utterly cherished.

He began kissing her neck as his hands cupped her bare breasts, kneading them, squeezing, even tweaking her nipples. The more he played with them, the more desire flared within her. Then his hand gradually slid down her belly. She knew its final destination and felt her breath quicken.

Slowly, Val ran the tip of his finger along the seam of her sex, causing a deep ache to fill her. She realized she needed him inside her—and told him so.

"Oh, I like that you are so open with me," he said, sliding a finger into her, stroking her deeply.

She mewled, her body shuddering, and he continued caressing her, adding another finger. Then he pressed against something, his finger slowly circling it.

"This is your pearl," he explained. "It is the point on your body which will give you the ultimate pleasure. Let me demonstrate."

He continued circling it, pressing it, even as his other fingers stroked her. She grew hot all over, the flames of desire filling her. Her hips began to move, meeting his fingers. A pressure built within her.

"I feel something coming," she said, breathless. "I don't know what it is."

"Let the anticipation build. Keep moving. Whatever feels good to you."

He continued his caresses, and his lips trailed along her neck. Kissing. Nipping. Soothing.

Then it was as if a volcano erupted. Tremors poured through her body as the purest of pleasure rippled through her. Eden cried out, bucking against his hand now, the feelings raw and real and wonderful. Finally, the feeling subsided, and she came back down to earth. Val turned her, her breasts now pressed against his hard chest as he kissed her.

"Let me bathe you, love. Then we will go to our marriage bed."

Lovingly, he took the soap and lathered his hands, rubbing them all over her body. It was a most unusual bath, and she told him it was the only kind of bath she would want in the future, causing him to burst out laughing. Then he allowed her to do the same, and Eden enjoyed exploring the planes of his body, watching his muscles bunch as she touched him. She grasped his cock, hard and stiff, and he closed his eyes, leaning his head against the tub's edge, groaning low as she rubbed her thumb along the shaft.

Then he took her wrist. "Enough, else I will explode and then not be able to make sweet love to you."

"I thought that was what we had been doing," she said.

"I want more of you. Dry, this time," he said, chuckling.

They stood and enjoyed toweling off one another. She was already getting used to seeing him without his clothes, admiring the sleek muscles, knowing his body now belonged to her as much as it did him.

"You are a handsome thing," she told him as he took her hand and led her to the bed.

Their bed . . .

For the next hour, they touched one another everywhere, kissing the entire time. Sometimes, on the lips. Sometimes, their lips grazed bare flesh. She began to learn what Val liked—and what she liked, too.

Then their fevered touching led him to lying on his back. He told her to straddle him, and she did so.

"Do you trust me?" he asked.

"Like no one else," she said solemnly.

"You are going to set the pace, love. You will have all the control."

"But I am only learning what to do," she protested.

He grinned. "But you like being in charge. Admit it."

"I do," she said grudgingly.

He had her rise to her knees and take his cock in her hand, saying, "You will lower yourself onto me."

Glancing down, Eden said, "You are too large, Val. You will never fit inside me."

He caressed her cheek. "A woman is made for this very thing. You will be surprised. Yes, I will fill you, but it will feel right."

She began to ease downward, her hand firm around his shaft, guiding it inside her. Eden took more and more of him into her until she was seated.

"Now move. Just a bit. A little wiggle will do it."

She did—and pleasure danced through her. "Ooh, I like that."

"Keep moving," he urged, having her do so in different ways.

They found a rhythm, and then they were dancing together in the most divine dance ever created. She gasped, that wonderful feeling from before coming again. Anticipation built within her, knowing now what lay ahead.

Suddenly, he flipped her somehow. Now, she was on bottom and he on top. Val began thrusting deeply into her, telling her how much he loved her even as he kissed her repeatedly. Then a shower of stars exploded inside her, and pure pleasure rocked through her. Their dance finally came to an end, and he collapsed atop her.

"I love you," he told her. "I will always love you."

Eden cradled his handsome face in her hands. "And I will love you, forever and ever."

Epilogue

Two months later...

"STOP THE CARRIAGE!" Eden cried.

Val quickly rapped on the roof with his cane before throwing the door open and jumping from the vehicle. He grabbed her by the waist, swinging her to the ground—and not a moment too soon.

She retched on the side of the road, and once more, her queasiness fled.

Her husband took her by the elbow, gently turning her. His eyes were filled with sympathy as he asked, "Better now, love?"

She nodded, allowing him to dab his handkerchief against her mouth.

"We can walk a bit if you would like," he offered.

"No. We are both eager to get home. We cannot be far now."

"I would say another half-hour or so."

"Really, I am much better. It just strikes so suddenly."

Val took her hand, bringing it to his lips and kissing it tenderly. "Just as love does," he teased.

He handed her back into the carriage and took a seat beside her, knocking on the vehicle's roof once more. The carriage began rolling along the road again.

Eden was ready to get home to Millvale. They had been gone almost six weeks now, spending almost a week at each of Val's properties scattered about England. He had said the roads were at their best during summer, making travel slightly easier. She had not expected a honeymoon, but that is what it had turned out to be. Time for them to be alone together. She had proven to be adventurous when it came to lovemaking. They had coupled in the carriage on several occasions. In gardens and various rooms throughout the houses they visited. Even in an abandoned cottage one afternoon. She could not seem to get enough of her husband, and he obviously felt the same about her.

But this sickness, because of the babe growing inside her, was driving her mad. She had begun experiencing it in the mornings when she awoke, and Val had learned to always have a crust of bread or a few bites of cheese on a nearby table. He would feed it to her in small bites, helping her nausea to subside. She hoped the entire time she was increasing did not affect her so.

When they made the turn and drove up the lane to the house, her heart sped up. She was still getting used to the fact that she was a duchess and that she lived in a grand house. Eden had yet to see Val's London townhouse, but she would do so next spring when they went to town for the Season. She thought she had become with child the first time they coupled, which would mean the babe would be born sometime in March. Next year's Season would begin about a month after she gave birth.

While Eden would have preferred staying home, she knew Val needed to be in town. Lia's and Tia's come-outs had already been delayed a year, thanks to their father's death. Both girls were eager to make their debuts into Polite Society, and Val would be the anxious brother, watching over them, helping them to arrange their matches. If she decided to stay in the country with their babe, he would never go to town. She determined to give birth and then go to town the next month. Naturally, they would bring the babe with them. She agreed with Ariadne and would always bring their children to town with them.

She was glad they had stopped in Surrey at Aldridge Manor before making their way back to Millbrooke. Ariadne had been incredibly sweet and kind to Eden, and she had fallen in love with little Penelope. Even Julian, who was quite possessive with his daughter, allowed Eden to hold Penelope. It had also been good to meet Lucy and Judson, who lived but a couple of miles from Aldridge Manor. They had visited them for a day at Huntsworth. Lucy was also increasing and would likely have her babe near the beginning of March. The Huntsberrys were looking forward to a visit from Lucy's sister. Dru was scheduled to arrive early next week. Con had gone home to Somerset to escort his sister to Surrey. While it would have been nice to also meet Dru and see Con again, Val had told Eden they could visit in a month or two. He was as eager as she was to return to Millvale.

The carriage stopped, and the door to the house opened. Out poured all four girls, with Her Grace and Lady Traywick not far behind them. The girls squealed and waved, and Justina even jumped up and down in excitement.

Val departed the carriage first, handing Eden down, and she was swarmed by the four young ladies, who all proclaimed how much they had missed her.

"I cannot wait to hear about your travels, Miss Snow," Verina said before quickly covering her mouth. "Oh, I am sorry, Your Grace."

She took her former charge's hand. "Please. You are to call me Eden."

"I do like your name," Verina said, "but it is hard to think of you as anything other than Miss Snow."

"Frankly, I feel the same way," she confided.

Eden moved to greet her mother-in-law and former employer. Both women embraced her warmly, and the dowager duchess said, "Tea is almost ready. Come to the drawing room." She slipped her arm through Eden's, and that gesture alone made her feel so very welcomed.

In the drawing room, she poured out alongside her mother-in-law since she outranked Lady Traywick. It felt right, however, to be acting as a hostess. After all, this was now her home.

"Tell us about your journey," Lia encouraged.

She and Val entertained them for an hour, talking of the places they had been and what they had seen. Then she looked to her husband and nodded imperceptibly.

"We have some other news," she began.

"We are going to be aunts!" cried Tia. "I knew it. I could tell from Val's face."

"Yes, a new little Worthington will make an appearance sometime in March," Val said. He took her hand. "If Eden feels like it, we will go to town for the Season."

"I would stay home," Lady Traywick advised. "The Season will always be there."

"But would my sisters agree to delay their come-outs yet again?" Val asked.

"No!" both cried in unison.

"It is important that Val be in town," Eden said. "The sisters to a duke will be highly sought after. Val wishes to inspect Lia's and Tia's suitors carefully."

He kissed her fingers. "And I would never dream of leaving my beloved wife and child in the country. We will go to town together. Mama, you and the girls are free to go earlier. I know you will have modistes to see. Hats to try on. That sort of thing."

"Won't Dru be old enough to make her come-out then?" Lia asked.

"Yes, she will," Eden said. "We called at Aldridge Manor on our way home. Not only did we see Ariadne, but we also saw Lucy. She shared that Dru is coming to visit her and Judson in a few days."

The two older women looked at one another, and Her Grace said, "We have some news ourselves. Now that you are home again, we all will be leaving in the next day or two."

Val frowned. "Where are you going, Mama?"

"It is time Lia and Tia saw something beyond Millvale. Agnes has invited us to return to Cumberland with her, Verina, and Justina," the dowager duchess shared. "We shall travel with them and stay for an indefinite period." She smiled at Eden. "This will give you time to settle in as the Duchess of Millbrooke, my dear. Your rooms are already waiting for you. You will be able to decide how you wish for the household to be run without interference from me. I can always go to the dower house when we return."

"No, Your Grace. I do not want that. Neither would Val. While I kindly thank you for turning over your rooms to me, you are family. Tia and Lia will be in the house with us. We want you here with all of us."

Her mother-in-law smiled gratefully. "Thank you, Eden."

They finished tea and discussed the trip to Cumberland for another hour. Lady Traywick, Verina, and Justina shared what Traywick Manor was like, and even Eden chimed in upon occasion, thinking she would miss her former home, but she was so happy she had a permanent one here with Val.

When tea ended, her husband asked, "Shall we go stroll in the gardens and cool off a bit?"

"I would be happy to do so."

She took his arm, and they left the house, entering the gardens.

"I cannot help but think of the wonderful hours I spent here with you before our marriage," he told her. "I know we will share many more happy times here together."

They stopped at the bench where they used to meet, taking a seat next to one another, and Val slipped his arm about her. She rested her head against his shoulder, and he placed a palm against her belly.

"I cannot wait to meet our child," he told her. "I hope they have your hazel eyes."

She glanced up at him. "And I wish they might get your chestnut hair. Oh, Val, will we always be this happy?"

He lifted his hand from her belly and cradled her cheek. "I believe we will be happier with each passing day."

Her husband kissed her, and Eden knew total bliss.

About the Author

USA Today and Amazon Top 10 bestselling author Alexa Aston lives with her husband in a Dallas suburb, where she eats her fair share of dark chocolate and plots while she walks every morning. She enjoys travel and sports—and can't get enough of *Survivor* or *The Crown*.

Her Regency and Medieval historical romances bring to life loveable rogues and dashing knights. Her series include: *The Strongs of Shadowcrest, Suddenly a Duke, Second Sons of London, Dukes Done Wrong, Dukes of Distinction, Soldiers and Soulmates, The St. Clairs, The de Wolfes of Esterley Castle, The King's Cousins, Medieval Runaway Wives,* and *The Knights of Honor*.

Printed in Dunstable, United Kingdom